a wedding invitation

Books by Alice J. Wisler

Rain Song
How Sweet It Is
Hatteras Girl
A Wedding Invitation

a wedding invitation

Alice J. Wisler

BETHANY HOUSE PUBLISHERS
a division of Baker Publishing Group
Minneapolis, Minnesota

© 2011 by Alice J. Wisler

Cover design by Jennifer Parker
Cover photography by Getty Images, Dimitri Vervitsotis

Published by Bethany House Publishers
11400 Hampshire Avenue South
Bloomington, Minnesota 55438
www.bethanyhouse.com

Bethany House Publishers is a division of
Baker Publishing Group, Grand Rapids, Michigan

Printed in the United States of America

Library of Congress Cataloging-in-Publication Data
Wisler, Alice J.
    A wedding invitation / Alice J. Wisler.
       p.   cm.
    ISBN 978-0-7642-0733-4 (pbk.)
    1. Female friendship—Fiction. 2. Marriage—Fiction. 3. Falls Church
(Va.)—Fiction. 4. Winston-Salem (N.C.)—Fiction. I. Title.
PS3623.I846W43 2011
813'.6—dc22   2011025211

11 12 13 14 15 16 17   7 6 5 4 3 2 1

For all who passed through those dusty classrooms
of that memorable place we called PRPC

What lies behind us and what lies before us are tiny matters compared to what lies within us.

—RALPH WALDO EMERSON

one

February 1993

When a pet goes missing, it's hard to concentrate on anything but where he might be. Missing a cat can cause his owner to lose focus, forget, and do silly things—even hang clothing in wrong places. Today this is happening to my mother.

As though she's walking through a fog, Mom stares into the distance and hangs the newest order of black dresses all together in a clump. The metal hangers clink against each other, and I wince, realizing what she's done. The size twos are next to the size fourteens, yet the entire point of Mom's store is that the small and large sizes are displayed conveniently on different racks, not all meshed together, tangled in a confused web.

Following behind her, I sort the designer dresses into their proper sections, wondering if I should remind Mom that she can't compromise her organizational skills—they are her strength in running her boutique, Have a Fit.

With two dresses dangling from hangers in her hands, my mother mutters, "Where could he be?"

Her cat, Butterchurn, has never left Mom's home before. Well, once, to chase a squirrel, but after realizing the fluffy creature could scamper up a tree trunk and escape onto the branches at a rapid pace, Butterchurn walked his rotund body back inside to rest by the fireplace, waiting for my mother to serve him catnip.

"Why would he leave? Where would he go?" Mom has a habit of muttering to herself, and this morning the habit has peaked. Since the boutique opened at ten, she's mumbled continuously about Butterchurn's possible whereabouts. I hear the distress in her voice as she says, "Three days, three days." She lowers her head as though she's praying. "Mrs. Low says I need to leave tuna outside. She said when her cat was gone, a can of tuna brought it back."

I've met Mrs. Low once but don't see her as the type to leave a can of fish around her property. Both her spacious lawn and the exterior of her house are carefully maintained.

"And I think she poured some blue cheese dressing on top because her cat has a fondness for blue cheese. I don't think I've ever given Butterchurn blue cheese."

Pausing from hanging size-three dresses with other size threes, I volunteer, "I could make a flyer."

"A flyer?" Placing a finger along the side of her nose, Mom contemplates. Her gray head, at last, bobs in agreement. "We could put it by the Scones-and-Shop poster." She's referring to the large green poster about our event coming up later this month—shopping while enjoying free scones. I created that poster with a mixture of colored markers and tenacity.

"I see missing-pet flyers when I'm out on walks," I tell her as I head behind the counter and open the drawer that holds tape, scissors, Sharpies, pens, Post-It notes, and other objects we need throughout our days in the boutique. I don't tell her that seeing those flyers always makes me feel sad that someone is missing his or her pet. When I come across flyers that offer large rewards, they inspire me to look under bushes and in other obscure places. Although I'd love to be a hero, I have yet to find a missing animal.

"What color paper do you want me to use?" I ask as I note the various colors in the drawer.

"Yellow. Yellow catches attention."

Luckily, there are two sheets of yellow construction paper, so I pull one out. "Do you have a picture?"

"Of Butterchurn?"

"Lots of flyers have pictures of the missing dog or cat."

"At home I have the one you took last Christmas. I can bring it tomorrow."

At the top of the paper I use a black Sharpie to form bold letters: MISSING CAT. I place a square in the middle of the page for the picture of Butterchurn I'll insert tomorrow.

With the feather duster in her hand, Mom walks toward me to peek at my work. "Make the words large. Some of our customers can't read small print." Then with a swift flick of her wrist she lets the duster's thick gray feathers fly across the phone. Moving toward the shelves that hold scarves, she begins to dust those.

When the flyer is complete, except for the picture of Butterchurn, I hang it behind the counter with a sufficient amount of tape. "Do you like it?" I ask as she reads aloud.

"Lovely. You have such good handwriting."

Smiling, I busy myself with the task of ordering summer clothes for our store. This is a job Mom has recently entrusted to me, and I've grown to enjoy it. A colorful catalog from one of our suppliers lies open on the countertop. I see a much-too-thin model in a bright pink skirt and satin blouse and wonder if these skirts are items worth offering to our customers. I'm about to ask Mom her opinion when I hear her mumblings turn into, "I don't know why Butterchurn doesn't come home. I hope no one has . . ." She pauses; I look up to see that she's taken off her glasses and her eyes are red around the rims.

"He'll turn up," I assure her. I hate to think of my mother's world without her pet that curls against her whenever she reads Dickens or Hemingway. She and Butterchurn are like the historical landmarks a few miles away on the National Mall—you can't imagine one without the other. I slip behind the counter to embrace her, but she brushes past me and goes to the shelf of hats and starts to dust them. My mother is not big on affection. Apparently her father was the stoic type and Mom inherited his genes, while Mom's sister Dovie in Winston-Salem got enough affection for three people.

Flipping the pages in the catalog, I see a short sleeveless party dress. Reading the details, I note that it's made of rayon and silk with a scoop neck and a zipper in the back. The model looks great in the dress, and as I imagine myself in it, I wish I had a party to attend. Something with jazz music and silver trays of those tiny hors d'oeuvres where you wonder just what you're getting and then end up pleasantly surprised.

Feeling guilty about my self-centered thoughts, I turn to Mom. "Cats are able to live a long time on their own. Dovie told me she saw a show where a cat lived by herself for sixty-two days, just feeding off the land."

"We're in a metropolitan region," Mom says as though she needs to remind me. "D.C. has no place for a cat to feed off the land."

Again I see distress in her eyes, but I have no idea what to do. I want to hug her and tell her I love her. But she never accepts that kind of affection from me.

With her glasses once more on her face, she asks, "Could you make a few more?"

"Few more?"

"Flyers. I'll tape some up to telephone poles in my neighborhood."

As I pull more sheets of paper from the drawer, Mom nods with approval, her dismal mood seeming to brighten a little. By the time two customers enter the shop, Mom's face shows its usual liveliness. Guiding them toward the newest slacks and turtlenecks, she speaks of the way polyester and wool are blended in the pants. "A must-have," she coos. Holding up a cream-colored turtleneck, she fingers the fabric. "This is the most comfortable shirt you will ever wear."

The shop closes at seven tonight, with Mom heading home to a dinner of crock-pot beef stew—simmering on low since morning and one of her cherished classics—at her ranch house in the suburbs, and me to my apartment complex just five miles down the road. I think there's a pack of hot dogs in the freezer that will serve as dinner.

"Why aren't you putting on your coat?" my mother asks as we walk to where our cars are parked. "You will catch cold, Samantha. You are not in the Philippines anymore."

I smile, walk a little faster, and wave good-bye. The temperature has dropped since this morning when a light rain washed over the region; I'm anxious to get home before the roads grow shiny with ice. With the heater warming my car, I drive cautiously.

At the stone entrance to my apartment building sit rows of metal mailboxes lit by a pair of towering florescent lights. After parking my car, I unlock box number 214 with a tiny key I keep on the key ring with the one for my apartment.

The wind whips through my cotton blouse, making me wish I didn't toss my coat in the back seat of the car instead of putting it on. The mailbox creaks open, and I pull out a handful of colorful flyers, a power bill, and a large powder-blue envelope.

Clutching the mail with numb fingers, I tackle the envelope. After tearing it open, I pull out another smaller envelope and from its glossy interior retrieve a soft aqua piece of card stock. Silver lettering is imprinted on its face. Shivering, I read. Avery Jones and John Mason request the honor of my presence at their wedding. My mind does a few cartwheels, happy that Avery has found a man to spend the rest of her life with.

As though in a deliberate attempt to snatch the outer envelope, the wind seizes it from my hand and flings it against the frigid pavement. I reach for it. Like a heavy breath, a current of air blows it north, toward a set of rusty garbage dumpsters.

After a long day at the shop, I have no energy left to chase this item around, especially in this weather. I clasp the pieces of mail to my chest and climb the flight of stairs to my second-floor apartment. Inside, coolness greets me, causing panic to set in. Last year the heating unit broke and the maintenance man repaired it at two in the morning as I sat waiting at the kitchen table in my heavy coat and two pairs of socks. I crank up the thermostat to seventy and am relieved when I hear air blowing through the vents. On the back of a chair I find my trusty wool sweater—as shapeless as a lump of yarn. Even though it has two holes and will never be a fashion statement, it feels comfy and keeps me warm.

In front of the living room window I stuff my hands in my sweater pockets and watch the first snowflakes begin their dance across the lawn. Mom always says that when snowflakes dance, it's because they're happy to be birthed from pregnant clouds.

Hungry, I heat two hot dogs, squeeze mustard onto my plate, and wonder if there's a good movie on the Lifetime channel. Halfway through *When Harry Met Sally* I'm thinking of days past, when Avery and I were roommates at James Madison University and used to dip Twizzlers into cream cheese frosting for midnight snacks.

She was dating Perry Lesterfield then, and thought she was in love. With a mouthful of Twizzlers she confessed one night that she wanted to marry Perry even though her mother thought his ego was larger than Australia.

I finger the invitation and wonder how Mrs. Jones feels about her daughter marrying John. I liked Perry because he always had a good story to tell, even though I think some of them were embellished. I've never met John Mason.

Dialing the only friend I've kept up with since my days at James Madison, I reach Dexter.

"Did you get invited?" I ask as I run my fingertips against the raised script on the invitation.

"To what?" His first name is Howard, but he prefers to be called by his surname of Dexter.

"Avery's getting married in May."

"Twizzler Girl? I hadn't heard."

Because he's a good friend, I say, "Wanna go to it with me?"

"To Avery's wedding? Who is she marrying? Perry?"

"No, the invitation says John Mason."

"Where's the wedding?"

"Winston-Salem."

"North Carolina? Why's she getting married there?"

"I don't know, but it's where my aunt Dovie lives. I'd love to see Avery again. Want to meet me there?"

two

May 1993

As long as I have Paul Simon CDs and my own concoction
of sweetened lemon iced tea, I can drive anywhere. Leaving
Falls Church, I pop the 1971-to-1986 collection of Paul's hits
into my Honda's CD player. Soon the nostalgic words to "Fifty
Ways to Leave Your Lover" entertain me as my southbound
trip expands down the highway.

The day is warm with a gentle breeze, and just to feel air
sift across me, I open the window. Clouds spiral over the
sky, looking like mounds of whipped cream on a slice of
blueberry pie.

"Hop on the bus, Gus," I let my voice bellow, glad that I
still remember all the lines. I hope that singing will distract me
from my guilt over not being at the boutique today. May is an
active month for the store as women look for spring clothes and
Mother's Day gifts. I owe my friend Natasha dinner at Native

Thai Restaurant—my gift of gratitude for her willingness to help Mom at the shop today.

When the WELCOME TO NORTH CAROLINA sign flashes in front of me, anticipation nips at my pulse. At a gas station, I put twenty-six dollars of regular into my car, then find the restroom nestled behind a stack of wooden crates and cardboard boxes crammed with rolls of toilet paper. As I wash my hands, my reflection in the glass above the sink shows the apprehension I can't hide. It's been years since I've seen my friends from JMU. What will it be like? I recall a tale Dovie told me about a woman who went to a college friend's wedding twenty years after graduating and no one remembered her. Perhaps I should turn back.

Just hop on the bus, Gus. Set yourself free.

"You can do this!" I say. Adding scarlet lipstick to my mouth, I tell myself I have to carry through with this. I sent back the RSVP card saying Dexter and I would be there. With a surge of confidence, I cry, "You are going to have fun!" Then I straighten my teal chiffon dress at the waist as uncertainty lines the walls of my stomach.

Embarrassment replaces the fear when I open the restroom door to find a middle-aged woman waiting to enter. By the woman's smile, I know she heard my pep talk to myself.

I must be my mother's daughter. I often talk to myself, just as she has for so long—especially on those winter mornings after Dad died. *"Now, Cecelia,"* she'd say in a tone a general might use on his platoon, *"we are not going to cry today. We are going to act as though life is merely but a dream."* Then she'd hum a few bars of "Row, Row, Row Your Boat," put on her L.L.Bean slippers, and walk downstairs to make her morning coffee.

I pay for my gas, thank the cashier who wishes me a nice day in her creamy Southern accent, and then head out of the station. I wonder if Avery will serve Twizzlers at her reception. It would be like Avery to do that. She is not at all conventional.

As I sail down the interstate with Paul singing "Still Crazy After All These Years," I imagine what it will be like to see old friends from college. I think of the four of us who hung around together our junior year when we all got roles in JMU's production of *Our Town*. Dexter was Mr. Charles Webb, and my role was Mrs. Julia Gibbs, although secretly I'd hoped to be cast as the star, Emily.

I lost contact with my college friends when I was in the Philippines. Between caring for Mom and all the hours I put in at her shop, my days are full. Natasha and I manage to go on walks so I can justify the pair of Nikes I didn't buy on sale, but most evenings after work, I only have enough energy to watch a movie on TV and then the news as I drink coffee. Often during those hours, Aunt Dovie phones to talk about Mom.

"Come down to the wedding," my aunt said as I studied the invitation shortly after receiving it. Dovie's Southern accent was like Christmas carols in my ear. *"It will be spring and my butterflies will be at their best. You'll get some good photos, and of course you will stay with me."*

Dovie's old white house with metallic green shutters has four bedrooms. But we've all learned that just because you're invited to stay doesn't guarantee you'll get to sleep in one of the beds. Dovie brings home boarders like dogs carry fleas; some of the people take up residence in her house for as long as a year. All are wanting, according to my aunt. She is fond of saying that each one needs *"a little bit of loving and some good nutrition."*

I look at the directions she gave me over the phone. Dexter and I plan to meet at the Congregational Church on Cherry

Street for the wedding, then we'll drive together to the Winston Avalon Club for the reception. With about seventy miles to go before I reach the city limits, I replay Paul's "Fifty Ways to Leave Your Lover" as my mind dips around the world, southeast.

three

July 1985

I'm not sure if they enjoyed seeing us protest or if they really wanted to hear their American teachers sing, but often the Vietnamese refugees would pass a microphone to a group of teachers and beg them to belt out a little karaoke. One night in July, at the neighborhood outdoor café, under a sky spotted with dim stars, Van, a young Vietnamese refugee with chunky glasses, handed me the mic. He pleaded, "Miss Bravencourt, please. Sing."

The music blasting from his tape player was Michael Jackson's "Thriller," a favorite among the Vietnamese, especially the children. I complained, saying that was much too hard a song for a novice like me.

Under a single-bulb light hoisted in a tree limb by a tangled cord, Van rummaged through his collection of cassettes. "I will find song for you," he assured me while I prayed that we'd either be hit with a downpour or the batteries would give out. Finding a cassette, he fiddled with his large boom box until Paul Simon's "Fifty Ways to Leave Your Lover" piped out through the speakers.

In the humid night air, Van's face was beaded with sweat. He took a sip from his bottle of Sprite and again said to me, "Sing."

I looked at my friend Carson, who was seated at the table next to me with several refugees. He and I had walked to this café together after dinner because Van, a mutual friend, had invited us. The night was just hot and sticky enough to mess with my better judgment.

Accepting the mic from the young man, I went over to a piece of plywood—the "stage" where others had stood to sing. Reaching out, I took hold of Carson's hand—those long fingers that mastered the saxophone so skillfully—and pulled him to his feet as Paul Simon sang. I smiled and asked Carson to join me.

Carson was in a jovial mood. I knew this because all night he'd been laughing. I wouldn't have asked him otherwise because I hated the way he resorted to sarcasm when irritated. He grinned at the audience—one of his lopsided smiles—and as we shared the mic, he sung out, "There must be fifty ways to leave your lover."

I threw in a few *oohhhhs*, making the crowd clap. When we got to the chorus, we sang together, "Hop on the bus, Gus . . ."

We laughed afterward as we walked back to our dorms, using the main road that ran between the two phases—the sections that divided the camp. Our staff housing was a six-minute walk from the café on a good night, built between Phase One and Phase Two.

"You have a right nice voice." Carson's tone was soft, but there was a sincerity to it that made my heart tingle. "You should sing more often."

I was flattered by his compliment but didn't know how to respond. So I changed the subject. "Did you see how those kids danced while we sang?"

"I guess we should start regular performances." He grinned.

"Next time, you could play your sax." Carson often entertained the rest of the staff with his music. The three teachers who had brought guitars would join him, and we'd sing for hours in his dorm's living room.

That night was warm, too warm, and I was tired, yet happy. When I'd met Carson on my second day at the camp, we'd talked about North Carolina for half an hour. He was from Raleigh, and although I was from northern Virginia, I knew a lot about his state since my aunt Dovie lived there and I visited her often. The other American and Canadian teachers within our agency liked to tease Carson about his Southern accent, use of colloquialisms, and the way he would say the words *right* and *nice* together. But I was used to hearing people talk that way.

As we walked back to our dorms, Carson shared a childhood memory about the time his brother was angry with him and stuffed olives into his saxophone. It was after nine o'clock and the curfew for the camp had kicked in, so our voices were the only ones whispering in the night. Carson told me that, to this day, he didn't eat olives.

"Black or green?" I asked.

"Neither."

"What a shame! I love olives."

We stood together in the dusk, two teachers at the Philippine Refugee Processing Center—a refugee camp near Bataan for Southeast Asians who had fled their troubled homelands— thousands of miles from home. We'd both signed one-year teaching contracts with a U.S.-based agency called World Concern. It was my second month, and Carson's fourth. We were supposed to teach the children the essentials they'd need to become Americans.

When we parted to enter our separate dorms, his arm brushed against mine. I felt my heart flip in my chest.

You are crazy, I told myself as I went into my dorm, the creaky screen door shutting with a bang behind me. I greeted two teachers, who were in our living room talking about how hard it was to teach "Amerasians," the term applied to children of American soldiers and Vietnamese mothers. They told me they'd heard that in Vietnam, these half-breeds were discriminated against so violently that often the young children were forced to live on the streets. I had yet to have an Amerasian child in my classroom, so I just listened to the conversation, feeling pain in the pit of my stomach for every one of the kids.

In my tiny bedroom with a twin bed and one opened window, I turned on my fan and sat at my little desk, letting the whirl of the fan's blades circulate the air and cool my face. Then I got my toothbrush and tube of Crest and walked down the hall to the only bathroom in our dorm. I brushed my teeth as I looked at my face in the little mirror above the sink. *Carson has a girlfriend back home, remember? You've seen her photo—the one pinned to the bulletin board in his room.* She had thick brown hair, full lips, and her name was Mandy . . . or Mindy. Perhaps I wanted to pretend I didn't know for sure.

Stop thinking about him. I brushed harder. *Take photographs, go on walks, spend time with some of the female teachers. You came here to teach and help others; don't get your heart broken so that you'll be the one needing help instead.*

I brushed until my gums bled.

four

There aren't many things that make a girl's palms sweat and skin prickle like when she realizes she's in the wrong place. Once, I waited for Natasha at the Lincoln Memorial, but within a few minutes I realized we'd planned to meet at the Washington Monument and made my way across the National Mall to the white edifice, my apology as heavy as my panting.

More recently, last month I thought the UPS truck was delivering stock to the boutique when the packages actually weren't due for another week. I'd canceled a doctor's appointment and wore my tennis shoes to work, prepared for a day of moving boxes and sorting clothes onto their proper racks.

"Why did you wear your sneakers?" Mom asked me as she fastened her apron strings around her waist and watched me. From the apron's pocket, she withdrew a black licorice morsel and chewed it with deliberate thoughtfulness. She has stared at me while sucking on licorice for as long as I can remember.

My mouth opened to say, You know I always wear my tennis shoes when our new stock comes in, but I sensed something was wrong. I walked behind the counter and looked at the calendar of store events. That day's box was unmarked. Nonchalantly, I picked up the feather duster and ran it along the phone. I felt Mom's eyes still on me. My own were studying my shoes. "They're comfortable."

"You know it's next week our shipment from New York arrives."

"Oh, yeah." I coughed. When I'm caught off guard or a little uncertain, a good cough puts me at ease.

But both of us knew I was a week off schedule.

Like that day, I don't want to admit I've goofed. This is probably one of the most embarrassing mistakes I've ever made. People like me don't fail to read instructions or omit details. I took a quiz about my personality once, and the results showed that I'm organized, precise, a bit of a flirt, and like to have fun.

But inside the sanctuary of the Congregational Church, quiz results don't matter. What does is that I've never before seen this tiny wisp of a woman with blond curls and an ivory veil. As the creases in my hands grow moist, I stretch my brain to come up with a way that I might know her—and a reason she might invite me to her wedding. I scan the heads of guests for Dexter's. But he's not here at all.

The groom, dressed in a gray tux and a golden cummerbund, looks like he might fall over from anxiety. He lifts his hand to wipe a beaded brow as I notice that the best man is tanned and fit; most likely he worked out yesterday and will do the same tomorrow.

Trying to appear casual as I turn to my left and then right, I scope out the scene for a familiar face. There is a woman with spiked hair who could be Annette from my sophomore year, but she's blowing her nose into a pink tissue and Annette never cried, not even when we all watched *Terms of Endearment*.

I pull at my earlobes to make sure my tiny pearl earrings are still in place. I fold my hands, sit up straight, cross my legs, uncross them. I got an invitation to this wedding, didn't I? In my mind I go over as many details as I can remember about the day in February when the pretty card arrived. Standing at my mailbox, I took it out and opened it. I read the words. Avery Jones was getting married in Winston-Salem on Saturday, May 15 at 4:00 p.m.

I cough—two times—and the man in a dark blue suit and avocado tie seated next to me hands me a pack of Life Savers from his pocket. I take the roll and pull out a cherry-flavored candy. My grandmother on my dad's side used to hand me Life Savers in church, but since her death eight years ago, no one has offered me any. I pop the sphere into my mouth.

The man smiles when I return the pack to him. His eyes are a creamy brown and match a pair of sandals I have under my bed.

As the organist plays and a robust soloist sings in a nasal soprano about loving through a lifetime—or she could be singing about living through a love time—I swallow my discomfort, keeping the Life Saver from going down my throat. I hear popping sounds in my ears. The man next to me is cute. Before shifting my gaze toward the front of the church again, I note that his left hand is sans ring.

As the bride and groom proceed with their vows, I attempt to relax, but one thought keeps reoccurring: This is what happens to other people. Actors get paid to act out a scene in which a woman ends up at the wrong wedding. I expect someone to jump out from behind the minister, who wears a black robe, and shout, "Surprise! You're on *Candid Camera*!" With the sense of humor Dexter has, I wouldn't be surprised if he is behind this.

I consider grabbing my clutch bag and exiting this place, taking confident breaths as I go. Mr. Cute beside me has three others seated next to him, and to my right there are three women and two men. I think the expression *sandwiched* could be used here. I am sandwiched between guests without any wiggle room, and regardless of which aisle I chose, I'd have to trip over people in order to make my escape.

I've already stepped on Mr. Cute. Before the bride flowed down the aisle with her father, her bouquet's fragrance leaving an aromatic scent behind her, I accidentally bumped the toe of my shoe against this gentleman's shin. I apologized. Quickly, he whispered, "That's okay," and I was reassured that it was.

When the ceremony ends, the organist plays a lively hymn that sounds like a rendition of "Joyful, Joyful, We Adore Thee." Folks stand to chatter. The man and I introduce ourselves to each other.

As he shakes my hand with a firm clasp, he tells me his first and last name, to which I respond, "I'm Samantha." I don't believe in bothering with last names.

After asking where I'm from, he says, "Is the reception near here?"

"I'm not sure." At this point, there's little of which I am sure.

"Are you going?"

I've come all this way, and this guy is so cute. Standing, I nod.

"Great!" says what's-his-name. I wish I'd listened better when he introduced himself. I've already forgotten what he said. He rises, touches my shoulder. "See you there."

His smile reminds me of a vacation Mom and I took to Emerald Isle, off the coast of North Carolina. The sun baked my skin and spirits as I spent mornings on the beach, making treks into the waves every half hour to cool off. Mom joined me once, got caught in a wild wave, took in a mouthful of salt water, and then laughed. She hadn't laughed since Daddy died. I remember looking up at the bright sky and thinking that we were going to be all right. Daddy was in Heaven, and we were going to be able to eat chocolate and strawberries with cream and laugh, even when adversity came in the form of a large wave.

As the wedding guests make their way through the packed sanctuary toward the door, I see a skinny man in a velvet top hat videotaping the guests. I like to look my best, so I give my so-glad-to-be-here smile.

Brown Eyes says that his father and Avery's dad were in the Korean War together. I want to say that Avery was my roommate during our first year of college, but I'm in church, and as my eyes shift over the stained-glass windows—scenes of Jesus feeding the hungry—I don't feel I can lie. Clearly, this is not the right Avery Jones.

His eyes flicker with light from the pillar candles that stand in each window. I am soaked up in warmth like when I see my mother's dogwood blossoms on a spring day.

"I'll see you at the reception," I tell him.

"Sure thing," he says.

I hope I remember where I parked my car.

five

After two glasses of champagne and letting the band's tunes from the seventies mellow my disbelief, I don't care that I know no one here. The day is like a dream—soft clouds, a faint breeze, and the sky is bluer than the coneflowers in Dovie's garden.

I'm seated at a table dressed in white linen under a canopy of more white. Taylor—I did have to ask him for his name again—and four couples share the table. Clear vases of day lilies, yellow carnation buds, and miniature roses decorate the center; the outside patio of the Winston Avalon Club is adorned with ceramic planters of impatiens and petunias.

So far I've learned that the bride and groom are from Winston-Salem. The farthest north they've been is Richmond, but that is about to change. Tomorrow morning they'll fly to San Francisco for their honeymoon. "San Francisco," chirps the bride, dragging out the name of the city into eight syllables.

I hope they'll think I'm Taylor's date and then won't try to figure out the real reason I'm here. I watch their narrow bodies swirl onto the dance floor like two twigs on a windy day. They are still in their wedding attire, although she's removed her veil, letting it hang in a bushy fir tree by the steps to the clubhouse.

Taylor asks what I do. He has a tiny mole on his left cheek, and when he smiles it scrunches close to his eye.

"Well . . ." I clear my throat, look into his eyes, and begin. "I work at a boutique in Falls Church, Virginia, with my mom. She owns the place, and we sell women's clothing and jewelry." I explain how my friend Natasha is covering for me so that I can be here today and that she and I like to walk for exercise and then buy chocolate ice cream from the vendors near the Washington Monument. I even toss in the fact that Natasha not only walks but also runs, and on a good day she can run a mile in six minutes.

"So do you ever jog?"

"No, not me. Jogging makes my teeth hurt." I tell a story about my great-uncle Charlie, who learned to sprint so that he could get away from the law. The police in Winston weren't fond of his moonshine operation. When he bought a Harley, getting away from the police became easier for him. "At least that's what they tell me about him," I conclude. "I saw him a few times, but he was pretty old by then. He'd been in World War II, and his war stories and those about escaping from North Carolina officers sort of got mixed together."

When Taylor laughs, I'm fueled to continue. I share another tale about my late uncle who once told an inquisitive cop that he was making molasses in his basement. As I pause, Taylor excuses himself and walks toward the fountain, avoiding a girl in pink bows and black patent leather shoes.

It is then that I realize I've been talking too much. I haven't asked him anything about himself; I only answered his questions about me. When will I learn? Flirty and chatty only go so far—after a while a guy wants to know that I'm interested in him. I walk along the stone pathway from under the canopy into the sunshine, blinking from the brightness.

A woman in high heels tries to chase a boy in a gray suit. The child runs toward the gurgling fountain, giggles, and turns to see if his mother is following. He shrieks as she attempts to get him, grabbing his collar. He slips from her reach and squeals as she cries, "Jeremy! Get over here now."

Walking farther, I pretend to admire the roses in the gardens that surround the patio. While the large yellow blooms look lavish and healthy, I like the tiny buds still waiting to expose their petals. A few of the buds have aphids crawling up their sides, and as I circle away from the gardens, I feel like those bugs, skittering about aimlessly. I consider going to my car to get my camera, and then, when a light wind scatters a candy wrapper along the stone walkway, a revelation hits me.

When I opened the wedding invitation months ago, the envelope it came in was blown away by the wind. What if that envelope was addressed to someone else? Of course it was. It was probably for the tenant who used to live in my apartment—the person who was invited to this wedding instead of me. Her name is Joanna Lawson, and she gets the good mail. Sometimes I'll scratch *No longer lives here* on the envelopes with a pen and slip them in the mailbox at the post office. What a coincidence that Joanna and I both know a woman named Avery Jones.

Back at my table, strewn with cloth napkins, half-eaten platters of finger sandwiches, and plastic champagne flutes, I'm aware of another revelation. I will never attend a wedding and reception solo again. It's too lonely. Dexter better have a good excuse for standing me up, I think, and then I wonder what

Aunt Dovie is doing. I guess I'll find out soon enough. Digging into my bag, I retrieve my car keys.

"Do you know when they plan to cut the cake?"

It's him—Taylor.

Pleased that he came back, I smile. "Soon, I think."

Shielding his eyes from the afternoon sun, he asks, "Would you like to dance until then?"

I blurt, "What do you do?"

Confusion lines his face.

"I mean, for a living. Work. I never asked."

He leads me onto the dance floor. "I'm a P.I."

"A what?" I lean in and wait for his reply. The band seems to have increased their volume as they play Chris de Burgh's "Lady in Red."

"Private Investigator." He places his arms loosely around my waist. "Licensed."

"Like Magnum?" My arms gently encircle his shoulders. It's been years since I've danced with anyone.

"Almost. I live in Baltimore, not Hawaii."

If he investigates for a living, can he tell I'm not supposed to be here?

"Well, you're still young," I tell him. "Perhaps you'll end up in Hawaii one of these days."

As he draws me closer to his chest, I rest my head against his shoulder, sleepy from the champagne. He's like an angel, saving me from heading back to Aunt Dovie's completely frustrated.

The next song is Madonna's "Borderline," and as the band belts out the words, "You just keep me hanging on," my throat grows dry. As I follow Taylor off the dance floor, I reach for another glass of champagne, flash a smile at the private eye, and watch those from our table rise to dance. Their animated bodies blur as my memory, like a descending elevator ride, takes me down to a time when I thought I'd never be able to let go.

six

August 1985

My first class of Vietnamese students was graduating. I'd attended other graduation parties at the camp, so I knew what to expect—laughter, noise, and an unsurpassed frenzied energy. But this night in August, I wasn't just a guest, I was the one in charge, responsible for keeping order.

The eight and nine year olds were wild with excitement as they rushed into my dusty classroom, their flip-flop-clad feet sliding across the slate floor. Mothers and fathers brought in trays of *chagio*, the spring rolls filled with minced pork that I'd grown to love, and vermicelli noodles topped with basil and mint leaves. Bottles of soda filled my teacher's desk. The classroom was electrified with children dressed in their best, racing around the benches. Music played on a large Sanyo tape-radio player, and some students chanted, "Dance! Dance!"

Bao, my teacher's assistant, was punctual, arriving just on

time at seven. He wiped his brow with a large handkerchief and stood in a corner under a chain made of strips of forest green paper. I told him that we would eat first and then hand out the graduation certificates. This was the protocol for the graduation ceremonies that took place after each nine-week course ended.

Bao stood silently, his stare somewhere over my head.

"Could you please tell the children?"

He sighed.

I wanted to sigh, too. I wondered why he'd been assigned this position as a teacher's assistant when for the past nine weeks he'd done little in the way of helping me teach. His eyes seemed distant, and one day when I entered the room and approached him with a question, he jumped, his whole body shaking.

I concluded he had some physical condition or that he was nervous. That was before I heard his story of his voyage from Vietnam. After I learned how his wooden boat had been seized by pirates on the South China Sea and his father murdered, I let him stand and be removed from reality. During break times, I encouraged the children to not give me so many bottles of Sprite but to take some over to him. They followed my suggestion only to have him refuse their offerings. Then the students would return to my corner of the room to place the declined bottles on the top of my desk, lining them up like a row of tragedies.

When Carson and Brice arrived at the graduation ceremony, I wanted to hug them. They were my sanity—other teachers, ones who spoke my language. My students scooted toward them and chattered in Vietnamese. Carson replied to their questions during the brief pauses. He'd studied Vietnamese from a college buddy at NC State. The friend tutored him in exchange for Carson's help with calculus.

Brice just smiled as the children watched him, and that was enough; the girls all thought he was "very nice teacha." It helped that his hair was thick and blond, and his eyes were the color of a summer sky over Virginia Beach.

The ceiling fan squeaked as I called the group to silence. I was wearing a mint green skirt and white blouse, my bare arms and legs tan from treks to the coast in nearby Morong. The flip-flops I had on were a gift from Avery Jones. The night before, I'd gone to one of the billets to get a manicure and pedicure from a young Vietnamese woman, the older sister of a student. She'd soaked my feet in a metal pan of cool water that soon turned brown. My feet were subject to dirt every day, and keeping them clean while wearing flip-flops was a feat I never mastered during my year in the Philippines.

"Welcome," I said after turning down the volume on the cassette player. "Welcome," I repeated and waited for the children to find places on the wooden benches. "First we will eat." Sweat moistened my armpits.

Carson grinned at me from where he sat next to Brice, and my arms relaxed against my sides.

"Dance, Miss Bravencourt!" Two girls in short skirts and smeared lipstick were adamant.

"We will dance after." I clapped my hands to get everyone's attention, a gesture I felt was the epitome of a schoolteacher, and the results were worth it.

The thirty-one students were silent until I said, "Let's eat!" Then there was boisterous laughter and wiggling.

We served the fried spring rolls and noodles in baby-blue plastic bowls and passed around bottles of Coke and Sprite. Seated on the wobbly benches, we enjoyed the meal. Later, there were pieces of candy and gum that seemed to come from nowhere, although I had a suspicion that fingers brought them into the room through the slatted wooden windows. Faces peered in to watch us from the narrow openings. Lien, one of the Amerasian girls, was among them. She entered the room once, but her brother Huy shooed her out. So she returned to observe us from the outside.

When dishes were cleared, it was time for the graduation certificates, followed by plenty of pictures taken by a man in the camp who had a camera. After developing these, he would charge a peso for each one.

I had filled in the name of each child from the roster I'd been given before the term started. I decided to let Bao pronounce the names instead of butchering them with my incorrect pronunciation. Handing him the certificates, I asked, "Could you please read the names?"

He withdrew his handkerchief, used it to take the moisture from his face, and said, "Yes."

I told him to read the names as I had written them—the American way—the first name, followed by the middle name, and then the last name, not the other way around as was the Vietnamese custom. We were, after all, trying to prepare our students for how things were done in the United States.

Bao's hand shook, rattling the certificates, and after reading the child's name from the first one, he gave me the document. The first student, Ma Le Tung, came up to accept it. She squeezed my hand and then we posed for a photo. The teacher's assistant coughed and read the next student's name— Huy Hong. With his black hair slicked back from sweat, the young boy stepped forward, his smile showing his pride in his accomplishment.

After the certificates were handed out, I asked the class to pose for a photo. "But before we do this," I said, pausing so that Bao could translate, "I want you all to know that I have enjoyed teaching you. Some of you will be leaving soon to go to America. Your family's name will appear on The List and that will mean you are set to go, done with camp life, and on to a new adventure. I wish you the best."

The students clapped then, a few of them shouting, "Thank you, teacha! We see you in American!"

Although their flubbing of the English language made the teacher in me cringe, I let them bellow out phrases for a while and then asked them to come to the front of the room by the chalkboard for the group photo. Instructing them to cram together until I could see them all through my Nikon's viewer, I said, "One, two, three!" and let my camera capture their smiles.

When the music turned loud, the children dispersed around the room, crying, "Dance now!"

As the teacher's assistant went out to smoke, some of the girls pulled Carson and Brice onto the floor, and then the kids yanked on my hands until I was on my feet. Madonna's "Borderline" shimmered off the wooden walls, the students enjoying the beat but having little idea what the words "You just keep pushing my love over the borderline" actually meant.

Under a squeaky fan we laughed and danced with the students. Carson and Brice caught my eye, clearly enjoying themselves. The rats in the rafters had grown quiet and remained that way. I saw only one scamper over the ceiling beams before hiding from my sight.

Lien again tried to enter the party, but Huy told her to go home. That much Vietnamese I understood. She exited the classroom, only to perch herself by one of the window slats and cackle like the hens in Dovie's backyard.

When Bao entered the classroom again after smoking a few cigarettes, three girls—my favorite students in this particular class—surrounded him. After a few minutes, he nodded and said to me, "They have gift for you."

From a secluded spot under a bench where discarded pairs of flip-flops were scattered, one of the girls retrieved a narrow cardboard box about the size of a wallet. Carefully, she came over to where I was seated being photographed by one of the camp photographers with six boys, who all scrambled to be in the picture with me.

Circling me, the children watched as I opened the gift. Lifting the lid, I pulled out a white piece of material embroidered with delicate yellow flowers that looked sort of like tulips. The material unfolded and I saw that it was a handkerchief. Looking into their sweaty faces, I said, "Thank you!"

The girls giggled, and then a boy asked a question.

The girls giggled again.

I stood waiting as the girls and Bao talked. Sure enough, a translation followed. "Her mother sew this for you." Bao indicated the smallest of the threesome.

"Oh, thank you." I fingered the cloth and attempted a bit of Vietnamese. "*Cam on ban.*" I hoped I'd pronounced the phrase correctly. "It's very nice." I smiled at the small girl. "Tell your mother thank-you for me."

But my words were overcome by the increased volume of the tape player. Michael Jackson was singing "Thriller." Again.

"Turn it down." I raised my voice to be heard. After no reaction from my students, I tried again. "Turn the music down. Please."

Huy rushed over to the bench where the tape player sat, and soon I could hear myself think again.

Before the curfew of nine, there was time for one more dance, and after Stevie Wonder's "I Just Called to Say I Love You" ended, I shut off the music. I sent the students home to their billets with their graduation certificates, wishing them a good night. A few were not eager to leave; they wanted to dance some more.

"We come back tomorrow and see you, teacha," a number of them said.

I just smiled, knowing that I had two days off since my classes had ended for the term. My new classes wouldn't start until Monday.

Alice J. Wisler

Later, after sweeping the classroom of candy wrappers and forgotten straws, Carson, Brice, and I walked home together, back to our dorms. Rain started to fall, and then it came down like a waterfall. We found shelter on a small roofed stage in a grassy area. The stage had been built for the performances that happened periodically in the camp.

Carson wiped water droplets from his face; a few glistened on his eyelashes. On the stage he began to dance and sing, "You just keep pushing my love over the borderline!"

Brice and I laughed.

"If your parents could see you now," I said. "They probably think you came here to be a dignified teacher, not a performer."

Carson sang a few more lines from the song and then looked my way. "I know what my mother would say."

"What would that be?"

"Oh, she'd tell some story about how I was born singing. No one else in the hospital thought my wailing was a song, but I was different from the other newborns. I actually sang."

I smiled as he talked, trying to imagine what he looked like as an infant.

"And your father?" asked Brice. "What would he say if he could hear and see you now?"

Looking at the floor of the stage, Carson replied, "Not sure. But I think he'd smile at me from Heaven."

I felt my stomach tingle.

Carson's eyes were soft, vulnerable.

"He died?" I asked.

Carson blinked a few times and lowered his head.

"How long ago?" I edged closer to him.

"Three years."

"That's just like yesterday!" The words flew out a bit louder than I'd intended for them to sound. "I mean," I quickly added, "it's so recent."

His tears did not shock me, but Brice had to look away. I reached into my skirt pocket and handed him my new handkerchief. I thought he might push it aside, but he took it and wiped a tear that was suspended on his cheek.

"I lost my dad, too," I said as the rain slowed its pace against the roof. "He was only forty."

Carson put an arm around me and drew me to his chest.

We stood like that for a few moments, and then when the rain relented, we all three stepped out from the enclosed stage and continued our walk home. The air was saturated with dampness. No one spoke. Even Brice was without his usual jokes.

As we approached our agency's main building where the admin staff worked, I asked Carson if he had a picture of his parents. He told me he had one in his room but first had to go into the admin building to get the lesson plan book he'd left there earlier.

I watched him go inside, noting the way his broad shoulders filled his shirt, and then, realizing I needed to use the bathroom, went inside after him. The women's restroom held two stalls, and I remembered to use the one that locked.

When I came out, I couldn't find Carson anywhere. Figuring he was waiting for me outside, I looked around for him. When I didn't see him, I went toward his dorm across the soggy grass.

The building was quiet. I heard a radio softly playing a song in Tagalo from someone's room. I walked down the narrow hallway, and when I got to Carson's room I paused. His door was ajar; I knocked, listened, and then pushed it open. I could wait for him in here. I sat on his bed, looked up at the photo of Mindy, and frowned. She had a perky smile, a wide set of teeth, and straight brown hair, giving her a model-like quality. I sat there recalling all the things he'd told me about her—her fondness for onion rings and Caesar salad, how she had a golden retriever named Ranch and a blue parrot from Peru.

My eyes roamed to the left of his single bed, to his desk that held a cassette player, a lopsided stack of paperbacks, and two red pens. We liked to kid him about his love of red pens, the ones he used to grade his students' papers. I stood to straighten the books, and as I did, I saw a lined sheet of paper crammed with writing. Something told me that I knew better, but I swatted that thought away like I swatted at flies and mosquitoes when they buzzed around my dorm room. I picked up the paper and read: *She's naive and, although pretty, she isn't intelligent.*

Curious, and yet at the same time hearing a warning signal rap against my mind, I continued. Above this line was my name—my name in Carson's handwriting. He always wrote in all caps, even when he wrote on the blackboard in his classroom. His Es were like backward 3s. This letter's penmanship was a little sloppier than usual, and each letter jarred against my heart.

But I couldn't stop; my feet were like lead, and although I knew I shouldn't, I read more.

Samantha's a big flirt, and you know how I feel about flirts. She's someone to hang out with when there's not much else to do.

My whole body grew hot. Shaking, I lifted one foot from the floor, hoping it would move. When my legs cooperated, I left his room. With a quick turn down the hallway I found the front door, bumping my forehead on the doorjamb.

It was the first night in a long time that I couldn't breathe due to tears. I could have used my new handkerchief, but Carson had forgotten to give it back to me.

The next day at breakfast, Carson asked about the bruise on my forehead. He also wanted to apologize. "After going to the administration building, I looked around for you, and when I didn't see you, Brice and I decided to play Ping-Pong."

"Oh? Who won?" I feigned interest.

"I lost."

So did I, I thought. The impact of the words from his letter to Mindy still punctured my heart. I wanted to discuss how his words had hurt me, but how could I admit I'd read his letter? So I searched for something else we could talk about—the New People's Army, the Vietnam War, the horrendous actions of the Vietcong, or, on a lighter note, how my aunt Dovie raised monarch butterflies. But, as I sipped my coffee, I figured it would all be wasted on a man who didn't find me intelligent anyway.

seven

As I drive to Dovie's after the reception, the sky is bountiful with pastry-puff clouds lit by a shimmering sunset. My feet are sore from dancing and I look forward to taking off my heels. At least in the Philippines the flip-flops we wore didn't hurt my feet, even after dancing or walking across the camp from one neighborhood to the other.

At her chalky white two-story I park my car in the gravel driveway. Milkweed, her overfed tabby cat seated on the olive green love seat on the screened-in porch, greets me like a purring Southern hostess.

I walk up the three brick steps and knock on the front door, which stands heavy against the right side of the porch.

Within seconds, Dovie appears in a periwinkle cotton dress and fuzzy polka-dotted slippers. "How was the wedding?" she asks after she kisses my cheek, tells me I've gotten taller, and ushers me into a kitchen smelling of baked bread.

Beanie, looking thinner than the last time I visited, stands in a pair of jeans, an oversized flannel shirt, and an apron, stirring a tall pot with a slender spoon. "Long time no see," she says.

"Hi, Beanie." I know not to embrace her; like my mother, Beanie resists affection. She claims it's the Chinese side of her that causes her to be this way. "Smells good," I say as I peer into the pot and see chunks of chicken and flat noodles in a velvety broth.

Beanie grins. If you compliment her on much else, she won't accept it, but she does believe she can conjure up a tasty meal.

It's nearly eight, just about dinner hour for Dovie and her boarders. Dovie collects people like squirrels store food. Young, old, wealthy, or miserly, my aunt takes them in. Beanie's history is long and dark, although I have never heard all the details in sequence.

"So, how was the wedding?" Beanie pauses from her stirring like she's waiting for a good story. "Tell us."

"It wasn't the right one." I place my clutch bag on a clear spot on the counter.

"What?"

"My friend didn't get married." Pulling off my heels, I sink into a cushioned kitchen chair. Through my panty hose, I see blisters on both of my big toes and wince.

"Oh," says Beanie. "Those kinds of happenings do happen, so I've heard. The bride gets cold feet and never makes it to the wedding."

"She made it. She just isn't my friend." Standing, I put my shoes over to the side of the room near Milkweed's food dish and begin to remove my stockings.

"You and her got in a fight?" Beanie's face lights up like one of the pillar candles I just spent an uncertain hour with. "That

43

can happen. There are times I know I shouldn't, but something comes over me that I just can't get ahold of and tame. Did you win? Must have because you still look pretty good."

"No."

Beanie frowns. "Are you hurt?"

"Only my toes."

"I hate it when someone steps on mine. Makes me all kinds of annoyed."

Beanie is like a train out of control. I put an end to all her illusions, something we often have to do when she wants to believe the nonsensical. "No, no fighting."

"But she's still not your friend?"

Moistening my lips, I start to explain. "I thought that my friend Avery was getting married and that she'd invited me to her wedding. But there must have been some mix-up. I didn't know anyone at the wedding and she wasn't even—"

Aunt Dovie interrupts. "*Catalina Afternoon*."

Beanie's brow is furrowed. "Really?"

I search their faces. Is this some kind of code? "What?"

"*Catalina Afternoon* is a movie we saw. Friends end up at the wrong wedding." She hands heavy pottery bowls one at a time to Beanie.

Well, I think, if I'd known that a movie title would set Beanie straight, I would have tried that tactic from the first.

Beanie takes a bowl and ladles soup into its deep opening.

Deciding I should make myself useful, I take the bowl and set it at the table.

Beanie hands me another bowl. "Those friends didn't realize they were at the wrong wedding until it was too late. Tragic, in an odd sort of way."

As we sit at the kitchen table with a spring breeze blowing through the opened window, my aunt offers a prayer of thanksgiving to God.

After her joyful "Amen and amen!" I ask, "So, you've seen a movie about someone who ends up at the wrong wedding?"

"Yes," says Dovie as she passes me a basket of sliced oat-meal bread—one of her homemade specialties. "Only there was violence at that one."

"Three die," Beanie adds. "Or was it four?"

Aunt Dovie refers to movies and TV shows as examples for just about anything. "Let's see," she says as she butters her slice of bread with swift motions. "There was the daughter. Then the sister-in-law."

"And the hamster." Beanie lets a laugh escape from her mouth like a secret.

"Two hamsters?" asks my aunt as she chews a crust of bread. "Wasn't one a guinea pig?"

"No, the neighbor with the John Deere had the guinea pig. It got caught under the wheels."

"Was that before or after the rehearsal dinner?"

Before Beanie can comment, I say, "Well, no one died today. In fact," I add, smiling, "I met someone."

"Ohhhh," says Beanie as she lifts a heaping spoonful of noodles into her mouth. Chewing, she says, "I've heard about that, too. Two people end up meeting at a wedding and then get married themselves right quick."

He did ask for my number. Beanie and my aunt discuss the plot of another movie they saw about a hairdresser and prison guard who met at a wedding and later married in the Grand Canyon.

I watch the lacy daisy-colored curtains billow at the window as a hefty gust of wind enters the kitchen. I close my eyes and think of the way Taylor made me feel as we danced. When I let my mind drift back to the conversation at the table, Beanie says, "Well, the church is full of hypocrites."

Dovie asks, "Now, what makes you think that?" It is not

the first time Beanie has said something like this. Last time I drove down for a weekend, she complained that church people wouldn't accept her due to three failed marriages, her crooked left eyebrow, and her past obsession with Johnnie Walker.

"Folks look at me like I shouldn't be there."

"Nonsense," Dovie cries. "The church is one place where everyone is welcomed."

"In theory."

In theory is one of Beanie's favorite phrases.

"In theory all should feel cozy warm at church worshiping God. But those folk choose who is welcome and who is not."

"Why don't you feel welcome?" I ask.

Beanie spits a fingernail out of her mouth. " 'Cause they don't like women who used to dance for a living."

"How do you know?"

"I get these vibes."

Beanie chews her nails, trimming the ragged edges with her teeth, and when a piece winds up in her mouth, she lets it dangle on her tongue and then forces it into the garbage can when she stands to get us dessert. I start to decline dessert because I had two slices of wedding cake, but then I see Beanie take a strawberry cheesecake from the fridge and know I must have a piece.

"What color am I?" asks Beanie as she stands at the counter with a knife in her hand.

"You are a mixture of everything." Dovie's words are warm.

She nods. "I am a product of a black father, Hispanic mother, and great-grandfathers who were Chinese and French. I should be welcome everywhere because I am every woman."

Dovie starts to hum "I'm Every Woman." Beanie laughs, her left eyebrow twitches, and then we all have a generous slice of cheesecake.

As we place dishes in the dishwasher, Beanie tells us she went for a job interview at the local Wachovia branch and "feels this might be my ticket to employment." She describes how the manager interviewing her kept sniffing and that finally Beanie offered her not only a tissue but some of her allergy medication.

"I helped her with what she needed and now I hope she'll help me."

"Do you like bank work?" I ask.

Beanie laughs. "I like having money in the bank. Right now my disability check is not big enough to keep me in underwear."

"Disability?" After I say it, I wonder if it's rude to ask why Beanie is on disability.

The phone rings, and since I'm standing beside it, I answer. Little, a woman who's been living with Dovie since Thanksgiving, has finished her shift at Wendy's, her bicycle has a flat tire, her head hurts something awful, and she needs a ride home—quickly, before any other parts of her world cave in. "We'll be there," I tell her because I know that's exactly what my aunt would say to her.

Under a moonless sky, the three of us pile into the cab of Dovie's pickup with the cracked windshield and begin the drive to the Wendy's where Little works.

We park in a spot by a florescent light that flickers off and on like a Christmas tree. After five minutes, a short, middle-aged woman with a round face and a crop of curly blond hair comes from the restaurant toward us. She's balancing a cardboard carrier in her tiny hands.

Beanie rolls down her window. "What you got?"

Carefully, Little hands her the cardboard through the window. The contraption holds three yellow cups with lids. "Frostys for you," says Little.

Beanie steadies the milk shakes on her lap. "Going to fire you," she warns, "if you give food away." She pops a straw into the lid of one of the cups.

Little smiles, the gap between her two front teeth extensive.

Squeezing into the back with me, she says, "Who says I'm giving food away? These, I found in the trash can." She speaks slowly, each word a feat to get out of her lips.

What I know about Little is that, growing up, she was constantly interrupted when speaking. Apparently, due to her speech impediment, it took her a while to get her thoughts out, and her six siblings and parents were not patient. Dovie and Beanie have learned to be patient, and Little seems to like that.

Little rests her head against the windowpane. From her uniform, the aroma of fried food fills the car. "I thought eleven o'clock would never get here." She eyes me and says with a smile, "Good to see you, Sammie Girl."

Beanie hands me a Frosty. Then she sips from another. "Pretty good for dumpster food. And trust me, I would know."

Beanie was homeless for a few weeks before she found sanctuary at Dovie's house. She claims that all she had to her name at that time were her cloudy reputation, a stale loaf of pumpernickel bread, and a folded dollar in her shoe.

I shove a straw into the hole in the plastic lid and take a small taste. The coolness of the contents is soothing against my dry throat.

As Dovie pulls her truck out of the deserted fast-food restaurant's parking lot, she passes her milk shake behind her to Little. "Take a sip."

"Oh, no," says the woman. "I don't want to get sick from dumpster food."

Laughter and slurping carry us back to Dovie's. Dovie and Beanie talk about some 1950s movie about milk shakes and a lovers' quarrel.

I think of Mom and feel a tinge of guilt that she's alone in Falls Church, so far from this happiness that I feel she could use. Yet I remind myself that Dovie always extends the welcome mat to her. Mom chooses not to accept, claiming she has a new life in Falls Church and wants to put her past in Winston-Salem behind her. I heard her tell Dad once that her childhood was not pleasant due to her parents' fighting and dysfunction. Now, as a woman in her sixties, she prefers to stay away from Winston and its many reminders. Dovie, on the other hand, tells me that Winston-Salem is the only place she feels at home. *"Why,"* my aunt has been known to repeat, *"Winston is where I feel the most alive and feel God's hand on my life."*

eight

I trail behind my aunt, sleep still in my eyes. The early service at her church this morning was lengthy because there were several prayers for a youth team preparing to travel to Haiti. After the prayers ended, I had to force my eyes to stay open. I longed for my grandma's Life Savers, always a sure way to keep me from dozing off in church. Now there's no time for a nap; we're preparing for a butterfly release.

In Dovie's fenced-in backyard are two matching wooden sheds—their only differences being the color of the roofs. Dovie rattles a set of keys as three hens scurry from our path, making their way to the apple tree. These clucking birds all have names—Breakfast, Lunch, and Dinner—affectionately given, but not with the intention of actually consuming any of them for the meal they were named after. Dovie purchased them solely for their egg-laying capabilities.

As the noisiest hen pecks at a tray filled with grain, Dovie unlocks the first shed with the sloping red roof. Gently, the door creaks open. We enter, shutting the door behind us.

The interior is damp and cool, with peculiar odors. A tiny window about two-feet square lets in rays of late morning sunshine. This hatch, as she calls it, holds a crudely built wooden table that is crammed with branches sticking out of dirt-filled pots. Large green plants spray out over the floor. In the early spring, this is the hatch that holds lots of about-to-change caterpillars. The larvae stick to these branches until they're ready to become butterflies. Today there are just a few late bloomers. One she studies and wonders aloud why it has not broken from the silky sack and tried its wings.

"Are you too cozy inside there to even try to come out?" she asks it as one would question a child. "Come out, now, honey. It's a fascinating world."

The next shed is a colorful wonderland. This is where Dovie keeps the monarchs that emerge in the previous shed. She takes them out of their first home and places them in this hatch—the same size but with more greenery and better sunlight. I quickly close the shed door and step into the beauty of life. Dovie stands with her fingers outstretched, and within minutes one of the insects has landed on her thumb. She smiles at me and then motions for me to pick up the wire cage on the left side of the room. Slowly, trying not to disturb anything, I reach for the tightly woven cage, open its tiny door, and place it on the table in the center of the shed. Dovie covers the butterfly with a hand and swoops it into the cage.

From the time I was small, Dovie taught me the cycle of the monarch butterfly, but all I fully recall is that each female lays her eggs on the underside of the milkweed leaf. After the egg is laid, the caterpillar is born, and basically goes through his short days and nights eating leaves and pooping. Dovie's explanation included that the caterpillar was then ready to pupate and form a chrysalis and spin a silky thread around him until it was time for him to emerge as a butterfly. When I was small I thought the words were *puke* and *crystal*, so for a long time I held an image of these minute, furry bugs puked into crystal dishes and then the puke magically turned into a silk sac that, for some reason, hung upside down, possibly because it was still too nauseous to stand upright.

I watch Dovie lock the shed door, place the keys in her pocket, and then pick up the cage filled with monarchs. We make our way to the driveway where her truck sits. With a gentle swing, she puts the metal cage into the cab. Then we hop in.

Little left for work about the time Dovie and I headed into town for church. As she drained her mug of coffee and finished two slices of toast spread with coconut butter—a product she discovered when she lived in Dundee, Florida—Little said she hoped not to be working next Sunday. "I can go to church with you then," she said as she wiped her mouth with a napkin. "I do miss it when I have to work the morning shift. Asking whether or not the customers want lettuce and tomato on their burger is not at all as glorious as singing hymns to Jesus." Then she stood in her uniform outside by the porch, waiting for a coworker to pick her up and take her to Wendy's.

Although Beanie has no plans for the day, she declined Dovie's invitation to join us for church, and now she refuses to come to the butterfly release.

"I don't do silly sentimental things," she states. "Besides, I have some potatoes I need to boil for dinner tonight."

"So where are we going?" I ask Dovie when we are about a mile out of her driveway. With a firm hand I secure my camera on my lap.

"Today it's the Amber Grove Cemetery."

I nod, recalling having previously heard the name of this

particular cemetery. Uncle Charlie is buried there, with a head-stone that has a motorcycle engraved in it. My great-uncle liked to ride fast, and my relatives tell me that his Harley out-sped any police car on the Forsyth County squad. He also made moonshine, borrowing a recipe from Scottish immigrants who settled in the Appalachian Mountains.

"This is a group of parents who have had children die," Dovie tells me.

My tongue freezes like one of the orange popsicles I ate growing up.

"They ask me to come to the cemetery every year for a but-terfly release. You'll see that parents of deceased children have a strong connection to the butterfly."

The truck hits a pothole; we steady ourselves. "Why is that?"

But my question gets lost as we pull into the cemetery and Dovie sees a mass of balloons. "Balloons, too," she says as her truck bounces along the uneven narrow road toward dozens of parked vehicles.

She finds a spot for her truck under the branches of a mam-moth oak tree and then turns to me. "Balloons and butterflies are free." Her eyes hold flecks of light. "And when they sail into the sky, they eventually disappear. But their beauty remains in our hearts. These parents feel the connection."

I sit a bit longer as she makes her way over to a group par-tially veiled by an assortment of colorful bouncing balloons. The people are all wearing dark blue T-shirts with white words and some sort of indistinguishable emblem. I watch Dovie speak to a woman and then my aunt comes back toward the truck, her strides long and purposeful.

She takes her cage of butterflies out from the back of the cab and smiles at me. "We're at the right place and on time."

Reluctantly, I follow half a dozen steps behind her with my camera strapped around my neck.

A woman in a white ball cap greets Dovie. They exchange words and then my aunt places her butterflies on top of a mossy tree stump.

As I get closer I see that the shirts this group is wearing read *The Compassionate Friends*. The design under the words is two hands with an image of a person above them. I wonder if this is some kind of religion. Standing beside my aunt as the others in the gathering talk quietly, I observe faces. If it is a religious sect, their god must not be too generous because no one looks happy.

Feeling awkward, I take a few steps back to see a fresh bouquet of red rosebuds, purple violets, and yellow daisies in a plastic vase by a tombstone. Lowering my eyes, I read the inscription: *Gone too soon. Kara, our beloved daughter.* The dates are too close together. I calculate that the girl lived only nineteen years.

One woman in the cult-sounding shirt makes an announcement. A man with a fuzzy beard reads from a sheet of paper, steadying it as the wind flares its edges. I strain to hear over the cooling breeze; it is something about how children live on in our hearts and in our memories.

Next, Dovie steps into the center of the crowd, carrying her cage. She tells about the monarch butterfly, its life cycle and how it has been silent in its silky sac but now is a beautiful creation. She explains how this new life is a testimony of God's creativity and of His love of nature. She lets the crowd know that these butterflies will be released soon and begin a journey just like the children who have died are now on a new adventure in Heaven. "And like each of you," my aunt says with a gentleness to her voice. "Each of you is becoming someone new as you learn to cope and adjust to a life without your precious child."

As she says these words, a few burst into tears. They are quickly embraced by others within the group.

When Dovie finishes speaking, she lifts the latch on the cage. Slowly, a lone butterfly emerges from the door. It flits toward a gray headstone, then makes a left, and relaxes on a vase of day lilies. Another winged insect sways out, unsteadily at first, and then gains momentum. When nothing else peeks out of the cage, Dovie rattles it a few times. We wait; a silence prevails like it does when a bride appears from the back of the sanctuary, ready to make her gentle way toward the altar.

There is a fluttering of wings and then, like a stream of wonder, a cluster of butterflies lift into the air.

Anticipating a great photo op, I poise my camera as the people raise their heads, point into the air, murmur. The ones who have been crying wipe their eyes.

With wings in motion, the insects sail into the waft, a scattering of orange and black.

Some of the creatures aim high; others simply circle the area. One lands on a woman's shoulder. A tiny one, appearing dazed by the sunlight, gently perches on a teen's head, bringing a few smiles from the crowd. I get a picture of that.

Observing the scene as a bystander, I try to take it all in—the program, the words, the tears, and the new realization that these people are not in a cult but part of a parental support group called Compassionate Friends. When a man stands directly in front of me, I see the rest of the wording on his shirt: *Supporting Family After a Child Dies.*

This is the first time I've been to a release this somber, and also the first time where the butterflies seem so energetic. Last time I was at an outdoor wedding with Dovie, the monarchs she hoped to release took over half an hour getting out the cage door. My aunt had to reach inside the compartment and take each one out individually because guests were growing tired and their catered lunch was ready to be served.

As I think back to that day, I see one of the black-tipped

monarchs coming toward me. I watch as it spins around my head, lingering. I hold out my finger the way Dovie does, hoping it will rest upon it.

Instead, it swoops around a small tombstone—a burst of color—and then is gone.

I look near my shoes to see: *In loving memory of Oliver Branch. Gone from us, embraced by God.*

The words on the tombstone are like a jab at my heart. Oliver. I bend down and touch the name. It was my dad's name. I feel my pulse race, like it has the energy of the butterfly. My throat fills and I cough—twice. Realizing that I'm kneeling at the grave of a person I don't know, I stand. My camera smacks against my chest.

Then, aimlessly, I step over the large, gnarly roots of the oak.

My attention goes back to the crowd and my aunt just in time to see balloons rise into the air. The round, colorful balls allow the stream of wind to boost them into the breeze, and then they are high above our heads.

I watch as a sobbing woman holds on to a balloon string. The man beside her secures an arm around her shoulder until at last she releases her balloon. Tied to the end of the string is a pink object; it looks like a miniature stuffed bear. A torrent of tears gushes from the woman, and I expect her to fall into a heap on the ground. I shuffle away, my back scraping the oak's trunk. Tripping on a thick root, I use my hands to brace myself against the trunk. The tickle in my throat has expanded, filling my chest.

As my breath comes in little gasps, I think perhaps it was not a good idea to come here today. Like Beanie, I do not do well with sentimental stuff.

nine

With my head bent I tread across the grass, the taller blades rubbing against my shins, to Dovie's truck. In the reflection in the passenger's window, I see a woman with smudged mascara. I rub the marks from under my eyes and wish it were time to go home.

As the oak's leaves banter in the wind, I watch the gathering of parents grow smaller. Cars and vans back up and head out of the cemetery gates, leaving behind the light aroma of dust.

The wind holds a lonely timbre; just half an hour ago I relished its coolness. Leaning against the truck, I consider getting in, hiding. Another part of me wants to run to a place where no emotion can find me, and certainly where my father's voice does not resound in my ear.

"My little Samantha, I love you to the Milky Way and back."

Footsteps cause me to turn and see a boy in a pair of faded

jeans and a *Chicago* T-shirt. I sense that he's been studying me. "Hello." A smile forms, and he steps closer.

He looks to be about fourteen, with eyes like chocolate kisses and a build that is slim yet muscular. "Miss Bravencourt!" he says with zeal.

I merely look down at my hands. Is he talking to me? No one calls me Miss Bravencourt. Not since—

With hope shining in his eyes, he asks, "You remember?"

Remember? I scan his face, and something jars within my memory.

"I was at PRPC with you." He takes out a worn leather wallet and from it produces a color photo filled with children. There I am in the middle—the only Caucasian. I'm holding a Coke bottle with a straw protruding from its mouth. Youthful Vietnamese faces surround me, including this boy's.

"Yes. Of course!" I cry. "You're Huy!"

I scrutinize the photo with intent. There I am. Smile wide, my light brown hair frizzy due to the humidity, purple flip-flops—a going-away gift from Avery. The wraparound skirt and a cotton blouse I have on are from the casual shop where Mom used to work before opening Have a Fit.

The boy eagerly says, "Come to Saigon Bistro tomorrow for lunch."

"What?"

"Please, teacha." Although his English has improved since he moved to America, I notice that this plea sounds just like it did inside the walls of the refugee camp, before Huy and his family ever saw a North Carolina pine. He continues, "My mother and father have a restaurant here. Saigon Bistro. You come tomorrow. You eat."

"I'm leaving for my home tomorrow."

"Then come tonight."

I haven't been in the remote village snuggled among mountains since 1986, and yet, right here and now, I feel transported back to the camp. It's as though time has not moved at all, as though we are still in that isolated region where the Laotian, Cambodian, and Vietnamese cultures intertwined, and, in my opinion, came nowhere close to transforming into Americans. We teachers tried to get the children we taught to see knowledge as a powerful tool. Often, as we showed visuals of American homes, describing how microwaves functioned and what a vacuum cleaner was, the children watched us like deer caught in headlights. We explained about traffic lights and subways while they remembered shiny rice paddies and corner markets with fresh chickens strung up by their feet. Even though the sounds of Huey helicopters and mortars rang in their ears as they recalled daily life in their war-torn countries, they still remembered the good about their homelands.

Huy was one of those kids who never gave any indication he would be able to adjust to life in America, and yet, now, here he stands. If this were a movie, either Michael Jackson's "Thriller" or another one of the many songs of the eighties that used to play on boom boxes across the neighborhoods would be on the soundtrack.

But this is reality; I know because anxiety finds its familiar place in my throat. I cough.

Pointing to his wristwatch, Huy says, "Seven o'clock."

I look at this boy and remember the feel of teaching him inside my classroom, and so much more. I observe him for a moment as the wind rustles a large maple's leaves. I wonder how life has been for him and his family. I want to ask more questions but feel a bit embarrassed since it must be obvious that I've been crying. "Okay. I'll be there." I nod, and when I do, he smiles.

A group of Asian boys hovering around a clearing that holds a park bench look our way. They call to Huy in Vietnamese.

"See you tonight," Huy says to me and leaves to join his friends. He is still smiling; I remember Huy is the type of person who smiles no matter what.

When Dovie makes her way to my side, she says, "Did you see a ghost, honey?"

"Yes. No. What?"

Tossing the empty cage into the truck, she tells me to get in.

A monarch butterfly dips around a weather-beaten angel statue. The insect is clearly one of Dovie's, still lurking, evidently unafraid to be alone. I wonder if it realizes the rest of its group has long since gone, flown off, away from this somber place.

Through the open window next to the driver's seat, my aunt calls for my attention. "Samantha! I'm fixin' to leave now."

Her voice jolts me back to this moment. With slow movements I climb into the truck. "What time is it?"

She peers intently at me as I secure my seat belt. "What happened to you?"

"What do you mean?"

"I just have this sense."

If there's one sure thing about Dovie, it's her ability to sense things. Once you know that she has a feeling about you, there's no choice but to tell her whatever it is she wants to know.

"I met a refugee." Removing the Nikon from its position around my neck, I place it on my lap.

"I know you did. I read every newsletter you ever wrote when you were over there."

"No, I mean here."

Her eyes study me just as Huy's did moments ago. "Here?"

Looking across a field of headstones, I nod.

"Well, my goodness."

As she starts the truck and backs out, exhaustion fills my body. I note the time on the dashboard: 3:34. Perhaps I'll be able to take a nap before my dinner event this evening.

Through the windshield I see Huy. Breaking from his group, he stands at the edge of the road near an ivy-covered stone statue of a man in a robe with outstretched arms—Jesus, I assume. We pass Huy, who waves and calls, "Bye, teacha."

"Is that the refugee?" Dovie asks.

I manage a small wave, still uncertain about the dinner I have committed myself to. "He was my student in the Philippines."

The truck picks up speed as she steers it out of the cemetery. "A good one?"

"What do you mean?"

"Did he cause trouble?"

I think of Huy and his sweet manners. His sister, Lien, was the problem, but I don't feel like telling Dovie about that right now. "He was a good kid."

"And now he's here in America. My, my." She chuckles and then starts to sing "In America" from *West Side Story*. She surprises me because she knows every one of the verses and she lets them carry us all the way home.

ten

september 1985

When my new class started at the end of August, Huy's sister, Lien, arrived the first morning wearing dark sunglasses, a white T-shirt with *Hello Kitty* printed in pink across the chest, a pair of gray pants that were loose on her slim hips, and a red ball cap that read *Saint Louis Cardinals*. Her orange hair stuck out from the brim.

We knew each other because of Huy and Carson. I often saw Lien inside Carson's classroom just a few doors down, talking with him in Vietnamese. Her boisterous laughter rang through the thin walls when he'd mispronounce a word or phrase. Many times from my wood-slatted window I'd see her traipsing from the marketplace with a bottle of Sprite or Coca-Cola in her hand. I always knew it was for her favorite teacher, the one she called "Mr. Borra."

But neither Carson nor I had ever had Lien as a student. Then in August her name showed up on my class roster. I asked our director if perhaps she could be assigned to another class, and he said, "Samantha, we cannot pick and choose."

Even after the class started, Lien spent more time with Carson. She literally clung to him, placing her arms around his waist and talking in her native tongue. I knew that the Amerasians in the camp had a tendency to be a bit unusual, and in our staff meetings we commented on how they drew attention to themselves with their behavior.

One afternoon, Lien, her sunglasses on the top of her head, seated herself on one of the benches next to the slatted window. After I told her to get rid of her gum, she swallowed it, opened her mouth so that her tonsils showed, and announced to the class that the gum was gone.

As I stood in front of the class teaching, she kept her gaze aimed out the window. When she saw Carson walking toward his classroom, she jumped up and ran out, calling, "Mr. Borra! Hello!"

The third time she did this, I reprimanded her. "Tell her," I said to my teacher's assistant after she returned to the classroom, "she can't act like this in America."

The TA looked at Lien, sighed, and then said to me, "She is Amerasian." His nose twitched as he said the term. "Amerasian is noisy. No good."

"She go to Monkey House," one of the boys seated on a bench in the back of my room chirped. The Monkey House was the camp's house of detention.

Lien heard this comment, and pulling back a clenched fist, rammed it into the boy's arm.

His reflex was to reach toward the wall to steady himself. Then he muttered in Vietnamese, threatening to hit her.

"Stop now!" I made my voice harsh. Walking toward the culprits, I commanded, "Sit down. Everyone. Now."

Lien gave me a hug. "Teacha, I no go Monkey House." Sticking out her tongue at the boy, she called him a liar. *"Sao!"*

"Enough!" I glared at her. "And it's Mr. *Brylie*, not Borra. Mr. Ba-rye-lee." I pronounced Carson's last name slowly but in a loud tone.

"He my friend," said Lien as she sat by herself on a bench.

"He is a teacher, and you need to respect him." I nodded to the teacher's assistant to translate.

He said something, but I had no indication whether or not he was interpreting the way I wanted him to. He was not Bao; Bao had seen his name on The List, the sheet of paper periodically hung in the camp, announcing the people or families soon to be released from the camp to travel to their new country. This new TA liked to talk, and I think he also liked to embellish whatever I needed him to translate.

Marching to the blackboard, I picked up the only piece of white chalk and wrote RESPECT, using all capital letters just like Mr. Brylie did.

The teacher's assistant said a few words that got the students to listen. I told them what it meant to respect another person, but as I looked at Lien, who was squirming in her seat and picking at a scab on her elbow, I doubted any part of it was getting through.

Later that night, Carson and I went out to dinner at the sandwich place in Vietnamese Neighborhood Nine. All of the neighborhoods carried a number from one to ten. Some neighborhoods housed only Laotians, others only Cambodians, but the majority of the neighborhoods were populated by Vietnamese.

Low tables were strung together, with a few chairs surrounding them. We ordered two bottles of Sprite and two

French-bread sandwiches. The baguettes were baked on-site and then slit open and spread with some unidentifiable meat paste, sliced cucumbers, and seasoned carrot strips. This meal was a welcome change from the food in the mess hall.

"Why does Lien have to be so unruly?" I asked as I slid onto a wobbly chair around a small table that shifted whenever I did.

Carson's long legs bent awkwardly as he tried to fit them underneath the table. Giving up, he stretched them out, away from the table. "Considering how she was treated in Vietnam, I think she's doing well."

"What do you mean?"

"Well, she was thought of as *bui doi*."

I desperately wanted to appear that I knew the meaning of those words, that I was as fluent in Vietnamese as he was. I'd had a couple of lessons from a young woman named Song, a name I liked because it was easy for me to pronounce, but usually after half an hour of teaching, she'd revert to English and say, "Tell me all about America," and I'd do just that. She'd come to the Philippines via the United Nations Orderly Departure Program, which meant her family had been able to legally and safely make their way out of Vietnam. She had no horror stories of being at sea and tormented by pirates during a rocky voyage.

I looked into Carson's eyes and said, "Explain what those words mean in English."

"*Bui doi* means 'dust of life.'"

"That's horrible! Why would they call them that?"

"Anger."

"At what?"

Our sandwiches were brought to us, wrapped in paper. Hungry, we began to eat.

After a few bites, Carson took a sip of his Sprite and then said, "The Vietnamese Communists were mad that the American soldiers slept with their women and then left behind a whole bunch of kids who didn't fit in. Kids that are mixed blood like Lien are unhappy reminders of the past."

Sympathy rose in my chest as I took in Carson's explanation. "But it wasn't the children's fault."

"No, it's never the fault of children. But they usually suffer the worst. I've heard from many of the Vietnamese here that kids like Lien are often raped and forced into prostitution."

I silently prayed that I would be more kind to Lien and asked God to coat me with a double dose of patience for her. I glanced over at Carson, thinking about how nice he was. He got along with everyone, even Lien.

A few of Carson's students came over to our table to talk, and as he broke into their native tongue, I quietly nibbled at my food. I hoped after we ate we'd go back to the dorms, play a few games of Ping-Pong, sit close and watch a video together. Perhaps he would recant the words he'd written in his letter to Mindy and whisper in my ear, "Sam, I was wrong about you."

My anticipation was destroyed when he finished his sandwich and said, "I need to get back to my room. I owe Mindy a letter."

I watched the way the light from a bare fluorescent bulb lit up Carson's hair and wished that he did not affect me the way he did. He's just a man, my head told me. Just a mere man.

Carson helped me to my feet and paid for our meal.

We walked past the market, closed for business until the next morning and, using the main road that ran behind the billets instead of the path that went past the living quarters, made our way into the next neighborhood. A young boy, distinctly Amerasian with a mass of white-blond hair, waved to us, calling, "Good evening! Hello! How are you today?" as though he was practicing his English.

In one of the Cambodian neighborhoods, we watched the women wash their clothes at the community faucets, located behind the row of wooden billets. Seated on their haunches, they scrubbed, their long colorful skirts hiked up to expose their calves. The water gushed out, spewing over their plastic flip-flops. Nearby, small boys and girls wearing only pants played with empty tin cans and string. A few bubbles from the suds floated into the air, and a girl chased one, crying out in Cambodian something that sounded like a musical chant. A thin woman in a rust-colored skirt stood to pin some wet clothes to a clothesline strung out between two bamboo poles. I'd taken pictures of scenes like this, fascinated by the way the refugees were able to function in the midst of these adverse conditions.

As Carson and I approached our staff dorms, I knew that he would soon enter his room and sit at his desk to compose a letter to Mindy. I remembered something Avery and my other friends at James Madison used to say about guys we found attractive: *"The good ones are usually unavailable."*

Carson's unfavorable assessment of me still caused me heartache, but I also believed that he had to care about me. His eyes often looked my way from across the room at staff meetings, or over the heads of others when the bus took us to our classrooms to teach. I wanted to believe that I meant something to him, regardless of my lack of intellect.

eleven

Beanie says she'll go with me. She listens as I retell the story of Huy and how hospitable his family was to me in the refugee camp. But perhaps she can hear something in my voice or see a dab of worry in my eyes. Mom tells me that I've never been good about hiding my emotions. And of course those who know me best know that when I cough twice, this is a sign that I'm feeling out of my range.

Beanie announces that the potato sausage casserole is ready to bake, but she'll wait until we get home to place it in the oven.

I try to dissuade her. "You're busy. I don't want to impose on your evening."

"Don't be a stack of hay. No imposing." She finds room for the casserole on a shelf in the fridge. "How well you know these people? Could kill you if you go alone."

"They were my friends," I say.

She just ushers me out the door. "You've already been to a wrong wedding this weekend. You don't need any more trouble."

In my hand I have the address. Shortly after getting home, I realized I could not fall asleep for a nap, so I checked the Yellow Pages for the location of Saigon Bistro. I scribbled it on a piece of memo paper from the pad Dovie keeps by the kitchen phone.

As we drive in my Honda, I breathe in, aware of the tobacco smell that permeates the air as we drive near the R.J. Reynolds factory. Although the odors were different in the camp, something about this night sends me into visions of rickety billets sprawled over the neighborhoods, women in sarongs, men in trousers coming out of the community bathhouse, children playing with bottle caps and string, and an occasional stray dog or chicken roaming through the marketplace. Fondly, I recall how much I enjoyed Vietnamese food—crispy spring rolls and bowls of thin, white noodles.

Beanie settles in the passenger seat once she finds the station on the radio she likes. As we thread through town, someone requests a song and wants it dedicated to his girlfriend. Billy Joel's "Just the Way You Are" fills my car. "Ahh," says Beanie. "This is the one song every woman wants sung to her."

"Really?"

"By the right man, of course."

I say, "Of course," and then wonder why. I've never cared much for Billy Joel, although I suppose I wouldn't mind if someone could love me just the way I am.

Beanie is in a thoughtful mood. "Sometimes we get so involved in our lives—you know, the tedious day to day. We lose our sight and push away what we want."

"You mean like our hopes and dreams?"

"Sort of." She scratches her neck and then chews on a fingernail. "It gets pushed underneath all our living."

I start to ask Beanie what she would like in her life when I notice we're almost there. I brake to make a sharp right turn into a parking lot. With my tires screeching I just miss an RV on its way out.

"Careful, Sammie Girl."

Pulling into a space by a tow truck and an apple red Mustang, I feel my stomach sink toward my knees.

Beanie says, "This where we need to be?"

I take the key from the ignition and squeeze it till my fingers are numb. "Yeah. This is it."

Exiting my car, we walk toward the restaurant poised between two others that have Vietnamese lettering on their clear glass doors. The silver and gold shingle—a bulky piece of metal that dangles in front of the row of stores, the left side raised higher—reads *Saigon Bistro*. As we walk by the sign, I have the urge to push up the right side to make it level. Mom always says I like the dress racks to look even.

"Saigon Bistro," Beanie reads, enunciating each syllable. "Sure hope they have something to wet my whistle."

I'm conscious of my labored breathing.

Beanie looks at me through narrowed eyes. "You can still run. I'll never tell."

I see the stern faces of Huy and Lien's parents from seven years ago when Lien was accused of stealing in the camp. The rift created from that incident will not leave my mind. Yet that was seven years ago. Perhaps that's been enough time for forgiveness and a clean slate. After all, we are in America.

"I'll be okay," I say.

Seeing her reflection in the bistro's glass door, Beanie fluffs her dark hair with a quick gesture. "I look a mess."

Swallowing nervousness, I say, "You look fine." Then I push on the door. It won't budge. I give it another attempt, pushing harder.

"Maybe you pull it."

I pull but still have no luck getting inside.

Just then a man in a white dress shirt approaches and unlocks the door from inside the restaurant. He smiles, exposing a set of uneven teeth. "Welcome. Come in, please."

Inside the sparsely lit interior, the faint aroma of fried pork greets us.

Immediately, I'm drawn to an object—a Vietnamese dress— a slim blue *ao dai* encased in a glass compartment, displayed on one of the stark walls. A cream-colored scroll with Chinese characters fills another wall, and below it is a metal shelf with five tiny faint-blue teacups. A watercolor of a lone purple iris hangs by a straw hat on the wall farthest from where we stand.

The man who met us at the door has disappeared. Beanie and I stand and look at each other.

Beanie breaks the silence with, "This reminds me of a movie where this family got trapped in a restaurant."

There's a rustling sound and a door opens under the metal sign that announces *Employees Only*. A young woman in jeans and a pink shirt saunters toward me. "Miss Bravencourt!" Her voice rings like Dovie's wind chime.

She is tall and pretty. Her nose, the one they call the American *mi*, is still freckled.

Grasping both of my hands in her slender ones, she giggles. "You the same!"

She's wearing silver earrings, two gold bracelets, and a chain with a cross around her neck. There is a dusting of gray eye shadow on her lids and a hint of sweet perfume in the air around her. Her hair is brown, wavy, and cut just above her shoulders. Gone is the dull orange color of her refugee camp days.

Huy appears from the same door. He's changed his clothes and is now wearing a button-down white shirt, with the sleeves folded halfway between his wrists and elbows—the same look he wore at the camp, along with hundreds of other Vietnamese. Behind him follow an older man and woman, their hair streaked with gray. I swallow to hold back the anger that tries to rise, the emotion I felt the last time I saw this couple. I greet them as warmly as I can—Lien and Huy's parents.

They smile, gold teeth glittering under the blush of the yellow lantern, a globe suspended midair above a large bare table.

"Nice to see you again," Lien's mother says, her words halted like Little's. "Sit, eat." She coaxes us toward the table.

A flashback zings though my mind to when she said the same thing when we were guests in her billet, scrunched around a coarsely built table as rain gushed down the alleyways and moths huddled for comfort around a single light bulb.

The man pulls out a chair and motions for me to sit. I oblige. Another chair is pulled out for Beanie.

I introduce her. "This is Beanie, my friend." I then slowly give Huy's name, pronouncing it as I learned so that it sounds like *Who-ee*. Motioning toward Lien, I say with emphasis, "And this is *Lean*."

"Nice to meet you," says Lien, her English sounding better than it ever did in my class.

They bring us each a bowl of hot noodles in a beef broth—*pho*. On a plate placed between us are four dainty fried spring rolls adorned with a few sprigs of mint and basil leaves. Little dishes of a pickled green substance arrive next.

"Thank you," I say. The little Vietnamese I once knew evades me under these circumstances.

Chopsticks appear, and glasses are filled with ice and Pepsi.

I cringe when Lien and her mother start to argue. Huy brings their raised tones to a halt and then sheepishly offers, "They want to know if you would like iced coffee."

Lien looks at me and says, "You don't like, right?"

She glares at her mother until I tactfully say, "Well, I did like it when I drank it at your billet." Then she frowns at me. I don't want them to fight here like they often did in the Philippines. So, thinking quickly, I add, "But I prefer this soda." I wrap my fingers around the frosty glass of Pepsi.

Huy translates, and when both women smile, I am grateful that he's done his job to smooth over any potential argument.

Beanie guzzles her Pepsi, tries to stifle a burp, and then mutters, "Excuse me."

I gesture to her to try a spring roll and then pick one up with my set of chopsticks.

Huy disappears into the kitchen and seconds later brings a shallow bowl. The smell tells me that it's *nuoc mam cham*, the fish sauce my students liked and were always eager to have me try when I was invited to their billets for a meal.

The spring roll is delicious, and to please Huy, I dip the end of mine into the sauce. The aroma of the vermicelli noodles entices my senses and I draw the bowl closer to the edge of the table to take a slurp.

"You like?" Lien is at my elbow.

"Yes." I pick out a slice of roasted pork with my chopsticks, chew, smile some more.

Huy tells me to add some fish sauce to my broth, so I take the spoon from the bowl and with it add a teaspoon to my broth.

Beanie tries one of the spring rolls, stabbing it with a lone chopstick.

I scan the restaurant. No one is here but us. "Where are your customers?"

Lien says, "We close on Sunday."

"We're at church every Sunday," explains Huy. His English has improved, too.

"I learn about Jesus at church," says Lien. "Forgiveness, and how do you say, grace?"

"Yes," I say. "Grace."

"And Grace is name of one of my friends from school, too," she tells me with a giggle. "She helped me change my hair."

Not understanding at first, I question, "You mean she helped you dye your hair."

Confusion lines Lien's face.

"Color," I say. "Change the color of your hair."

Lien laughs, lightly massaging the tips of her hair. "Yes, I use Clairol."

"So, how is school?" I ask after a moment.

Huy explains that he's in seventh grade, a bit behind where others his age are due to his "bad English."

"Lien, and you?"

"I try but I take long time."

She has to be twenty or older now. "Have you graduated high school?" The second the question slips from my lips, I want to take it back.

But there is no need for me to worry. Proudly, Lien replies, "Last year."

"That's great!" Years ago I never dreamed that this wayward child would ever complete anything but a fistfight.

Lien excuses herself while her parents grin and refill our soda glasses. Lien's father, Minh, wants to make sure we are not too hot or too cold.

Speaking for both Beanie and me, I say that we're comfortable. To Huy I say, "I thought you were scheduled to relocate to Chicago." Lien often told me that she and her family were headed from the camp to Chicago, where a relative was waiting for them.

Huy says, "Chicago was too cold. We have an uncle here, so after one year, we live in North Carolina."

Chi, whom I recall being rather quiet, boldly uses her English and says, "Chicago too much snow."

"Yes," I agree. "Chicago can get bitter in the winter." Then

I wonder why I chose the word *bitter*. Perhaps I am still trying to teach English as a Second Language.

I continue to eat, knowing all eyes are on me. I glance at Beanie to see that she's fussing with her chopsticks.

Lien returns to us. "He's not in town," she says as she flops onto the chair beside me.

"Who?"

"Carson."

"What?" My stomach flutters like the wings of Aunt Dovie's butterflies.

"I leave him message." Her face transports me back to seven years ago when she told me that she'd skipped class to hang out with a twenty-year-old Vietnamese boy her father forbade her to see. "He not home so I talk on his answering machine."

"You called Carson?" Every pore feels warm.

"Yes."

I stop eating, my pair of chopsticks suspended over my bowl. "But . . . why?"

"He wants to see you. He your friend, right?"

Was. I feel the word in my mouth, tasting metallic. *We used to be good friends, but things change. You certainly know about change, Lien, so let's just leave it at that.*

But Lien continues, her hazel eyes bright. "Miss Bravencourt, I never thought I see you in America! We get Carson here and we can have party."

I fake a smile. It stretches across my face like putty, but it's still not genuine.

"Mr. Carson want to see you, I'm sure."

"Isn't he married?" Certainly by now he has made his vows to Mindy from Raleigh.

"No, not married!" She giggles. "He single. Like you."

Single. The word stings. When the refugees used it back in the camp, it was suited for me. Now, at age thirty-one, the word feels wrong for me. I should be married by now, my days busy with mopping the floors, making crock-pot dinners, changing junior's diapers and reading to him from the pages of *The Pokey Little Puppy* and *Goodnight Moon*.

I ask Huy to get a fork for Beanie. She has struggled with her set of chopsticks long enough. But once the fork is in her hand, I decide she's not too fond of her Vietnamese meal by the way she only rearranges the pieces of pork and vegetables in her bowl. I suppose she's saving room for her sausage potato pie.

"Miss Bravencourt," Lien says after she and her parents have exchanged a few strident words in their native tongue. "You live here now?"

"No. My friend and aunt live here. I live near D.C."

"Washington, D.C.?"

"Yes."

Beanie twists a lock of her black hair so tightly that I see her finger turn blue. She sips from her glass and then plays with her straw paper. Seeing that she's not going to eat any more and that my bowl is empty, I say that we must leave now.

Beanie nods and a softness returns to her face. Quickly, she stands.

Lien says, "Thank you for coming." Then she asks Huy to take a picture of the two of us together. She wraps her arm around my waist and laughs as Huy uses the Kodak camera. "One more," she tells him, and this time she presses her cheek against mine. The flash goes off again, causing dots to float across my vision.

Their parents thank us for coming in the best English they can muster. Even the man who opened the door for us enters the restaurant to thank us.

As I drive back to Dovie's, my mind is crammed with memories. I want to talk about my days in the camp, the meals similar to tonight's that I enjoyed in the billets, the tales of anguish I heard from many of the refugees, the excruciating heat, the respite at the beach in Morong, the walks in the neighborhoods, and the thrill of hearing a student pronounce a word correctly in English. My memories take me to the administration building, where we teachers often sat at tables under a fan that never provided enough cool air.

As Beanie studies her fingernails, I say, "We used to have staff meetings each Tuesday afternoon. They went on for hours because our director, Dr. Rogers, loved to tell us how we needed to be extra careful about the New People's Army hiding in the brush." Nearing Dovie's neighborhood, I continue, "Once a group of us wanted to go to Mindanao for a vacation, but he stopped our plans, saying that area of the country was no place for Americans because of the NPA's activity being heavy in that region." Shuddering, I wonder why I'm thinking of this military wing of the Communist Party on a night like this. As Dovie has been known to say, our minds can be strange places.

Beanie is still thinking about the meal served to us at Saigon Bistro. She says, "My ancestors are Chinese, but I don't care much for their food."

The next day I set out to leave early. I told Mom I'd be back at the shop by noon. Natasha will need to go to her office, unable to cover for me. When the clock radio alarm goes off, I feel it is one of those mornings that I could literally sleep until noon.

As I carry my suitcase downstairs, I see Dovie on the porch with Milkweed. Her opened Bible rests against her lap, her reading glasses perched on the bridge of her nose. The whole scene is Norman Rockwellesque. I shed my suitcase and open the screen door to join them on the porch.

Smiling, she closes the book and puts it aside. "Morning, love. Did you sleep well? I heard you up early."

"I slept well, thanks. Thanks for letting me come here."

"You know you are always welcome." Rising from the love seat, she reaches over to the small bamboo table where a large Tupperware container sits beside a thermos. She hands me the container.

As I look through it, I see bologna sandwiches on thick slices of oatmeal bread with Swiss cheese. "Oh, Dovie, this is so sweet of you."

Milkweed purrs, jumps off the cushion, and nuzzles my leg.

Dovie takes the box from me, picks up the thermos, and says, "Hope the tea isn't too lemony. I must have squeezed three whole lemons in there."

I now know that the drive back to Falls Church will be delicious and that makes me smile.

"Nourishment is vital for your long trip," she says as she follows me to my car. I often wonder why Dovie never married or had children. I think her maternal nurturing instincts are strong.

"How has your mother been?" she asks. I think she's asked this at least twice already over the weekend.

I reply as I have before. "She's doing really good." I know that's not proper English, but there are times I get tired of hearing myself use the word *well*.

"Now, if that cancer comes back, you make sure I'm the first one you call. I know Cecelia won't be calling to tell me."

The sun is just rising over the two sheds in the backyard. I hear the hens cackling.

I place my suitcase in the trunk and the food she has given me in the passenger seat. "Thank you for everything." I make my embrace tight.

"Love to your mother. Drive careful now. Call me when you get home." She kisses my check, and I catch the faint scent of peppermint, cloves, and worry.

twelve

It feels *right nice* to be back at the shop with Mom. As much as I often want a break from these walls and from customers who can be hard to please, whenever I return from time away, I know I'm where I'm supposed to be. There is something almost magical about running your own business, especially when that business is successful. The man who runs the business next to ours, Sanjay, calls it "the American dream at its best."

I drove straight to the boutique, not even stopping at home first, and made it here by eleven fifteen. During the trip from Dovie's, my thoughts flitted like her monarchs—waves of color that soared into memories—some nostalgic, some bothersome. I saw Taylor's face in my mind and felt his arms around me as we danced at the reception, and smiled just thinking of the way he smiled. Shortly after that, Carson's face crept in, and although I tried, I couldn't push away the array of emotions I felt the last time I saw him. The details of the day he left the camp wouldn't release from my thoughts.

Once I arrived in the southern tip of Virginia, I saw Huy and Lien's faces and went over bits of conversations we had at the cemetery and restaurant. When I stopped to eat a bologna sandwich at a rest area and drink from the thermos of lemon iced tea, I grabbed a mystery from the trunk of my car—the fourth in the series called *The Busboy Mysteries*—and became engaged in its chapters. Two hours outside of Falls Church, I used the dingy restroom at a gas station that reeked of sour milk and then continued my journey as the sun rose higher in the May sky. I tried to think about the pages I'd read, attempting to use my sleuthing abilities to figure out who killed the redheaded busboy, but the memory of Carson kept me from fulfilling that desire. So I quit listening to Paul Simon. Yet Carson's smile and the way he made me feel when we were together still seeped in through the vents of my car and mind.

At one point I shouted. "Oh, just go away!"

And that worked. For about half a mile.

Now, at the boutique, I debate whether or not to tell Mom about seeing Lien and her family again. I fill her in on Beanie and Little, and as she listens she drinks from a bottle of flavored water. Looking out the large store window, she says, "Dovie was always the creative one. The one who helped out in every soup kitchen and church function. So I'm not surprised at all."

"About what?"

"That she continues to house those hooligans."

Biting my lip, I arrange shelves of scarves. Some of these have been in the store for a year, and I know we need to move them. There are some more trendy ones in one of our suppliers' catalogs that I hope Mom will let me order soon. "And you, Mom?"

"What?"

"You said Dovie was the creative one. How about you?"

"I kept to myself." She fills her lungs with air and lets it out slowly, like one does when a doctor is listening to her chest. "I never ventured far. You know I told you that my childhood was spent in my room reading so that I could avoid my parents' arguments."

Mentally, I kick myself. I would never have asked if I'd known she was going to delve into her sad childhood. It tears at my insides to learn of how distraught she felt as a child.

My spirit soars when I hear her say, "Until I met your father."

"Things changed for the better after that, right?"

"Oh, yes. Your father helped me see that I was adored by him."

Warmly, I pat her hand. "He did adore you. I remember."

After some browsers enter and leave, Mom says she misses Butterchurn. "Still no sign of him." Minutes later, she says with enthusiasm, "What about a scones-coffee-and-Elvis night?"

"Here?"

"Yes, here."

"What does Elvis have to do with fashion?"

"He wore clothes."

"That makes him an icon for us?"

"I always liked Elvis. My dream was to ride in a black limo with him." Mom puts a hand to her heart. "He died on my birthday." She stares over the rack of tartan skirts.

"Did Daddy like Elvis?"

"He would have joined us in the limo, should my dream have worked out." Smiling, she says, "Your daddy tolerated him because he knew I liked 'Hound Dog' and 'Love Me Tender.'"

Each time "Love Me Tender" played on the radio, my mother sang along in her alto voice. Daddy, with his broad shoulders and whimsical smile, would just close his eyes and listen.

Mom chews a piece of licorice and sniffs. "So will you make a poster for Elvis Night?"

Soon our walls will be filled with posters. As I fold the last scarf, I say, "We could have a sale on scarves. Elvis wore those."

"Did you know that I had a friend who met Elvis?" Her eyes widen as she offers a coy smile.

"I bet after the concert, he kissed her cheek." I've heard this story more times than I've heard Beanie complain about hypocrites in church. The event with Mom's friend took place backstage at a concert long after Uncle Charlie met General McArthur in Japan. I think of the two occasions together because each time one is mentioned, the other story typically follows.

"Yes," breathes Mom. "Elvis kissed her cheek."

The shop's bell jingles as customers enter. Mother straightens her apron bow and welcomes them. Her smile seems weary this morning, but I push worry from my mind as though it is a piece of debris. I told Aunt Dovie that Mom's fine, and as of yet there are no signs the cancer has returned.

But I also know that she has a yearly physical in three weeks. These checkups are to test for one thing above all else. And when Mom returns from the clinic, it can be a miserably cold day, Wall Street stocks at a low, and the House and Senate arguing in the Capitol, but none of that matters when my mother tells me that the cancer cells have not come back. When she gives me that news, my whole world feels like a walk in a park on a golden autumn day.

As I add a few more strokes of green to my poster for our Elvis Night, there's the sound of rushing footsteps at our back door. First we hear a male voice holler, "Fire is here, fire is here!" and immediately we are relieved that it's only Sanjay, our Indian tenant to the left of our shop. "You must see this, you must see!"

"What?" I swear he watches too many reruns of *The Love Boat* and *Three's Company*.

Rounding the corner from the back storage room, I see him fully. His thin body shakes like a tree in a windstorm.

"What is it?" I ask, growing concerned.

He sputters, "There—there is fire rising."

"Where?"

Mom casts him an uncertain glance. "Do you mean there's a fire?"

Sanjay motions for me to follow him. I do, and he runs out the back door into the sunlight. Outside, when he's convinced that I see flames coming from the large metal dumpster the tenants in this strip mall all share, he stops. Violent shades of orange and red flicker from all angles. I watch the tops of cardboard boxes crinkle from the heat, their beige sides charring into shards of black.

Sanjay continues to moan, "This is not good, not good."

Running back inside the shop, I call the fire department.

"Is there really a fire?" Mom takes her hands from her apron pockets.

"Go see for yourself," I tell her.

"Who would do that?" Mom asks when she enters the store again ten minutes later. "I don't know why people have to create such havoc."

When the fire truck and police car pull into the front parking lot, Sanjay is waiting for them, guiding them to the back. Mother and I watch like little kids from the store's restroom window as firemen squirt the dumpster with a hose. With his arms in the air, Sanjay talks. Suddenly, he points to our shop's back door.

We see a large policeman make his way across the rear area toward our door. Quickly, Mom and I exit the restroom through the storage room and stride into the shop.

I stand behind the register and grab a catalog while Mom questions a lemon-colored necklace on the jewelry rack. "Do you think this will ever sell?" She holds it up to the light. "It looks like a piece of candy."

When we hear the anticipated knock on the back door, Mom lets the policeman into our store.

"Did you call about the fire?" he asks. He is large in width and height; I calculate about six-feet-four. Most men are too short for Mom, but he has a good four inches on her.

"I did," I confess.

He wants to know my name. I spell both my first and last names for him as he writes on a pad of paper. With a surname like Bravencourt, I've learned that it's easier to spell it right from the first.

"We've had a number of dumpster fires around this area lately." He brushes fingers over his chin before continuing. "Seems to be in vogue."

"Do you have any idea who is starting them?" I ask.

"Kids." He looks up from his pen, frowns. "Playing hooky." His eyes are blue, like the new line of pencil skirts we just received.

"Officer Branson," Mother says, taking a few steps closer to him. She prides herself on calling people by the names on their tags and badges. "If they need work, I'll let them unload merchandise."

This surprises me. It sounds like something Dovie would say. Dovie, who wants to help the world—not my mother, who is suspicious and keeps her distance.

"Thank you, ma'am," says Officer Branson as he rubs his mustache. The congeniality leaves his voice as he says, "I don't think you want these kids in your store."

"Oh?"

"Pretty devious bunch from what I can tell." He inserts his

pen into the pocket of his uniform. Puts the memo pad under his arm.

"Are they the types"—we wait for my mother to finish—"to steal a cat?"

At first I think he's going to laugh at her, and gritting my teeth, I pray he won't.

But instead he looks her over, his sympathetic eyes resting on her face. "Ma'am," he says in a gentle but firm tone, "these deviants will do anything."

Mom nods solemnly and then shakes his hand. I think she's had enough for one day and is encouraging him to go.

thirteen

November 1986

I t was the day Lien almost went to the Monkey House. We
wondered why she and her family never showed up at the
wedding held at the community chapel; it was her mother's
cousin who was marrying a thin man with a nervous twitch.
The new couple would relocate to Los Angeles, where family
and a Vietnamese nail salon were waiting.

Carson and I drank from lukewarm bottles of Sprite and
helped ourselves to crisp *chiayo* inside the chapel. Other guests
spoke to us, some in English, but mostly in Vietnamese. Carson
asked the bride where the Hong family was. She shook her
head and then turned to smile for the photographer, who told
her to turn to her left so that he could get a side view of her in
her silky traditional Vietnamese dress, designed with gold and
orange butterflies sailing up the front of it.

"You wear white gown in America?" the bride asked after

the photographer took his lens off of her and focused on a group of teens.

"Sometimes," I said and then took a bite of the spring roll.

"Sometimes?" Carson's eyes suddenly were like darts, ammunition, ready to act against me.

"Not all brides wear white gowns."

Carson dismissed me with a roll of the eyes, and then he and the bride chatted in Vietnamese and I realized that he could very well be saying that all brides wore white. I wanted to say, I was invited to a wedding where it was the bride's second marriage and she wore a floral dress with fuchsia stilettos. But neither of them seemed concerned with what I'd seen.

The groom, decked out in a solid blue shirt, the long sleeves rolled up at the cuffs, and a pair of brown pants with a leather belt, came over to our table and joined in the conversation with his bride and Carson. Getting the attention of the photographer, the groom asked him to take a picture of Carson, the bride, groom, and me. We had to move to get the pose the groom wanted. His eye twitched as he positioned Carson and me on the left side and then stood with his arm wrapped around his bride's shoulder. After two shots like that, he asked the photographer to snap a picture of just Carson and me. Carson and I were seated again, and Carson moved closer to me as we both smiled for the camera.

Later, in Carson's classroom, under a dull fan, he and I sat on benches and talked about effective tactics to teach cultural orientation to our students. Carson said he liked to use the visual aid of the American house, pointing out each room and explaining what people did in each one. Then, slowly and with strain in his voice, he shared a memory of his father at Thanksgiving. His father insisted on slicing the turkey at the meal, but he always took so long that his mother would end up taking over the task to appease the table of hungry family.

"That was our tradition," he said. "Knowing Dad would be taken over by Mom. Yet every year he wanted to be the one to cut the bird." Carson produced a slight smile, and spontaneously, I grabbed his hand. He let me hold it as I absorbed the excitement of the moment, but once I started to talk about our Thanksgiving traditions, the few I recalled from when my dad was alive, he let my hand go. I assumed that Mindy was on his mind.

When the door banged open and a distraught Huy entered, I was in the middle of talking about one of my Cambodian students who, as we studied the letter *P*, had said she wanted to live in a house in California with movie stars, an outdoor pool, a poodle, and plenty of pineapples.

Using Vietnamese, Huy spouted a large amount of words. Sweat glistened on his face. He paused as Carson said to me in English, "Lien's in trouble."

I was not surprised. The Amerasian could be nicknamed Trouble. Now that she was no longer in my class after having received her graduation certificate, I tried to avoid her. In the marketplace, she'd call out to me, "Miss Bavecoo, Miss Bavecoo!" Her energetic wave made everyone turn and look.

Carson said, "They are accusing her of stealing money and jewelry from the billets."

"How much did she steal?" I asked.

Carson's eyes were cold and didn't indicate he'd heard me. I waited while he said a few things to Huy and then to me, "Lien wouldn't steal."

When Huy left the room, I said, "I think she would."

Carson's jaw was like the barbed wire at the guard's gate at the entrance to the camp. If I touched it, I was certain that my fingers would bleed.

"She isn't like that."

"She is, Carson."

"How can you be sure?"

I thought of how Lien was once in the marketplace with a lacquer bangle brought over from Vietnam and some of my students were trying to catch up to her because the jewelry was not hers. Three girls approached me as I paid for two carrots and a head of cabbage. They announced that Lien had taken the item. I recalled the scenario for Carson.

"She was only playing," he said. "I later saw her with that bracelet and she gave it back to the proper owner."

"Well, she stole my watch once."

Bleakly, he looked at me. "She did?"

"She picked it up and took it."

"Off of your wrist?" Sarcasm was evident in his tone.

"No. I always remove it and put it on top of my desk when I teach."

"And she saw it and was playing with it?"

"No." I steadied my voice. "She took it."

"Took it away? Put it in her pocket?"

Today, Carson's Southern accent grated on my nerves, like fingernails on a chalkboard. Just moments ago I had held his hand and now I wanted to walk away from him. Why was it that Lien could do no wrong in his book? What was it about the Hong family that he revered? Accusingly, I stated, "She had it in her hands and was walking away with it."

He pointed to my Citizen watch, sitting securely on my left wrist. "And she gave it back."

"But she picked it up and held it."

"That's not stealing!"

Carson's tone shocked me. It was loud and seared my skin. I hadn't seen this side of him before.

"She had no business taking it!" I gulped, reminded that I had prayed to have patience with Lien, but now patience and understanding seemed miles away.

"That's not stealing." Carson's eyes looked like dark valleys, no room for light.

"She took scissors from my desk and kept them for two days."

"But she returned them, didn't she?"

"Carson!" Then my words spilled, toppling over each other. "You protect Lien all the time. You can't ever see her faults. She isn't perfect! If you're so in love with her, then just go off and have a happy life."

It was a stupid thing to say. I regretted it later.

I regretted a lot later.

fourteen

When I finally get Dexter on the phone, his apology is profuse. "Sam, you have to forgive me. My car wouldn't start. Crazy, huh? I cranked the key over and over, but it was dead. I got a friend to come over and try the whole jumper cable routine. That didn't work."

"So what did you do then?" I'm admiring the recent photos I took of Dovie's butterflies at the cemetery. I dropped off the roll of film after work and waited the one hour for the drugstore's lab to process it into glossy prints, which are now spread over the kitchen table.

"He drove me to Sears to get a battery, but even with a new battery it wouldn't start. I had to have it towed to a repair shop."

"Did you find out what was wrong with it?"

"Yeah, it was the water pump."

"Ohh. That can be expensive to fix."

"I'm sorry," he repeats. "Really. I bought a gift and everything. How was Avery?"

When I tell him it was the wrong Avery Jones, he laughs so loud I have to move the receiver from my ear. "Now that is funny," he says, and laughs some more. "You went to the wrong wedding, Sam? Just like you went to the wrong lab that time in chemistry. Remember?"

I think he must feel there's a pattern here, but really, I am not as ditzy as I seem.

Taylor calls me and he is as sweet as he was at the reception. He wants to take me for a boat ride on the Potomac River next Sunday afternoon. Jokingly, I ask if this is part of an investigative job he has to do.

"No," he says. "I leave my work at home."

"So this is for fun?"

"Unless you get seasick."

"Are we going as far as the sea?"

"Actually, no." I hear the rustle of some papers. "I have this brochure here that describes a cruise down the Potomac River on one of those old tour boats. Don't tell me you've already done that a million times."

"A cruise down the Potomac?" The idea sounds intriguing. During all the years I've lived in this area, I've never boated on the Potomac River. "That sounds fun."

When I tell Mom the news about my date, she wonders if I need a new outfit. "Something pretty?" she asks.

I think the word *outfit* is a funny English word, like it should describe a Halloween costume rather than something we choose to wear to work or to church. I recall one of my students in camp wondering why the words *out* and *fit* together meant an ensemble of clothing.

"He said to dress casually," I tell Mom. "We're going out on a boat."

"Shorts and one of the Liz Claiborne cotton V-neck sleeveless shirts," she suggests. I know exactly where those shirts hang and am grateful when she lets me choose the light purple one to wear.

On Sunday after church, I park my car at the wharf along the bank of the Potomac. The day is sunny with no visible clouds, the temperature hovering around ninety. After putting on a pair of sunglasses, I watch a sailboat glide across the water. As sweat glistens on my skin, I'm tempted to take a splash in the river to cool off.

Instead, I walk, meandering along the docked yachts, reading off their given names. There's *Enchanted Sea*, *Chesapeake's Charm*, and sillier names like *Little Putt-Putt* and *Sight Sea*. Their fiberglass hulls sparkle in the sunlight as waves lap gently against them. Realizing I've been here a while, I hope that I'm in the right place at the right time today. I followed the signs for the *Potomac Jewel* as Taylor instructed me to do, and unless there is more than one steamboat by that name in Arlington, I should be okay.

When I hear, "Hey there, Samantha!" I smile with relief.

Taylor, dressed in a pair of khaki shorts and an aqua T-shirt, approaches me. He gives me a warm hug and a smile so wide I can't see his mole at all. "Ready?" he asks. "We have to get our tickets. The tour starts in thirty minutes."

After purchasing our tickets, Taylor buys us cans of Sprite and we wait in line to board. He looks for a restroom as I read the brochure to learn more about this large apricot-colored steamboat docked in front of me. *The* Potomac Jewel *is a triple-decker masterpiece*, I read, and looking at the boat, I see that it does have three layers to it, like a wedding cake. The top deck is considerably smaller than the others, but my adventurous side yearns to climb to the very height of it.

Taylor returns just as the line starts moving. Children cling to their parents' hands, excitedly anticipating the ride.

"Daddy, do you think it will go fast?" asks one boy.

His father says, "I think it's a slow boat, but we'll be able to see far."

The boy seems pleased. "I hope I can see all the way to China."

Once on the *Potomac Jewel*, I note how majestic it feels. This is going to be romantic, I think as I give Taylor a smile. We stand close together on the promenade deck as a whistle blows and the vessel groans away from the dock.

We watch the wharf grow smaller, and the men standing on it, who have untied the heavy ropes from the vessel, shrink into toy sizes. The docked yachts now resemble white candy-coated Chiclets.

As the tour guide welcomes us aboard, Taylor comments, "That wedding reception was fun, wasn't it?"

I consider telling him that the funniest thing was that I was at the wrong wedding, but I'm not sure I should reveal my ditzy side just yet.

He launches into a story about a man who hired him to find his missing wife, a woman who really was not missing; she just didn't want her husband to find her. "The woman was angry when I located her," Taylor tells me. "She threatened to burn my house down."

"Are you threatened often?"

"Once a man let his pit bull chase me. He was angry that I told him he needed to appear in court the next day."

"Were you okay?"

"I got away. Did the whole 'throw the stick one way and run the other' trick. I use that on my dog sometimes."

"What's your dog's name?"

"Van Gogh."

"Like the painter?" Names for pets often amuse me, such as when my mother christened her cat Butterchurn because he's yellow, she said, like butter.

"He looks like a Van Gogh because one ear is smaller than the other."

We laugh.

"He's a seven-year-old Boxer I've had since he was a pup."

"Ah, must be nice to have someone who looks forward to your return each day." *No lonely nights.*

"It's great. He greets me when I come home from work with a tennis ball in his mouth. Just waiting to play. Boxers have great faces," he says over the tour guide's voice that is directing us to look out the starboard side of the boat.

"Faces?" I try to picture the face of that breed.

"Their large eyes and expressions make you feel they are really listening to you when you talk, and you feel that they understand you."

"Sounds like having a good friend."

"Until your Boxer licks his rear and walks away."

I giggle. "I might get a dog one of these days." I think of Milkweed and Butterchurn and add, "Or a cat."

"Cats can't fetch a ball or a Frisbee."

"True. Maybe a dog, then. I've never owned one, but yours sounds fun." Growing up, we had cats because Mom claimed that her personality was more suited toward having a cat. Thinking again of Butterchurn, I say, "Can you find missing animals?"

"What?" he asks as a gust of wind blows over us, tousling our hair.

"Aren't you a private investigator?"

"For people, Samantha," he says and then laughs.

"Let's go up to the top floor."

"You mean the top deck?"

"Whatever it's called. Come on." Grabbing his hand on impulse, I take us toward the signs for the upper deck.

After threading through the throng of people, we climb the stairs to the third tier of the steamboat. With a hand on the wrought-iron railing, I anchor myself and gaze to my left, where a milky marble President Abraham Lincoln sits in his columned memorial. The boat glides under the Theodore Roosevelt Memorial Bridge, and I get a glimpse of both the Korean War Veterans Memorial and the Vietnam Veterans Memorial. Up ahead, the Washington Monument towers like a beacon of national pride.

To the left is the Pentagon, sprawled out like a set of large building blocks.

When Taylor puts his arm around me, I catch a whiff of his cologne. A man who smells good is a plus in my book. We stay on the top deck, enjoying the break from the tour guide's microphone voice that is much louder on the lower levels.

When the tour ends and we're safely on land again, Taylor takes me to a little Greek restaurant near the Thai embassy, and we enjoy lamb gyros and slices of toasty pita with hummus. He talks about a case he's working on, and after I ask a few questions, he tells me about another.

We part around eight. I thank him for a lovely time and wonder if he'll kiss me or ask to see me again. As though reading my thoughts, he says, "I'd like to go out again."

"I'd like that, too."

"Have you ever been to Donatello?"

"Once." I recall going there with Natasha and Mom years ago.

"Why don't we go there sometime? It'll have to be later in July. I'm going home for Canada Day."

"Canada Day?"

"July first. Right before your Independence Day."

Hesitantly, I ask, "You're Canadian?"

"Through and through. Moved here when I was out of college. My parents still live in Toronto."

"Do you ever say 'eh'?" I tease.

He produces an awkward smile; I hope I haven't offended
him.

"Well, have a good time there." I give him my cheeriest smile
as we hug good-bye. Again I wonder if there will be a kiss, but
we break our embrace without one.

As I drive back home, the radio playing softly, I relive snatches
from our date. Stepping into my apartment, I switch on the
lights and then realize how tired I am. Thankful for a working
air-conditioner, I turn down the thermostat a few degrees to
compensate for the muggy night. As I pour a glass of lemon
iced tea, I listen to the message on my answering machine.

"Hi, Samantha. This is Carson Brylie. Lien gave me your
number. I hope we can talk soon. Bye."

For a second I don't breathe. Then when the shock wears off,
I put the pitcher down, walk over to the answering machine,
and play the message again. And again.

fifteen

On Monday morning, I wear my tennis shoes because I remember that it's delivery day from one of our suppliers. The UPS truck brings us seven boxes of clothes, the driver huffing as he carts the last one into the back room.

Since there are no customers in the shop, I begin to open the boxes. Feelings of happiness flit around my heart like Dovie's butterflies when I think about yesterday with Taylor. I recall how his arm felt around my shoulders as the boat skirted across the water.

Mom notes my smile and asks about the date. "Do you like him?"

"Hmmm," I say and then, looking at the boxes, decide I better step away from my cocoon of recounting Saturday and get busy.

"Just be careful."

I know that Mom's warning has nothing to do with the boxes of clothes. She knows something happened in the Philippines and wants to make sure my heart doesn't get trampled again.

Nodding to appease her, I get on my knees, pull a box toward me, and dig into the contents. The first thing I pull out is a pair of silky florescent pink underpants encased in plastic. The next item is the same.

"I didn't order those," says Mom, a blush the same color as the underwear tinting her cheeks.

I open each box, but none of the contents is what we ordered.

Mom's convinced that these are for that *other boutique* on the edge of town. She asks if the address is ours.

"Yeah, they even got the zip code correct."

"Well, it's a drastic mistake."

After being put on hold for twelve minutes, I reach an operator at the company called Bannerfields. "This is Have a Fit in Falls Church, Virginia. We just received the wrong shipment of clothing."

The woman at the other end can't believe that a mistake has been made. "Are you sure that you didn't order those?"

I look at my mother, one of the most modest women I've ever known. She's still blushing from the dozens of pairs of lacy panties, some with polka dots, others with tiny red bows. "We did not."

Per the operator's instructions I call UPS to pick up the unwanted boxes. The promise is that a driver will be at our store by five today to take the boxes away.

Mom sighs. I see heaviness in her movements and a dullness to her eyes. Panic fills me, my mind reeling back to the days she spent in the hospital getting treated for breast cancer.

"Why don't you go home?" I suggest. "Get some rest."

"What do you mean?"

"You must be tired."

"Samantha. I will run this store. Don't start telling me it's too big a task for me." I see her eyes plead, *Don't take this away from me. If you do, what will I have to live for?*

I put my arm around her shoulders.

She winces. "I will not let you or Dovie baby me."

I pull her close. "I know. I know that, Mom." I kiss her cheek, then release her.

She starts to sort dresses, putting the long in with the petite.

I don't say a word. I just take a marker from the counter and, for the next five minutes, add a few more lines to the *Shop with Elvis* posters.

In the microwave, I heat a bowl of noodles for dinner, first adding water and then sprinkling on the chicken flavor packet. I break apart a pair of wooden chopsticks from the takeout at Joyful Dragon and am about to sit at my kitchen table when the phone rings.

Setting down the chopsticks, I lean over to grab the cordless.

The voice on the other end is like a summer day at the beach, familiar and brimming with anticipation. "Hi. Is this Samantha?"

"It is." I feel my heart pole-vault in my chest. "And is this Carson Brylie?"

"It is."

I can tell he's smiling. "I can't believe it! How are you?" My words gush out like water from a faucet turned on all the way.

"Pretty good. How about you?"

"Good. Yeah. Doing well. I just made some noodles for dinner." Immediately I feel silly for saying that.

"Lien told me I could call you."

It sounds just like Lien to try to run the show. Even after

all these years, I still don't know how to handle her. Covering my thoughts, I say, "It was fun seeing Lien again. She's taller than I am now."

"She told me all about it. Showed me the photo Huy took of the two of you."

"She did?" I hope the photo is flattering. I hate to think that after all these years, Carson's first encounter with me was an unflattering picture.

"She couldn't stop talking about how Huy found you and invited you to the restaurant."

There's so much I want to tell him—about Mom's illness, my job, the fire in the dumpster, how often I think of him. Instead I mumble, "Yeah, she's grown up a lot."

"So, what are you doing?"

"Oh, not too much." The heat from the bowl and from Carson's Southern accent have warmed my face. "And you?"

"Just mowed the lawn. It's my day off."

I feel like a silly schoolgirl who's gotten a call from a guy she likes. *After all this time, you still hold a piece of my heart, Carson.* In the pit of my stomach, a disturbance flails. Swallowing, I steady my voice. "Where do you work?"

"A little radio station."

"What do you do there?"

"D.J."

"You're a D.J.?"

"Yep. You know, all that singing in the camp must have made me do it."

I feel my heart soften even more. "What kind of station?"

"Music from the seventies and eighties."

"Do you take requests?"

"We do."

Vaguely, I recall the voice on the radio station Beanie turned to when we were driving to Lien's family's restaurant. Could that have been Carson? At that time, my mind was preoccupied with seeing the Hong family again; I had not paid much attention.

"How about you?"

I think of everything that's happened since I last saw him, all the things God has brought me through. "Life is good," I say after a moment.

"It is, isn't it? Where are you working?"

I wonder if Carson still has that sense of humor I adore. I decide to give it a try. "Well," I begin, "I married a rich sheik who owns oil wells and we live in the Mediterranean with our seven children."

Carson's laughter is rich, taking me back to the evenings when we would sit outside the cafés in the camp, drink from bottles of Sprite, and confide in each other about our dreams.

"Actually, my mom owns a boutique in town and I work there."

"I thought you were going to become an ESL instructor and get your certification. What do they call that?"

"TESOL."

"That's it. Teaching English to Speakers of Other Languages. Wasn't that what you said you were going to work on doing next?"

Mom got sick, I want to say. The store needed help. As my thoughts churn, I imagine my dreams from my past, my lofty dreams, turning into puffs of smoke. "Things don't always work out."

"I know," he says. "I never expected to work at a radio station. So I guess life's turned out a little differently for us both."

I want to ask about Mindy, but I hold back. Later, I think.

Then he says he has to go. "Dat and Yung are here. We have a Bible study."

"Well." Reluctant to end our conversation, I say, "Thanks for calling."

"It was right nice talking to you."

When we hang up, I let my fingers linger on the phone as Carson's voice lingers against my ears. Quickly, like my mother would warn, I tell myself to be careful. *You were young back then in the camp. You gave away your heart too quickly.*

Ten thousand miles from Mom, in the Philippines, I disregarded the warnings she'd imbedded in me and became spontaneous with my emotions. I never told my mother how hard that was for me to do, shedding all the stories she had shared about her own childhood—tales of relatives who lied, stole, and cheated. *"Be careful about where you put your trust,"* she often advised. *"There are some who should never be trusted. Hold on to your heart. Do not be quick to give it away."*

sixteen

Three nights later, I've got another bowl of Asian soup in front of me, this one containing dried mushrooms and carrots. I'm seated at my coffee table watching *Casablanca*. I think this marks the seventh time I've seen it. I dream of Humphrey Bogart sometimes, the way I imagine my mother dreams of Elvis.

As I bite into one of the two carrots from the styrofoam bowl, the phone rings. If I were watching a movie I'd never seen before, I might let the answering machine pick up the call, but tonight I leave the living room and grab the phone in the kitchen.

Carson says, "Hi, Samantha."

"Hi again. How are you?" I suppress the desire to gush over how nice it is to hear his voice.

"I was thinking that you should come down to Winston."

My heart lurches; he wants to see me. Cautiously, like a robot, I ask, "Why?"

"Why?" His laughter is just like in the old days. "It's been a while since I've seen you."

Carson's words knit themselves into the corners of my heart, a fabric that is thin from being torn over the years. I see his face, feel his breath. In between these pleasant emotions, anger threads through my veins. I should say that I never understood so many things that happened at the camp. I should say that there is a box of photos from our days together that I have sealed in my closet under other boxes because I cannot bear to make that trip down memory lane. Instead, I try to focus on the here and now.

"When?" My voice sounds tinny. "When do you want to see me?" I walk over to the TV and turn down the volume just as Ingrid Bergman is about to walk into the bar, the scene that makes any romantic swoon.

"How about this weekend?"

"What?"

"Why don't you come to Winston this weekend? What do you say?"

I think of how I recently told Natasha I need to be less spontaneous, think of my mother more, and less of me. I think of what Ingrid Bergman would say if she were in a moment like this one. Finally, I come up with, "The drive is long. My car is old."

I hear Carson laughing. Again. "I'm sorry. 'The drive is long, my car is old' sounds like a Dr. Seuss rhyme. Like that book—"

"*One Fish Two Fish Red Fish Blue Fish?*" When I used to volunteer at the library for story hour, that was a favorite.

"Yeah, that one."

Silence saturates the air. I note that my toenails need a fresh coat of polish. With everyone else, I always want to get rid of the quiet moments out of discomfort. Yet, even after all this time, tonight's silence with Carson feels like it did seven years ago—acceptable.

"Could you hop on a plane?" he asks. "I can pick you up in Charlotte."

My heart twirls as I try hard to calm it and put it back where it belongs in its safe and guarded place. "I work."

"Can you get some time off?"

I feel the stickiness of an afternoon in the refugee camp, right before the air filled with the aromas of dinner cooking on portable stoves outside the billets. Closing my eyes, I recall our walks together.

"Do you think you could come for a visit soon?"

My teeth dig into my lower lip. I swallow and see scenes from the past sashay before me like the dance the bride and groom did at the wedding a few weekends ago. I wonder if Carson's hair still falls into his face after he's been caught in a downpour. I wonder if his eyes are as bright, flecks of green and gold dotting his irises. I wonder if his hands would still feel as good massaging my neck, easing the tension with just a few deep movements into my muscles. I wonder— "No."

After a pause he says, "No?"

"I really have a lot going on now."

"You do?"

With a final swallow, I say, "Thanks for calling. Bye." Then I disconnect us. I try to eat my dinner, but the noodles are rubbery and the steam from the broth mixes with my tears and burns my eyes.

I think about calling Natasha and telling her what just happened.

But what would I say? I'm not even sure I know what happened.

seventeen

Natasha thinks I should go to see Carson. On this Sunday afternoon, we walk around the Washington Monument. The June day is too hot for a walk, but Natasha is one of those avid exercisers. During the colder months, she goes to a gym and sweats on a treadmill. She knows she's unusual because she actually likes to sweat. Once she even had a personal trainer, but when she fell in love with him and he didn't reciprocate her feelings, she told him she no longer needed his help. She switched gyms.

Never stopping her quick strides, Natasha says, "Take a few days. You know that my schedule at the office is flexible. I'll help your mom at the shop."

"Why?"

"So that you can go see Carson."

"Why?" I pick up my pace to match hers.

"Why not?"

I pant and then push my drooping cloth headband up over my forehead. She's adorned with long legs; I'm long-waisted and my legs don't ever move quickly.

She stops for a moment, looks at me in her deliberate way, and states, "You're in love with him."

I raise my right hand to stop her and pause at her side. A flock of tourists crowd around a woman in a navy suit carrying a miniature flag of Turkey. With my hand still in the air, I say to Natasha, "Not anymore. I was once in love. Once."

Natasha shrugs. "I don't know why you think you can keep fooling yourself."

"I got over him."

"Really?" She starts to walk again, heading down the pavement away from the towering historical structure, dodging a group of kids playing in the grass with a Frisbee.

"Yes." I make a dash toward her, shielding the afternoon sun from my eyes, wishing I'd remembered to bring my sunglasses with me. "Besides, I went out with this guy I met at the wedding."

"Oh yeah, the cute one you told me about. So how was the date?"

"Great!" I cheer, but we both know I am exaggerating. "Look," I say as I feel a cramp developing in my calf, "I don't want to talk about it anymore."

We walk in silence. Natasha comments about her father's recent trip to Morocco. He works as a dignitary in the Clinton administration, but I can never remember his exact title. I feign interest and ask a few questions. She then says she's ready to date again, but there is no one she likes. "Well, one guy at the office. But I found out he's married." She mutters, "Why do men try to hide these things?"

We sit by the National Mall on a bench so that Natasha can re-tie her shoelaces.

I look out over the strip of water and say, "Wonder why he didn't marry Mindy."

Wiping sweat from her neck, she says, "I thought we weren't discussing this."

"You're right; we aren't."

As we start walking again, Natasha says, "But if we were talking about it, I'd say Carson wasn't really in love with her."

"I was really rude when he called," I admit.

"Rude to him? Why?" She turns to give me a quizzical stare.

"I just want him to go away."

"Away?"

"I don't need him back in my life."

"Really?" She squints at me.

"Yes, things were going well without him."

"They were?"

When I get back to my apartment, I check my mail at the row of boxes and pull out a power bill, a water bill, and a flyer for a new Italian restaurant in Arlington. I'm not hungry since Natasha and I had chocolate Häagen-Dazs popsicles after our walk. I don't feel like turning on the TV or reading, so I gaze out my window for a few minutes as the maintenance man cranks up a lawn mower. Then I water my two planters of ivy. I can't stand it when houseplants wither on my watch. But since I don't have a green thumb, sometimes they end up dying no matter how loving I am when I talk to them.

In the kitchen, I immerse four tea bags in a saucepan of boiling water, and after ten minutes, remove them and add a cup of sugar. Stirring the mixture, I make sure all of the sugar dissolves, and once it has, I squeeze lemon juice into a pitcher and then pour in the thick concoction. I fill half a glass with ice cubes and then top it off with tea. As the sweet liquid cools my throat, I see that my answering machine light is flashing. With a press of the play button, the messages begin. The first one is Dovie, inviting me to come down to see her again. "I'm having a dinner party on July fourth and have a surprise for you."

Message number two begins with, "Hello, Sam. This is Taylor. Sorry to miss you. I'll call again later."

My stomach does a little happy flip.

I hope he calls back, but by eleven I give up my childish notions and get ready for bed, reading the last chapters of *Deceived in Denmark*, one of the newer Busboy Mysteries. As usual, the author gives just enough clues to make me think one character is the culprit, but by the second-to-last chapter I'm suspecting another.

I met the author, R.C. Longjay, once at a book discussion and signing. At first I didn't recognize her because she had gray hair, wrinkles crisscrossed her forehead, and she wore horn-rimmed glasses. She didn't look at all like her glamorous book jacket photo. The elderly woman seated next to me had *Cornered in Cairo*, the just-released mystery by R.C., opened to the author's photo. To me, this stranger whispered, "Guess this picture was taken when she was in college or something."

I was about to comment when the woman must have read my thoughts, because she said, "I suppose she wants to remind us that she was young once." After smiling, she closed her book, rested it against her heavy thigh streaked with varicose veins, and sighed. "I don't blame her at all."

eighteen

We always close the shop the week of July fourth. Mom says it is patriotic to take time off and not be intent on making a buck off the holiday.

I create posters that we place around the front door of the boutique, letting customers know that we'll be gone. We also make sure to tell each customer who comes in before that week. Although Mom tells me her philosophy on not working, she contradicts herself by wanting people to think it's a working week. To those who raise their eyebrows and say, "A whole week off?" she gives them the sense that she'll be heading to our suppliers to check out new products. But the reality is that she drives to Virginia Beach with her friend Maralinda, another breast cancer survivor. They eat seafood, drink chardonnay from skinny glasses, and take walks on the beach in bare feet. They have been known to be noticed by single men. Perhaps, if the weather is cloudy, Mom might venture to a wholesaler in Richmond to see what they have in stock, allowing plenty of time for lunch along the way. But that's the extent of her "working week."

Five days before the fourth, Mom's lab results from her annual physical are in.

"Well?" I watch as she places the shop's phone in the cradle. My mind spins as the back of my neck grows clammy.

"I'm fine."

"Really?" I swallow.

She pops a licorice morsel into her mouth. "Well, he says I eat too much licorice. Stains my teeth, you know. He isn't happy about that." She's talking about her oncologist, Dr. Burgess.

"What else did he say?"

Mom looks at me with her hands in her apron pockets. "I suppose I'm going to live a while longer."

My smile is broad. I dive into her arms.

She pats my back. "So," she says, stepping back, "I guess we'll be carrying on with our plans, then."

"For what?"

"Take your dad's old camera when you go."

"Go where?"

Mom takes off her clip-on silver earrings and adds them to her pocket. "To Dovie's. You always have fun there. Dovie loves having you visit. Take the camera and get some pretty photos of the butterflies."

"What do you want them for?"

"I'll put them around the shop. You know, spruce it up a bit."

"I have to use Dad's camera?"

"You have one?" Mom's eyebrows rise.

"Mom, you gave me a Nikon for graduation."

"That was ages ago."

"I still have it."

She watches me. I know she's questioning whether or not it still works. I have been known to break a few items in my lifetime.

"Send Dovie my love but know that Maralinda is counting on me to join her at the beach house."

Softly, I say, "I know." Those two have a bond like glue. In fact, although I insist, Mom won't let me drive her to her physicals; she only lets Maralinda do that. Dovie invites her to Winston, but Mom rarely visits. "She should come up here," Mom tells me. "This city has so much to offer. I could take her to the Smithsonian, and then there's Folger Theater."

Once, just to play the devil's advocate, I asked if I could come with her to the beach house.

"Of course, you are welcome."

"I didn't ask if I would be welcomed. I asked if I could spend a week there with you and Maralinda."

"Oh, there are only two bedrooms."

"I have a sleeping bag."

"Her children usually stop over."

I didn't pursue it after that. Beanie told me, "Sometimes folk just want time away from their kids. Nothing personal, Sammie."

On the third of July, after we close up the shop at noon, Mom leaves for Maralinda's. She hands me a crumpled piece of paper with a phone number written on it. "The beach house has a phone, and if you need me, you can reach me there."

I want to say, What if I just want to talk to you but don't really *need* you? Will that be all right? But I just take the paper, give her a hug, and watch her take off her apron. She puts on a billowy hat that flops over her eyes. "You like it?"

It's from a shipment we received the other day from a whole-saler my mother has been eyeing. "Looks good, Mom." There are times I know Mom orders certain products because she wants them for herself.

I head home, can't decide what to pack, make a turkey sand-wich, clean out the outdated milk and sour cream from my fridge, and eat the sandwich. Within an hour I start my drive to Winston-Salem.

Leaving Falls Church, I say aloud, "If I were married . . . Yep, things would be different." I'd fly to Cancun this week with my charming husband. But I'm not, and although Natasha invited me to her parents' condo in Cape May, I'd rather visit Dovie for the holiday.

When I called Dexter last night to catch up, he told me that I should be glad that I have time off from work. From the sound of his voice, it seemed he was going to have to be working.

"So no time off for you, then?" I asked.

"No, and no sunny warm weather for me, either. Where I'm going, I'll need my parka and lots of hot coffee."

"Where is that?"

"Our team is headed to the Arctic to study the vocalizations of the beluga whale."

One of the things I love about being friends with Dexter is that he has fascinating tales. His job as a marine biologist has taken him all over the world.

"I never even heard of a beluga whale," I said.

"You've heard of white whales, right?"

"Oh, yeah."

"Beluga is a white whale."

"Well, make sure your car is running well," I tease, thinking back to the day of Avery Jones's wedding. "And have fun."

Dovie has a new boarder who sleeps in the little cove bedroom that has the dormer window. I expect my aunt to say that I'll have to sleep on the couch in the den since all the bedrooms are currently filled, but she tells me that I can have the basement. In the sterile-white lowest portion of the house, I place my suitcase on the double bed that is covered in a floral quilt. Aside from the plaid sofa that sticks out like a wayward appendage, there's a Kenmore washer, a Whirlpool dryer, and a set of sinks, their basins stained with rust. Above the sinks is a row of cabinets, also white, with little brass knobs that are in the shape of butterflies. The scent in the basement is a mixture of Pine-Sol and sweaty socks. I use the tiny bathroom off to the left, a room just big enough to hold a shower, a sink, and a toilet. Towels of red, white, and blue hang on the rack by the shower door.

Pearl, her new tenant, actually pays Dovie rent money. I asked Dovie about her when I arrived, and Dovie sat with me while I drank a glass of iced tea at the kitchen table. "She's newly widowed, and her children wanted her to move into a retirement home, but Pearl fought that."

"Really?" I said. "Not interested in a retirement place?"

"Not in the least."

As Dovie swept the kitchen floor, she told me that she met the eighty-five-year-old woman at a gardening party, and seeing her need, invited her to live with her. Pearl crochets, tends to Dovie's herb garden, feeds the chickens, and takes a nap every afternoon at three after drinking a cup of orange pekoe tea with three-and-one-half teaspoons of sugar.

Shortly after that, I met the short, plump woman with glossy white hair and she filled me in on her history, including that her husband had been in the Marines. I was about to ask a question about him when Pearl excused herself so she could catch *Jeopardy* on TV.

"I watch it every night," she told me. "Then I take my vitamins."

Seeing that it is almost dinnertime, I enter the aromatic kitchen. There is a plate of fried chicken on the counter, and my mouth waters. Beanie is making stuffed eggs, and my aunt is frosting a wobbly chocolate cake.

Dovie pours me a glass of iced tea and sets it on the kitchen table. She thinks I need iced tea all the time; a fresh pitcher of it is always available. "We're having a dinner guest tomorrow," she tells me.

My aunt likes to entertain. During the warmer months, she puts two tables together on the porch, covers them with pink linen, and serves a feast. Before I can ask who the guest is, the two pies cooling on the counter grab my attention. Each has a lattice crust just like you'd see in a fancy cookbook. "Who made those?"

"Pearl," says Dovie. "That's her specialty. Which is nice since neither Beanie nor I are any good at pies."

"What kind are they?"

"Rhubarb with strawberries. Secret family recipe." Beanie wipes her hands on a terry-cloth towel. "I think she puts nutmeg in it, and lemon juice."

"And a pinch of tapioca," Dovie says.

"Tapioca! Why would she put that in there?" Beanie arches her brows.

"Perhaps she knows something about pies that we don't."

"No wonder ours don't turn out right." Beanie covers the eggs with plastic wrap.

I take a sip of my iced tea and admire the cake.

"Thanks," Dovie replies to my compliment.

"Can I help with anything?"

Dovie looks at the chicken. "That's for dinner. We'll have some biscuits, too."

"And mashed potatoes are on the stove," says Beanie, turning toward the Kenmore. "And green beans. Oh, I need to add some butter to those now."

"We're set then," says my aunt as Beanie opens the fridge and takes out a stick of butter. "Dinner will be soon. First, we need to get some things taken care of for tomorrow."

Beanie pours a glass of tea.

"Carson is invited." Dovie says this like she says the day is overcast.

"Car . . . Carson?" My tongue trips over his name.

"Yes."

"Carson?"

"Yes, that man you know."

"But . . . How?"

"I hollered out the window. Would have used my phone I rigged up, the one made of soup cans, but the rope broke." Dovie tries to disguise her smile by covering her mouth.

Beanie laughs, the glass in her hand shaking from her movement. "Does the city girl think Southerners don't know how to invite folks over for dinner?"

Stammering, I say, "What I mean is—how did you get his number?"

"Carson's?" My aunt licks the knife she's been using. A dollop of icing drops from it to her chin.

"Yes. How do you know him?"

"He lives nearby."

"You think I believe that you know everyone who lives nearby?"

"I could." My aunt wipes her chin.

"She could," says Beanie with a wink. "In theory, we could know everyone in all of Winston—one big happy Mayberry family!"

I leave them cackling like the chickens Aunt Dovie has

running around her backyard. I head out to the porch, sit by Milkweed, let her flick her tail in my face, and read the first chapter of *False Identity in Finland*, the next mystery in the Busboy series.

Of course, at the end of the chapter I have no idea what the book is about. It's hard to concentrate on a murder mystery when the past shoves its way into my thoughts.

nineteen

I can't sleep. At first I tell myself it's due to the lumpy bed in the basement, the sheets that smell of cedar, and the dripping of a faucet, but I know better. I'm going to see Carson tomorrow. I don't know what to wear. I don't know what to say. My heart dances as I warn it to calm down. I wonder if he still looks like he does in my memory. I wonder how it will feel to talk while looking into his eyes.

In the kitchen, I forgo my usual iced tea and drink warm milk. When Milkweed purrs, I fill her white porcelain saucer that has *Spoiled* stamped on the side. I listen to the wall clock tick and watch its pendulum sway like a nervous cattail in the wind.

The next morning I head out for a walk, wishing Natasha were here to join me. The stress building in my head releases, and after walking ten blocks through the neighborhood and having a dozen homeowners either wave at me or wish me good morning, I'm convinced that it isn't hard to make friends here and eventually know everyone.

By a brick house on the corner, children play a game of croquet. Their mallets slice across the manicured lawn at the colored balls. The squeals and clapping bring smiles to parents seated on plastic chairs on a nearby patio.

An hour later I'm ready to go back to my aunt's. I'm perspiring and eager to get into the shower.

After my shower, I stand by the bed in the basement, a towel around me, and look at what I have to wear. My choices are limited to the packing decision I made yesterday. There's a jeans skirt, the purple cotton shirt I wore on my date with Taylor, a green shirt, a pair of jeans with holes at the knees (Mom is never impressed when I wear them), a pair of khaki shorts, and three cotton T-shirts all in varying shades of pink. If I'd known that I was going to see Carson, I'd have brought my sundress with the Thai print. I like the way it shows off my shoulders and is pleated at the waist.

"You are going to have fun," I tell my reflection in the bathroom. I smile—one of those smiles I often see at the boutique from a customer when she tries on a scarf or hat, strikes a pose, and thinks that no one is watching. I wonder if the jeans skirt and green shirt were the right choices and wish I was wearing the sundress. Mom tells me I look good in green, which brings out my olive complexion and brown eyes.

As I continue to hide out in the bathroom, I wonder if Carson will even show up. He's from Raleigh. He could have plans to go home for the holiday.

I frown at my reflection. *You sack of hay*, I almost say aloud. *You could be worrying for nothing.* I smooth my hair, then fluff it up around my temples. I hope that the tension in my neck will ease.

Leave it to Beanie to find me. "What are you doing down here?" she asks, knocking on the bathroom door.

"Busy," I say.

"Well, come on out and quit your foolishness."

I press my nose to the door. "I'm not being foolish."

"Come on out now."

"Why?" With my eyes on the stained ceiling, I wonder why this bathroom has to reek so heavily of Pine-Sol. With the amount she uses to clean, I think Dovie must have stock in the company. Closing my eyes, I try not to breathe.

"You are needed upstairs."

"Now?" Could Carson already be here?

"Hurry."

"I'm busy," I say and wince at my own deceit.

Beanie tries a soothing tone. "Come on, sugar, you can't miss out just 'cause you're nervous."

I turn around and swing open the door. "I am not nervous."

She eyes me, her small hands against her hips, a stance I've never seen her hold. "Sure you are."

"I am fine." I enunciate each word like I did when teaching English as a Second Language.

"Well, I would be if I were you."

I square my shoulders and walk toward the staircase.

"You can't hide from life. Even I know that."

I want to say so much—but not to Beanie. I want sympathy, not reprimand.

She follows me like the conscience I can't get rid of.

I march up the steps, almost run into Milkweed, and abruptly stop as I come face-to-face with the past standing before me— just as handsome and inviting as he was way back then.

"Sam." Carson's deep voice takes me back to the camp,

during the early mornings when he'd stop by to wake me for a walk to the market.

"Carson, how nice to see you!" I say a little too enthusiastically. My smile is pasted on my face, unable to come off even if I wanted it to. I know it's not wise, but nevertheless I look into his eyes—eyes greener than I remembered. My ears feel like they've been stuffed with cotton; it's hard to hear when your heart bangs against your rib cage like a noisy hammer. At last I find my voice. "Who would have thought we'd both meet again in North Carolina?"

He hugs me then, all warm and smelling of a fresh spring day.

Dovie tells us to make ourselves comfortable on the porch, where Pearl sits with a ball of rust-colored yarn and her crochet needle. My aunt and Beanie carry plates of food in from the kitchen.

I motion to a wicker chair to the left of the love seat. Carson sits down as I slip onto the love seat beside Pearl.

I introduce Carson, and when I say his name, Pearl puts her yarn and needle aside and tells him that she had a brother named Carson. As the two make small talk, I place my attention on the ceiling fan, the floor, anything but Carson's beautiful eyes. When there's a break in the conversation, I ask what he's been up to, and as he shares about a local Moravian man who makes the best cheese soufflé, I think that I must have missed something. "Do you know this man?" I ask.

He grins. "Like I said, he's my neighbor and works in Old Salem. You know Old Salem, right?"

"Of course," I say too quickly. I've only visited the famous Moravian section of Winston once as a child and don't remember much about it except people wore old-fashioned clothing and talked in a funny dialect.

"My neighbor is taking part in a soufflé contest today."

Carson continues to talk as I realize all I've been concentrating on is my breathing and making sure that I'm poised and looking relaxed. But I'm not relaxed because Carson is looking me over; I know he must be because he hasn't seen me since 1986, seven years ago. I would like to look him over, but my gaze is glued to the right of me, on Pearl. Pearl's worn eyes are safe to look at; this old woman will not coax my heart from its safe place.

The ceiling fan creaks as Pearl says, "I've never made a soufflé, but I do like to make a rhubarb pie every Sunday." With a chuckle she looks around the room and adds, "Sometimes I forget family tradition and make pies on other days of the week, too."

I can't recall the last time I had rhubarb. I know that Pearl's pies will be served for dessert tonight, along with the cake Dovie iced.

"The family recipe uses half a cup of white and half a cup of brown." She giggles as though she has told a funny joke.

"My mother always made rhubarb pies in the summer."

"I hated rhubarb when I was a child," Pearl confesses. "I think it's because it reminded me of celery, and I don't like celery."

I wonder if I've left earth and am now hovering around the twilight zone. This is ridiculous. Who doesn't like celery?

Carson smiles at me. "Sam, remember the time you and I made a pie for one of our potluck dorm dinners?"

I do remember that time. "It was an *ube* pie."

Carson explains the purple vegetable to Pearl as the older woman listens intently.

"A purple yam," repeats Pearl. "Sounds colorful. Now what is it called again?"

"Ube," Carson says. Then he jovially asks, "Sam, have you made any fried onions and green peppers lately?"

My first reaction is to laugh, and I do. "I don't have that skillet, so you know, without it, I can't cook." I see the skillet in my mind—it was a heavy object that once caught fire when I left it on a burner without any oil. I know Carson is remembering that scene because he was there to put out the fire with a bucket of tap water.

"Do you ever hear from anyone?" Carson leans closer toward me.

"From PRPC days? I get a letter from Brice about once a year. Christmas card, actually."

"I get those. I can't believe he's married with four kids and still living in the Philippines."

Once I got letters from you, I want to say. Then you stopped writing to me. I almost feel bold enough to ask him, What happened? But I just smile until my face feels like it might crack like dried Play-Doh.

When Beanie returns to the gathering from the kitchen, we stop talking to hear her tell us, "Wash up now because dinner is nearly ready." The aroma of food is enticing, although my stomach is tighter than Pearl's ball of yarn.

Carson and I head to the little bathroom by the front door as Pearl joins us, her orthopedic shoes heavy against the wooden floor. We let her go first and stand by the opened door as she insists that we use the decorative soaps in the glass canister beside the sink.

"I never knew why people buy these pretty things only to display them and never wash with them," she tells us as she pulls out a peach-colored ball in the shape of a seashell. As the water runs, she lathers with the soap ball. She rinses, dries her hands on the red, white, and blue guest towel that displays an embroidered American flag, and says, "I believe in enjoying life, I guess."

Carson and I smile discreetly at each other, and taking her advice, wash our hands with the pretty soap. Then we leave the fragrant room for the porch, where dinner is served under the wobbly ceiling fan.

Carson is the epitome of good-natured. His memory must be shorter than I realized, forgetting the distance that was once between us. "Sam, it's good to see you."

I swallow the desire to be sarcastic. How easy it would be for me to blurt out something about how he refused my advances one night after we watched a video together. How he wanted nothing to do with me for some time after that and how embarrassed I felt. How we disagreed over Lien's accusation of theft. How he avoided me.

When Dovie appears, we seat ourselves at the table, noting the aromatic spread that lay before us. There is a plate with stuffed eggs, another with watermelon, grapes, and melon slices, and a platter stacked with grilled pork chops. A green salad filled with Boston and romaine lettuce, cucumbers, dried cranberries, tomatoes, and slivered almonds is to the left of my elbow, and in front of Carson are trays of twice-baked potatoes and homemade oatmeal bread. An inviting dome of whipped butter sits in a ceramic dish.

Dovie asks us all to hold hands around the table, and then she says her usual prayer of thanksgiving. Once she says her "Amen and amen," we lift our heads and start passing platters of food.

I spoon small portions onto my plate and hope that no one comments on how little I've taken. As I cut my pork chop, I also hope that no one notices my shaking hand.

Beanie asks Carson about the radio station where he works, and after he's told us about that, I jump in to ask the question I've wanted to hear the answer to. "How do you all know each other?"

They look around and exchange sly smiles.

"I needed bail money and your aunt helped me out." Carson says this like it's a joke, but knowing how many people my aunt helps, it could be the truth.

"Really?" I scan their faces and realize Carson is kidding. "Tell me the truth now."

"It was at the soup kitchen," says my aunt. "Last December, wasn't it? His radio station was raising money for the kitchen, some sort of fund-raiser." She lifts a forkful of potato and eats.

"And he interviewed you," Beanie adds.

"That's right. I said something about being proud to give of my time." She looks at us and shrugs. "Something pretty lame."

"Oh, no!" cries Beanie. "You did just great. I was . . ." Her eyes focus on her hands. "I was proud of you."

I look closely to see that her eyes are moist. She blinks, looks back at her hands.

I want to reach across the table and say, "There now, Beanie. You can be sentimental after all."

Carson looks my way. "Then last week, I learned that Dovie is Sam's aunt."

"That's when I got the notion to invite Carson over for dinner with y'all tonight." My aunt is proud she could pull off this meeting, I can tell. Her face is radiant with the satisfaction of a well-kept secret. "I knew Sam would be coming here for the Fourth."

Dovie knows I'll always make my way down South when she asks; her home is like a respite from a weary world.

"I was the one who was listening to the radio station when Carson was announcing a song, remember that?" Beanie says. "He said it reminded him of his days in the Philippines at a refugee camp. I called him right then. I knew that Sam spent a year there."

"Same camp?" Pearl asks.

"Same camp," says Carson, his smile directed at me.

"And was the song Madonna's 'Borderline'?" I say with a knowing grin, because it had to be either that or one of Michael Jackson's.

Carson laughs. "It sure was."

"Since you work at the station," says Pearl, "could you have them play a song for us?"

"A song? Now?"

"I mean, this is quite a reunion we have here. You and Sam together again after all these years." Beanie tosses me a sly smile that I try to ignore.

"We do need a song sung," my aunt chimes in.

"Which one?" asks Carson as he sips his iced tea.

Beanie thinks aloud. "Now, we want something peppy, and yet not too loud."

"How about an oldie?" Dovie's eyes are bright. "I like lots of songs by Peter, Paul, and Mary."

"I like Frank Sinatra," Pearl informs us. Her smile is generous, exposing her tiny teeth. I wonder how she chews food with the miniature enamels. "Or is he too old for this group?"

"Everyone knows Sinatra," says Carson, his words making Pearl beam.

"I met him once." Pearl looks like she's trying to recall just where that meeting took place.

"You were in Manhattan," says Dovie.

"Oh yes, I must have told you about it already." She nods. "Yes, I was."

"Really?" Carson looks impressed.

For the first time I'm relieved that Mom's not here. She'd certainly jump into her old story of how her friend was once kissed by Elvis.

"We need a song that commemorates us." Dovie's mind is searching, I can tell by the way her eyes are squinty. "We need it to have a line in there that describes how we're feeling."

I can think of plenty of songs that deal with love that has gone sour, but I doubt anyone would understand why I feel a song like that would be appropriate right now.

Pearl has been concentrating with closed eyes, and now as they spring open, she cries, "Celebrate."

Beanie claps her hands together. "Celebrate!" She laughs as the older woman smiles. "By Kool and The Gang!"

"That's perfect!" says Dovie.

Beanie starts singing the chorus. "'Celebrate, come on!'" Then she insists that we each have a wedge of chocolate cake and rhubarb pie.

twenty

After dessert, Dovie gets the phone from the kitchen and hands it to Carson. From memory, Carson punches in the numbers as we wait with broad smiles.

Pearl whispers, "This is the first time I've ever requested a song on the radio." Her excitement is like a little girl's as she does something she has heard about but never had the opportunity or the nerve to try.

"Hey." Carson's voice is warm when the station answers the phone. "It's Carson. Hi, Jason." We are quiet as Jason talks and then hear Carson say, "Happy Fourth to you, too. The group I'm with wants to request a song. 'Celebration' by Kool and The Gang."

Pearl nods as Beanie rubs her hands together in anticipation.

"I don't know," Carson responds to whatever he's been asked. He looks around at us. "I guess we're Dovie's dinner guests."

"Dovie's exclusive dinner guests," Beanie says with authority. To the rest of us, she adds, "I always wanted to be part of an exclusive party."

After Carson hangs up, we resume our conversation as the radio provides background noise.

Dovie tells about a butterfly release she had a few weekends ago, where the butterflies refused to get out of the cage, even after she banged on the top a bit with her hand. She then explains how she plans to overnight some butterflies for a release in Florida.

The song "Yesterday" by The Beatles comes on, its melancholy tune reminding me of so many yesterdays, of time slipping away. Then we hear Jason announce that the next song is dedicated to "Dovie's exclusive dinner guests," and we grow quiet with expectancy. As the music begins, we grin at one another. Beanie taps her foot against the porch floor. Pearl rises from her chair, her belly knocking a spoon onto the floor, and twists her arms a bit, resembling a Hawaiian dancer.

Carson meets my smile and says, "Doesn't this remind you of the Philippines?" And I agree that although it's an older crowd tonight, the desire to sing and dance is just like during those camp days.

Beanie turns up the volume and sings with the musicians, "'Celebrate good times, come on!'" Then she pushes aside a few chairs and flexes her arms and shakes her thighs in an energetic move.

Dovie stands, her tall apron-clad frame looking like a telephone pole next to Beanie's short body. She wiggles her hips and snaps her fingers, not at all in sync with the music, but no one seems to mind. Pearl grabs her hand and the two shuffle about the room in between the furniture.

I envision plates being hit by swinging limbs and torsos so, maneuvering around the dancers, stack up a few to carry into the kitchen. Carson grabs two and follows me.

In the kitchen, beside the loud ticking clock, he says, "You know what?"

"What?" I say as I begin loading the dirty dishes into the dishwasher.

"Lien said you are the same, and you are."

I think that the years have made him mellow.

"Well . . ." I suck in air. "It's unbelievable that we are standing in the same space again."

He smiles, and I note that his light green shirt makes his eyes appear even greener. They are like emeralds almost, and I remember that when I used to look at them closely, I saw flecks of green, brown, and amber.

Seeing that the group on the porch is still dancing, Carson and I sit at the table.

"Is your family still in Raleigh?" I ask.

"They are. My brother and his wife bought a house off of Glenwood. My sister just got married."

"We were so worried about her. And you."

Carson's voice is soft. "Yeah. I'm glad she's okay."

"What was her diagnosis?"

"Breast cancer."

The words sting inside my heart. "My mom went through breast cancer."

Carson frowns. "How is she?"

"She had a mastectomy. Now she's fine. Well, you know, checkups every year where they run a bunch of tests."

"And you hold your breath and pray that the results are negative."

I nod and feel that bond between us fuse again, like all the years we've been apart never existed. "Exactly."

Laughter rushes from the porch into the kitchen. Beanie is still dancing. From the sound of scraping movements, she's possibly moving chairs to make for more room.

Carson's smile captivates me, and although I try, I can't look away. "Seems like they are having a good time," he says.

"Beanie with more talent than the other two."

"Your aunt is good for her. Good for all of us in Winston. Like our own Mother Teresa."

"Like you were in the camp."

"Me?"

"You helped everyone. Everyone knew you and liked you."

"Except for Minh. Remember how he was angry with me for sticking up for Lien?"

I'm about to ask how his relationship is now with the Vietnamese man when Carson reaches for my hand and runs his finger along my thumb. "Sam." His voice is low.

Warmth rises from my stomach and spreads over my limbs. Carson's face is inches from mine.

With feeling he says, "It's so nice being with you again."

"Oh, I almost forgot!" I pull my arms away from the table.

"What?"

"I have to take photos of the butterflies for Mom."

His look holds disbelief. I know that look well. "Right now?"

I don't meet his eyes.

"Sam?"

"And I have to make a phone call. Will you excuse me?" Darting out of the kitchen, I climb the stairs to the second floor. Once upstairs, I wonder where to go.

The bathroom is not in use. Inside, I lock the door. Leaning against the white door, I trace the wood with my fingers and feel my breath against my hand. I will not come out. I will not. Carson is not going to win me over.

Ever.

If that's what he's trying to do.

And he's not.

Eventually, I find that I can open the bathroom door and return to the porch. I decide to avoid the kitchen in case Carson might still be seated at the table. When I hear his voice from the group outside, I let myself enter the kitchen. Grabbing a glass from the cupboard, I fill it with water from the faucet and take a long sip. The water soothes my throat.

Just then I hear pounding on the back door. I open it to see four neighborhood kids standing there.

"Daddy's going to do fireworks," the tallest boy announces. He looks like he could be seven or eight.

"Where's Miss Dovie?" asks a girl. She has no front teeth.

"Out on the front porch," I say.

"Tell her to watch the fireworks."

The boys are in shorts, and the girls are wearing red, white, and blue sundresses.

"Will you tell her?" The tallest is demanding.

"I will."

"We're doing them on the cuddle sack."

I note the dots of perspiration on his tiny nose. "The what?"

"The road," says the girl with bouncy blond hair. Pink bubblegum pops off her lips. She catches it in her hand, shoving it back into her mouth. She then slides her hand across her sundress a few times.

"Cuddle sack is what you call the end of the road," says the shorter boy, wisdom flowing from his young words.

"Okay. I'll let everyone know."

Neighbors arrive carrying lawn chairs. They set them on the edge of the road in front of Dovie's porch. Dovie greets them all by name and asks if they would like either chocolate cake or rhubarb pie. Each one declines her offer but thanks her.

The family with the fireworks has its clan seated on a large fluffy blanket on their lawn at the end of the road. The children shriek and clap, begging their daddy to start the show.

Carson is near me. I have no idea where anyone else is; I just know that Carson is seated to my right, inches from my elbow. If I look down, I can see his left black Adidas with the milky white shoelaces.

The first firecracker launches. As it crackles into the darkness, it exposes each face with light. The next one flares, sending rockets of color into the dark sky.

The audience claps. The children cry for another.

I get a glimpse of Carson's face, that sturdy nose, that chin that juts out a little, and those eyes that squint when he's puzzled. But when he catches my gaze, I turn and study the sky once more.

One by one, the fireworks boom into the air. I've always been mesmerized by the beauty of these things. There is so much noise and color packed into one small container. I recall how Daddy would let me choose which cellophane pack to buy from the display at the grocery store. As a child I wanted the assortment that would bring the most sizzle. "Which package makes the best noises?" I recall asking my father. "That's what I want!"

Now I prefer the rockets that cause the air to tingle with romantic notions. I once told Natasha, "Fireworks are romantic."

She agreed and confessed, "I always pretend they scare me and then I have an excuse to grab the hand of the guy I'm with."

I feel Carson's legs stretched out near mine, his broad hands within holding distance. But even as a boom of fire rapidly sails into the sky, I can't reach for him. *You did that once, remember?*

He leans in and whispers something about the fireworks. I can't hear him over the chattering children and adults around us.

When three rockets pop into the sky, the children squeal. White stars crackle in the air, each one louder than the previous one.

"Daddy, make the next one hit the moon!" one boy shouts after the residue from the cardboard has subsided and the last hiss has left the sky.

Carson turns to me, his arm brushing against mine.

The urge to kiss him has never left me. As Beanie would say, it just got "pushed underneath all the living."

twenty-one

November 1986

Van came into my classroom with two other Vietnamese men the minute my afternoon students left. Standing beside my desk, they presented me with a bottle of Coke. I thanked them and asked how they were doing.

The men—older men with solemn faces that I'd never seen before during my visits to the neighborhoods—formed questions, questions directed at me for Van to translate. Van stressed that I must be truthful. As Lien's teacher, I needed to tell them what I thought of her. I agreed that I would be honest in my answers and so admitted that, yes, Lien came to class with items that did not belong to her. Yes, I thought she could steal. She had taken a pair of scissors from my desk drawer and had taken them home, secretly returning them a couple of days later; a fellow student had seen her slipping them into my drawer and shouted that Lien was a thief.

After the questions stopped, the men nodded, thanked me, and left. The room suddenly felt eerie, making me wonder what had just taken place.

Due to the questioning session, I missed the agency's van that afternoon and had to slowly walk the half mile back to my dormitory. I had a Bible study to attend, which lasted a long time, making me not get to the mess hall for dinner until almost eight. I looked for Carson, but he must have already eaten or was with students. I couldn't find him.

The next afternoon I found Carson alone in his classroom. We had both missed the van back to the dorms.

"Did they question you?" Carson's tone was low. He shoved his lesson planner into a knapsack he often carried around camp.

"Who?"

"Van and the councilmen."

I thought of the two men who'd entered my classroom with Van yesterday. I'd had no idea they were councilmen. From the look on Carson's face, he had some bad news to share. I hoped that Van hadn't conveyed to him what I'd shared with the men. "They did. Did they question you, too?"

His sigh lifted from his lungs and then he sat down. "The council members from Neighborhood Nine agreed to search the Hongs' billet."

"And?"

"They didn't find any of the jewelry and the only money was in a tin can and it amounted to a measly thirty pesos. Lien didn't steal anything. I don't know why her reputation makes everyone certain she would steal."

"So, since they found nothing, this means she's not guilty, then?"

Carson shook his head. "They think she stashed it somewhere else."

Maybe if she held a better rapport among her people, I

wanted to say, they wouldn't be so quick to accuse her. But then I realized that the dust or dirt of the earth would never be thought of as innocent. Regardless of whether she had the behavior of an angel, she would always be looked down upon. *Some things do not change, Samantha.*

Defeated, Carson laid his head against his folded arms on his desk.

I wondered if he'd let me hold him. I placed a hand along his back. When he didn't protest, I put both arms around him and laid my face on his shoulder.

"Mr. Hong told Lien that she can't come by this classroom to see me anymore. He's not letting her go out freely. He's keeping her on a tight rein."

"I'm sorry," I breathed into his shoulder.

A warm November wind pelted the tin roof, and the rats along the overhead beams grew quiet. I felt a cramp in my leg but didn't want to move away from Carson. I wondered if he cared more about the Hong family than anyone else in the camp. His capacity to wrap himself around the four of them was amazing to me. Sure, I felt a fondness for many of the refugees, but I knew my devotion could never match his. It set me in awe—and it frustrated me.

Carson's breath brushed against my encircled bare arms. I had this feeling that if he moved his lips, they would brush against my skin. I held my own breath, the longing growing with each moment.

Suddenly, the door to his classroom opened and Brice walked in, a smirk on his face.

Carson got up and stepped away from me, leaving me to catch myself from falling by grabbing the edge of his massive desk.

Brice sauntered over to us. "Want to go get dinner? I'm starving."

"Sure," said Carson.

"Did you hear that Lien's not allowed to come visit you anymore?" Brice shrugged. "Just as well. She's a handful. Do you think she really stole all that stuff?"

"Just a jade necklace and some bracelets," I said.

"That's not what I heard. I was told that she took a few dozen pieces of jewelry from five billets in the Neighborhood Nine, and at least seven hundred pesos."

Carson looked pained.

I wanted to tell him that it would be okay, that I was here, that I'd be glad to sit with him and just listen to the wind.

He looked at me and said, "Let's go eat."

My heart lurched.

Slowly, I followed him and Brice out of the warm classroom, into the damp evening air. But my longing stayed, sticking onto my skin more tightly than Dovie's butterfly cocoons wrapped on tree limbs.

twenty-two

Dovie, Beanie, and I clean up the kitchen, removing dishes from the dishwasher and placing them in the cupboards. Little calls from her daughter Liza's in Florence, South Carolina, where she's spending the holiday weekend. Dovie answers the phone and talks a bit and then repeats to us what Little just told her. "Says Liza wants to join the convent and become a nun."

Beanie rolls her eyes and mutters, "Has she lost her mind?"

"Well, well," my aunt says after listening a while longer, "I suppose that might work." To us, she says, "Little says that Liza wants to study overseas. Maybe Paris."

"Why does everyone want to go to Paris?" Beanie says to me.

"It's romantic," I tell her. I've always wanted to see the Eiffel Tower and dine outside at a street café under the stars. And just maybe, be with someone who touches my arm, causing fire to pulsate through every vein.

"I've seen all those movies that are set in Paris. Don't look like a place a person like me would fit in."

"Aren't you part French?" I ask, setting a plate atop the stack of others in the cupboard.

"Sammie Sugar, I am part everything, but that doesn't mean I understand it all."

When the kitchen is "put back into place," as Beanie says, Beanie, still murmuring about Paris, heads up the stairs to her room to listen to the radio. Dovie hangs a dish towel on the rack by the sink and tells me she's going outside to check on her butterflies and make sure the hens are rounded up and secure in their coop.

Knowing that I need to sleep because I can't be up like I was last night, I stick to my nightly ritual and brew a pot of coffee. As the crickets and bullfrogs serenade each other across neighbors' lawns, I join Milkweed on the porch's love seat.

The silent porch only makes me think of Carson. I sip from my mug of coffee, and although its aroma is strong, stronger still are the fumes from the fireworks. They filter through the air like the scent of a woman's perfume lingers even long after she's departed.

"Dovie?" I ask after she returns from making sure all her insects and chickens are safe. I know that ideally she'd like to believe that the chickens would go to their roosting spots by themselves each night without assistance, but there has been a spotting of a fox in the neighborhood, and Dovie doesn't want to subject her possessions to an attack.

"Yes, dear?" Dovie's voice has that lovely Southern charm to it. My own mother works hard at hiding her Southern accent. For whatever reason, she doesn't eagerly admit that she was born and raised in Winston. I think it's because, once she married Daddy, they lived in various northern regions and people teased her about her drawl.

With my legs stretched out on the ottoman, I ask my aunt, "Did you ever think of becoming a nun?"

"As a matter of fact, yes, indeed I did."

"Really?"

She plops her tall body onto the space beside me on the love seat. "Yes, I also wanted to be a Dallas Cowboys cheerleader and an interpreter for the United Nations."

I search her face to check if she's serious.

Her laughter is loud. "Me? Can you believe those dreams I once had?"

"I can. I once wanted to be a secret agent."

"Is that so?"

"After our trip to Scotland. Daddy told me I'd make a great agent, and he was sure that Scotland Yard could use me." I never made it to Scotland again, or London. But after traveling to the United Kingdom during our family vacation, I did yearn to live and work overseas. When I read about the need for teachers at the refugee camp years later, I eagerly applied and hugged Mom a few times when my application was accepted.

Dovie pats my leg like one would pat her child's, only my aunt has never had children. "I want you to know that you shouldn't worry so much."

"Worry?"

"Yes, I see those worry lines on your forehead."

I rub my forehead with my index finger.

"Samantha?" My name hangs from her lips like a cloak from a hanger.

"Yeah. I know."

"Know what?" Her brow wrinkles as her eyes look into mine.

This time I pat her leg. "That God loves me and wants me to trust so that I have no need for worry."

She relaxes. "I know you have a lot on your plate."

"You mean Mom and the shop?"

"And the past and the future."

I inhale and nod.

"I'm not sure what that boy meant to you in the Philippines, but you are here now. Release your fears to God."

In my mind I see a mass of orange and black decorating a field, beginning a journey. "Like the butterflies?"

"Exactly."

The crickets chirp wildly through the trees as the ceiling fan sputters, casting a breeze over my legs. I think of how we miss so much of nature's offerings because we're too occupied with our own dilemmas, yet if we listened to her music more, we might find the solace we desperately need.

"Release and be still," my aunt says.

"I loved him." Once the words leave my mouth, I wonder who has spoken. I think about clarifying or retracting them, but I'm too tired to try.

"I know."

"I won't get hurt again."

She places an arm around my shoulders. "No, you won't. You won't be hurt twice."

I rest my head against her arm. "How can you tell? How do you know?"

"I've been in love. Never found a man who could handle being my husband, but I know about love."

"How do you think Mom ever got so she could trust a man?"

"You mean your father?"

"Yeah. She says the two of you lived in an environment where there was little love and trust."

"You know that's true, Sam. She's not making up the ugly incidences of lies and deceit and abuse that infested our child-hood. But as I got older, I refused to let it keep me from living. God had to do a load of healing in me." Squeezing my shoulder, she continues. "Gradually, I learned that not everyone is out to get you. Your mama just is taking longer to see the same."

At this point in her life, I doubt my mother will ever change and soften like her sister, Dovie. Suspicious and cautious, she has become old before her time.

"She loves us, though, Sam. She may not want the affection or tell us that she loves us, but she does. Believe that."

My eyes well as I long for the days with Daddy when Mom smiled more often and I felt the strength of family.

Dovie kisses my cheek and gently wipes a tear that has criss-crossed my face.

We sit together as dogs bay in a neighbor's yard and a few firecrackers pop into the distant air. Then, after commenting on the brightness of the moon, we leave the porch and head inside. I wait as Dovie locks the front door and then watch her climb the stairs to her bedroom, Milkweed trailing closely behind.

Dovie pauses to say that she hopes I sleep well; I tell her the same.

twenty-three

Beanie makes me blueberry pancakes and sausage links for breakfast. She insists that I try the new syrup shipped from her friends in Vermont. "It's the real stuff, Sammie. None of that artificial sugar substance. You have not lived until you have tasted real maple syrup."

I'm not sure why she assumes that I've never had the real stuff before. But I play along. Lifting a large piece of pancake with my fork, I watch the syrup drip onto the plate. The morsel fills my mouth. "Wow, it is good."

"Better, right?"

"So much better." I take another bite.

Beanie smiles and pours herself a cup of coffee. "Want a cup?" She reaches for a mug as I answer, "Please."

"Someone made a pot of coffee last night and didn't bother to wash it out." Beanie's gaze hovers around mine.

Guilty, I confess, "It was me. Sorry."

As she hands me a mug, she says, "Coffee at bedtime. I don't know how you do that and actually sleep."

I take a sip; the warmth from the strong liquid glides down my throat. "In theory," I say, borrowing her phrase, "caffeine is supposed to make you not able to sleep. I guess I'm wired wrong."

She laughs. "I suppose we all have our little quirks. Dovie thinks it odd that I listen to WKLV every night."

The call letters for the station sound familiar. "Carson's station, right?"

She adds more sugar to her coffee, then stirs the beverage with the handle of a wooden mixing spoon. "Sure is. And by the way, he is a good D.J."

I don't want to keep the conversation on Carson. He already occupies way too many of my thoughts. I focus on the mosaic that decorates the wall behind Dovie's stove. The pattern is a monarch butterfly, marigold wings spread, ready to fly.

"He has a lot of fans."

"That was fun dancing," I say, changing the subject.

Beanie stares at me over the counter. After a moment she says, "Until it reminded me of the old days."

"Old days?"

"When I lived in New York City and was a dancer."

"Do you miss New York?"

"Never." She spits the word.

"Where's your family? Do they live up there still?"

"I'm from all over."

"That's right. You're every woman." Eager to learn more about her past, I lean on my elbows and say, "Were you really homeless?"

She nods. "The rumors are true."

She seems sad. Perhaps I've gone and opened a can of

memories she'd prefer to keep shut. I try to mask my own discomfort by asking if she got the bank job she interviewed for weeks ago.

"No."

"Sorry."

"Not a problem." She wipes the counter with a cloth. "In theory, I want to work. But then there's my health issue."

"Your health?" Oh no, I think. What is wrong with Beanie? Please not cancer, please not cancer.

But Pearl enters the room before Beanie can answer. The elderly woman is dressed in a flowered duster, her head covered by a brimmed straw hat, her black shoes firmly on her tiny feet. "I was going out to take care of the garden and feed the hens."

Beanie takes one look at her and says, "I'll come too." I'm not sure why she feels she must supervise the old woman. It's only the garden, I think. Pearl is not going combat fighting.

Beanie challenges my thoughts. "Those hens can be a handful," she says. "Dinner is an exceptional bear." She opens the back door and waits for Pearl to join her outside. They'll water the herbs, feed the chickens, and no doubt converse about the old days like all good Southerners do.

I finish my breakfast as the hens chatter outside. I consider calling Mom at the beach house. She should be awake and drinking her coffee, sweetened with a teaspoon and a half of sugar. I can see her in a straw hat, a little less worn than Pearl's, and adorned with a few flowers she's picked on a walk to the beach. She and Maralinda are probably deciding where they'll eat lunch. A wave of jealousy sweeps over my heart. If they would invite me to join them, I'd accept the invitation in a second.

Minutes later, when Carson appears at the back door, my mind is still on Mom. In fact, the cordless kitchen phone is in my hand. "Carson!" Here I am in a frayed T-shirt and pair of cutoffs and without any makeup.

As he grins through the screen door, I run a hand down my uncombed hair. "What are you doing here?"

"I was in the neighborhood."

I don't know whether to let him in or make him wait until I feel more presentable.

He opens the door and lets himself in. "How are you?"

"Good." I place the phone back in its cradle. "And what are you up to? Breaking and entering?"

His smile is genuine. There were times in the camp that his smile was clearly fake, only used to appease Dr. Rogers, our staunch director, or an irate student. I also remember that at the camp, he just waltzed into my dorm to see me whenever he pleased. "I was thinking we could go over to the bistro," he says.

"I don't think so." The words come out unfiltered, but once they're said, I stand behind them.

He doesn't leave, just grins, his eyes shiny and knowing. It's that knowing look that gets to me. Like he can see into my soul or read my mind. I'm not sure which is worse.

We are no longer at the Philippine Refugee Processing Center, I want to tell him. Here, people call before coming over. This is the South, and as a Southerner he should know that there are invitations, rules and regulations. Even in the Philippines I questioned his motivations when he'd knock on my dorm room door Saturday mornings and tell me I needed to go with him to the market for a breakfast of Vietnamese sandwiches or spicy noodle soup. Why did he want to spend so much time with me when he was saving his heart for Mindy?

"It's Saturday, Carson," I'd tell him at the camp.

"I know," he'd whisper. "The day's not hot yet. Plus, you like to walk."

Today I mumble, "I have . . . I have . . . things . . . to do." I know Dovie is headed to the homeless shelter. Who's to say I wasn't planning to go there with her?

His look of disappointment surprises me. Stuffing his hands into his jeans pockets, he confesses, "It doesn't have to take long."

I want to say that I'm sorry, that he will have to go without me, that I am a busy woman now and not at all able or willing to respond to his spontaneity. "Okay," I say. "But can I take a shower first?"

"Sure, that would be acceptable."

"You can wait in the den. Dovie's in there with Milkweed watching *The Price Is Right*."

At Saigon Bistro, the only table available is in a corner near the restrooms. I hate sitting by the restrooms. As customers walk to and from the lavatory, my hope is that they wash their hands.

Lien comes from the kitchen to greet us. Her dyed-brown hair is in a ponytail and her makeup adds sophistication to her round face. She looks Carson over and says, "You look handsome like movie star."

Normally I would laugh at such a line, but I'm at a loss for words.

Carson seems unmoved. Casually, he says, "Thank you."

"What you want today?" she asks, running fingers down her white apron with *Saigon Bistro* embroidered in baby blue over her chest.

We know what we want; there is no mulling it over. Carson orders two bowls of pho with pork.

Before heading back to the kitchen, she sticks around our table to tell us how she thinks movie stars came to eat at the restaurant yesterday. "They very nice and very beautiful."

"Do you know who they were?" asks Carson.

"Maybe Lady Diana. And someone else."

"Lady Di is not a movie star," I say.

Lien produces a small smile at Carson. "To me, she is."

When she leaves us alone, I let out the first thing that comes to mind. "She still adores you. Clearly."

"She's appreciative."

Huy brings our lunch on a black lacquer tray. Seeing we have nothing to drink, he cries, "She didn't get you anything?" Frowning, he asks what we'd like.

We agree that water is fine, even after he suggests soda. Carson tells him to wait on the other paying customers, not to worry about us.

Steam fills our nostrils and eyes as Carson and I lean over our bowls with identical pairs of chopsticks.

Later, Lien smiles down at us as we eat. "Like PRPC," she says, refilling our water glasses from a metal pitcher. "Just like days there."

Carson smiles, I smile, and Lien giggles. I feel silly.

She insists that we eat the sweetened rice concoction that she's invented. It's a cross between the Indian kheer that Sanjay makes and Scottish oatmeal with brown sugar.

"You like?" Her eyes are hopeful.

Carson responds in Vietnamese.

"Good," I say, but I suspect that Lien has not heard me at all. She tells us that she wants to open another restaurant in High Point and serve hamburgers.

"Why?" I ask.

Gazing at Carson, she replies, "Americans eat hamburger more than bok choy." Her laughter continues; it hasn't changed since she was a rambunctious student in my classroom. I expect that she'd take a swing at a customer who got under her skin.

After our bowls are empty, Carson looks at me. "Want to walk a bit?"

"Where?"

"There's a park near here."

I think of the summer heat that rages outside these doors. But then I recall how we managed to walk and talk all over the camp during the sticky days and nights of our time in the tropics. "Okay," I say.

This will be my chance to talk with you without anyone else vying for your attention. Mentally, I form my questions, and as we stand to leave, a certainty takes over my mind. I'll ask about *her.*

Although he knows that the gesture is futile, before leaving the restaurant Carson hands Lien a twenty-dollar bill for our lunch.

"I tell you no pay," she says, waving his offer away. "How you say? On top of the house?"

"On the house." My teacher side comes out.

"I get it." Slowly, she says, "Santa Claus goes up on top of house, but when you give friends a meal, it is on the house."

We smile at her manner of memorizing the English language, and then in Vietnamese thank her for our lunch, Carson's gratitude a bit more lengthy than mine.

Washington Park is about two miles from the restaurant, near the North Carolina School of the Arts, an area filled with elite homes and well-groomed gardens.

"I think Dovie's taken me here before," I say when I see the two stone columns holding up the wrought-iron arch displaying the name of the park. "Some organization held a butterfly release."

"Most likely," says Carson. "It's a right nice place. Lots of history here." He parks his car near the entrance and then leads the way under the arch. Soon we are walking along a path under large oak trees, their leaves sheltering us from the sun.

151

Squirrels pounce and run up tree trunks as birds flit around us. The sky is a brilliant blue with white cumulus clouds that sashay across it, driven by a light wind.

Walking usually gives me the freedom to think and even say things I might not say in a living room. Perhaps I feel that if I mess up and say the wrong thing, I can easily take off down a side street or walk off in the opposite direction from whomever I'm walking with. I've never actually done this, but perhaps just knowing I can provides me with some kind of tranquil assurance.

"Why aren't you married?" I blurt while keeping pace with him, looking straight ahead.

"What do you mean?"

"What do you mean what do I mean? It's a simple question."

"Is there a simple answer?"

"Yes."

We continue down the dirt path and then pause at a playground. I eye the swing set as Carson volunteers, "Want me to push you in one?"

"No. I want you to tell me what happened to Mindy."

Standing across from him, I study Carson's expression. Part of me wants to watch him squirm as he realizes he can't ignore my prodding.

"Let's see." He acts like he can't quite remember, like he's trying to recall who Mindy is. "I think we grew apart."

That's a lame response, and I tell him so. "There has to be more."

"Does there?"

"She was your life! You talked about her all the time."

His eyes are somber, as though going back to a place far away. "She was. We were together for a long time."

We stand next to each other under a hot sun as we did many times in camp. Just like during those times, I want more. He

152

knows this; he knows so well what I want to hear, yet he will not budge.

I relent. "Sure, you can push me in the swing." I climb on one of the metal seats, plant my feet on the ground, and wait for him to get behind me. His hands are gentle yet strong against my back. I watch the ground grow farther and farther away from my feet, the breeze cooling my moist and warm skin. Suddenly, I miss and long for a world of yesterdays; I wish to be a child in a swing again, with my daddy pushing me.

"I love you to the Milky Way and back, Sam."

The swing slows as the pushes from Carson become less frequent. Soon, my feet are once more on the surface of the playground.

"What's wrong?" he asks when I don't get off.

"Just thinking of my dad and how we'd go to this park in Falls Church."

"And there was a playground with a swing set?" Carson's warm tone makes me nostalgic for a man whose love I never doubted.

"Yes. Rickety and old, but Dad pushed me high." Getting off the swing, I go to Carson's side. "I guess you never stop missing those who've died."

Carson's embrace is powerful and catches me off guard. I resist the urge to bury my nose in his shoulder, to breathe in the fabric-softener scent that clings to his T-shirt and bawl. Pulling away, I put my hands in my pockets.

"I'll race you," he says.

"To where?"

Pointing ahead, he says, "That tree."

"Which one? The tiny one by the path or that larger one?"

Still pointing, he says, "That big one on the right. See it?"

Without hesitating, I take off running, knowing I'll hear him complain that I've cheated.

Sure enough, he cries, "That's not fair, Sam!" Then he is at my side, both of us racing toward the tree. Laughing, we touch the thick, gnarly trunk. "I won," I boast.

"You are disqualified."

"No." I catch my breath.

He playfully touches my chin. "You are a cheater."

No, I want to say as we head back to the parking lot because it is almost time for his shift at the station. You are the cheater. You will not give me a straight answer. Instead, I ask if he remembers the surprise birthday party I gave for him when he turned twenty-four. I had the mess hall bake a chocolate cake and bought six flavors of ice cream, including fruit ones made of mango and ube.

"That was a nice surprise," he says as his eyes graze my face. "You were good to me there."

Back at Dovie's, I help with dinner preparation, chopping vegetables for Brunswick stew. Beanie has the broth seasoned and simmering as I add onions, potatoes, and carrots. She browns cubes of beef in a skillet and then spoons the beef into the pot with the vegetables.

With slices of buttered oatmeal bread, we fill up on the stew, talking about butterflies and the possibility of creating a new brochure for Dovie with the pictures I've taken of the insects.

"I want to have something nice to hand out to folks who want to hire me out," my aunt explains.

"You don't charge enough," says Beanie. "For all you do, you should have higher fees."

Little comes home on her bike at nine thirty, and we warm her up a bowl of stew. Slowly, in her halting manner, she tells us about her day at Wendy's, complaining about an irate customer who turned his Frosty over onto the floor and then demanded a refund. Dovie rubs her feet as Little cries.

Dovie soothes the woman's feet and tries to ease her mind. "Sometimes people are already angry when they come into a store. Something completely unrelated to you has made them feel ugly. So they act mean. You have to believe that it wasn't your fault."

I agree. Working in retail, I do know this happens. Women angry about jobs or spouses, or lack of jobs and spouses. They come into the shop hoping an afternoon spending spree will make them feel better, but I know no satin blouse or black party dress can permanently remove weeks of tension.

"Got bunions," says Little, the words slurring into each other. "They hurt like fire."

"Need my herbal balm?" asks Beanie. She opens a cabinet above the sink.

Little holds up a hand. "No, none of that for me, thank you. I'm allergic to it, I think."

I peer into the dark cabinet, wanting to see what Beanie's herbal balm looks like, but I only see a bottle of Dawn dish soap.

Soon Dovie and Little join Pearl in the den to watch a movie. I take a seat on the couch by Pearl, who is crocheting a turquoise bootie. I know she completed the matching one earlier today before her nap. This set is for her great-grandchild, due after Christmas. The movie has James Dean in it, and I watch until Beanie calls me into her room. "Hurry, Sammie girl, hurry, hurry!"

I leap up the stairs and enter her room just as the voice on the radio says, "So here it is. For Samantha." Then the music plays, and of course I recognize it: "Still Crazy After All These Years."

Beanie has flopped onto her bed, her dark hair a stark contrast to the white pillowcase. She watches me as the words fill her room.

" 'I met my old lover on the street today. She seemed so glad to see me, I just smiled.' "

Beanie shows an ample smile as I stand at her door and listen.

When the song ends and a commercial for tires comes on, Beanie turns down the volume to her radio and says, "You didn't tell me you were in love."

I'm admiring the candles she's made. She has six of them in candleholders on a shelf in her bookcase. Last summer when I came to visit, she taught Dovie and me how to create homemade candles from beeswax. I bend over to sniff a thick one with a strong gardenia scent. "That one smells great." I step back and finger each candle. "These are so pretty."

"Ignoring me isn't any good."

"I'm not ignoring you."

"Well?"

"We aren't boyfriend and girlfriend if that's what you mean."

Beanie raises an eyebrow and says, "Then why did he choose that song to dedicate to you?"

"It was one we sang. Together. Once."

Beanie lets out her signature huff. "What else can you tell me?"

I know I could say that I think he played Paul Simon's song because of today and how we acted crazy at the park. I could tell Beanie that, but I don't.

Muttering, Beanie says she's tired and going to sleep. She pulls back the quilt on her bed, exposing sheets with a floral pattern. Fluffing her pillow, she says, "I was hoping for a nice love story."

"There isn't one."

I leave her room as she calls out, "Radio station's number is 103.9 in case you want to listen."

I head to the basement. Dovie comes down the creaking steps with Milkweed to take a load of clothes out of the washer and heave them into the dryer. Once she turns the dryer on, I have to crank up the volume on the radio.

Carson's voice announces another dedication, this time America's "I Need You" from Hilly in High Point to her man, Billy.

"Hilly and Billy," I hear him say. I know he's trying not to laugh.

Milkweed leaps onto the bed and settles against my arm. As the words and music to the song play, I think of how we made fun of this song in high school, calling it sappy. *"Like the winter needs the spring, you know I need you. . . ."*

Now, it rates right up there with Billy Joel's "Just the Way You Are," carrying with it a hope that someday someone will play the lyrics just for me.

twenty-four

I dream I'm dressed in a feathery blue ao dai and trying to escape from a snorting bulldozer at Washington Park. The bulldozer's grunts grow less threatening when I hear faint noises overhead. Dovie comes down the steps into the basement with Milkweed trailing after her. I'm not fully awake and still grappling with why I couldn't outrun the machine. I hear a cheery, "Good morning!" My eyes open just as she hands me the cordless phone.

Milkweed jumps onto my bed, her tail brushing my face.

My fingers wrap around the receiver as the soles of Dovie's slippers scuff up the stairs. "Hello?" Clearing my voice, I try again, "Hello."

"Good morning." Carson's voice is like candy.

"Hey." I push Milkweed's tail off my nose. "What's up?"

"Lien wants us to come over to the restaurant."

"Again?"

"She wants to see you before you go."

I stretch my legs and look at the digital clock radio Dovie placed on the counter near the dripping faucet. Eight fifteen. "I'll be here all week," I say, and then regret that I admitted that to him.

"Great! She'll be glad to see you many times while you're in town, I'm sure."

"It's Tuesday, right?"

"Yeah."

I yawn and then clear my throat as Milkweed nestles against my thigh and lets out a purr. "So what are you doing today?"

"Laundry. Playing the sax. I need to practice a piece I'm supposed to play next Sunday at my church." As he speaks of his saxophone, I can almost hear the tunes he played at the camp, and once more I know I must safeguard my heart.

"Where do you live?"

"I bought a house here a year ago." As I'm imagining what type of house Carson would live in, he says, "I work the afternoon shift at the station today. How about dinner?"

"What?"

"Can I pick you up for dinner tonight?"

"I don't—"

"How about six-thirty?"

"I don't really—"

"Great! I'll see you then."

I start to protest, but he's already hung up.

Milkweed closes her eyes as I shake my head. Just who does he think he is? Aloud I gripe, "What if I had plans?" Stroking the cat's head, I tell her, "I could be busy tonight. Do I seem like the type of girl who would just drop everything for a man?"

The cat raises her head as though she's going to tell me what she thinks, and for a second I wish she could. Her gaze darts

toward the radio alarm clock. She probably wants to say, *Be
sure to tell him how much the song dedication meant to you
last night. I saw you smiling. Wasn't that the first time anyone
has ever dedicated a song on the radio to you?*

He takes me to Old Salem. I'm amused that someone who
lives in this tourist town actually goes to this old Moravian
community. A friend of mine from James Madison grew up in
Las Vegas and claimed he hated going to the Strip. "Tourists
are always pushing and congesting the place," he said.

But Carson doesn't seem to mind that there are plenty of
tourists here in Old Salem. He walks along the cobblestone
streets comfortably, not bothered like I am by a couple with a
double stroller stopping right in front of us, blocking our path.

The woman points to a house that belonged to a tinsmith
and is now open for the public to view. She shouts, "I thought
you wanted to go in here now."

"No, I never said that." The man has walked past the store.

"Yes, you did," she continues loudly.

"I said I was hungry and wanted to eat."

"No, you said we'd eat later."

Meanwhile, their two kids in the stroller both start to cry,
and the smallest one flings her stuffed bear onto the street, the
bear hitting a passerby in the shin.

Carson guides me past the whole scene as I shake my head
in disbelief.

He waits as I pause to watch a gentleman by a candle shop
put on a demonstration of dipping string into hot wax to form
layers for a tapering candle. I think of how Beanie showed us
how to do this ancient art at Dovie's kitchen table.

Three young women in flowing dresses with white aprons

saunter past us. With their bonnets secured under their chins, they remind me of a Moravian doll Dovie gave me for Christmas one year. A man tips his Paul Revere-like black hat at them, greeting them in Old English. He carries a bushel of apples and slips past me to enter a clapboard home surrounded by a lavish vegetable garden.

"We should have told the refugees that this is real American life," I muse as Carson and I start to walk again. I breathe in the aroma of boxwoods and gardenias.

"Sometimes I wish it were," says Carson.

"What would you do?" I ask. "There were no radios back then. You'd be out of a job."

"There's a gunsmith not too far from this street. I'd work there."

"Not me. I'd work close to the Moravian cookies." Just the thought of the paper-thin cookies makes my stomach growl.

"I don't think making those cookies was a full-time job back then. You'll have to pick something else."

We stroll past more gardens, including one where a woman in a straw hat and baby blue dress is bent over with a hoe. She thrusts it along the dark dirt near a patch of white daisies.

Before Carson can suggest that I could take care of the fields, I quip, "No, no garden work for me. I can barely keep my ivy inside my apartment alive."

Watching the scene for a few more moments, I wish I'd brought my camera.

"How about teaching?" Carson asks as we continue our walk.

"In a one-room schoolhouse?"

"It would have been no harder than teaching in the refugee camp."

"I'd like to teach again one day." As I make this confession, Carson nods.

"You're good at it," he tells me as I give him a wide smile of appreciation. "You have that teacher ability running through your veins."

"Right after I got back from the Philippines, I was hired part-time to teach at this small language school near the Japanese embassy." I remember how I always had trouble finding a place to park when I went to my classes; the streets seemed to be filled with No Parking signs.

"Did you like doing that?"

"It was a fun job, but it made me miss my Vietnamese students from PRPC."

Carson takes me to his favorite restaurant—one with a shingle out front that reads *Ye Ol' Dogwood Café*. The interior of the building is large and airy with high ceilings. The beams in the rafters are oak and from them hang various old kitchen and fireplace utensils. Carson ushers me inside, his warm hand against the small of my back.

Once we're seated at a table by one of the windows, I say, "I heard that you dedicated a song to me."

"Did you? I was wondering if you were listening."

"Beanie always has your station on, and she told me."

"I thought about calling you to tell you to listen, but then I felt that was a bit silly." He grins. "I'm glad you were listening."

I smile into his eyes as I lean into the table. "It was nice of you. Even if you think I'm still crazy."

The waitress asks us how we're doing.

I wish she could ask Carson to tell me about Mindy and why they broke up, because I can't seem to do it. But she's in a hurry and dashes from us to a table of twelve. She asks for their drink orders and then explains the specials of the evening.

I'm so hungry, I could eat the tablecloth. When our food comes, the portion looks small, like it won't be enough to fill my groaning stomach.

Carson's ordered a rib eye and garlic mashed potatoes with a side of fried okra. He licks his lips in comical fashion. Then he eyes my plate of seafood. "Is that what you ordered?" His voice shows concern.

"Yep, squid brains and eel hearts." He laughs with me at our joke, one of the many from our days together at camp.

After a few bites, my tummy quiets, and I'm able to enjoy the buttery texture of the stuffed trout in a cheese sauce. The tablecloth is no longer appealing.

"Do you think about it?" asks Carson.

"About what?"

"The refugee camp."

"All the time. I think about my past students and often wonder how they're doing in America. I often think about how good those Vietnamese sandwiches were."

Although he nods, his wistful look tells me that that is not all he had in mind. I won't let myself believe that he's reminiscing about the fun we used to have together. About the talks under the tin roof of his classroom, about the walks at night through the neighborhoods. "I miss it."

I want to say so much more, but instead I choose to say nothing.

He tells me, "The last refugees left PRPC and then it shut down just last year."

"I heard that somewhere."

"The camp's deserted now. I suppose it looks like a ghost town."

Something I have read about Amerasians in the *Washington Post* suddenly comes to mind. "Do you know how the refugees that came over under the Amerasian Homecoming Act are doing?" I expect Carson to be surprised that I have studied up on what is going on in our country, that I know all about the more than 23,000 Amerasians who were able to immigrate to

163

the United States in 1989 based entirely on their mixed-race appearance.

"People have abused it," he says. "The government is allowing relatives to come over with the Amerasians, and people are pretending to be relatives just to get a pass over here."

"Selling visas for large sums?" I read about this, as well.

"Yeah, and using the Amerasians as their ticket to America. Dat told me that one kid was told he could go to the U.S. if he said the four traveling with him were related to him. He came here, and then although the four said they'd take care of this kid, they left him all alone once they went through customs." Carson shakes his head. "The other side to it is that there are those who are clearly Amerasians—you know, they look different from full-blooded Vietnamese—but for whatever reason, they are rejected a visa and forced to stay in Vietnam."

"Sounds like a bunch of corruption."

Carson agrees. In camp I thought his knowledge about the Amerasians could be annoying, but here I respect his love for this abandoned and ridiculed population.

Carson insists that we order dessert, claiming the restaurant's apple strudel is the best he's ever eaten. I'm full from my dinner of trout and suggest we share the strudel. He agrees.

As we enjoy the tart apples in a rich syrupy sauce, I say, "How do Minh and Chi feel about you now?"

"What do you mean?"

"About the past. When Minh wanted you to not have anything to do with Lien because she was accused of stealing?"

"That was a tough situation to be in." Carson's face shows some of the pain he felt during that time. "Minh didn't like it because I stuck up for Lien. He felt it was none of my business as a non-Vietnamese."

"You put your neck on the line, so to speak." I recall the

agony Carson went through during that time when he was forbidden to associate with or help Lien.

Chewing, Carson nods. Thoughtfully, he says, "I learned later that it was not my place to intervene between the neighborhood leaders and the Hong family."

"And now? Has all been forgiven and forgotten?"

A smile plays across Carson's lips. "It has."

How nice that there are those who can forgive and forget, I think. I wonder if this would be a good time to let Carson know that I still harbor an ill feeling about how he treated me in the camp. Boldly, I begin. "You know, there were times I was mad at you."

Carson looks confused, like he doesn't have any idea what I mean.

Back off, a voice inside my head says. *Stop trying to dig up the past.* Relenting, I say cheerfully, "You were right; the dessert was delicious."

After Carson pays the waiter for our meals, we head to Saigon Bistro. I don't know why we have to go there so much. But Carson is unwavering. "You'll see, Sam. Just trust me."

Carson drives us across town to the restaurant as I think of how comfortable being with him feels. It's like sitting on Dovie's porch when a warm wind blows. We've picked up where we left off. *Yep*, says the voice in my head. *Just where you left off years ago—the same old confusion and frustration and so many unanswered questions.*

When we arrive at the restaurant, the kitchen crew is washing up. Lien gives us each a hug—Carson's noticeably longer than mine—and asks what we'd like to eat.

"We already ate," answers Carson.

She serves us moon cakes and hot tea anyway. Then she sits across from us at the table as her arms move from her lap to the table and back to her lap, her bracelets clinking against each other.

I see that there is a new painting on the wall, one of a rice field, its green blades and muddy waters being lit from the ginger and red hues of a setting sun. "Where did you get that?" I ask.

"You like?" she asks with a nervous grin.

"It's peaceful." I wish I felt as peaceful as it looks.

"I give to you."

"Oh, no!" My protest is adamant. How could I have forgotten that one needs to be careful when admiring something that isn't hers around the Vietnamese. I ended up with so many trinkets when I told refugees their possessions were pretty or nice. *You like?* I'd be asked, and the next thing I knew, the ring or picture or piece of cloth was mine.

"Thanks for the tea," I say to change the subject, and then take a small taste.

Smoothing a tuft of hair from her face, Lien says, "I am getting married."

My eyes almost pop out of my head. "You?"

Carson gives me one of his *you better be careful* looks.

"I mean . . ." I cough and continue. "Really?"

Lien's head bobs up and down.

I sputter, "Congratulations, Lien."

Carson smiles, seemingly pleased with my reaction. "When did Jonathan ask you?"

"Jonathan?" I am out of the loop. "Who is he?"

"He American," says Lien. "He go to my church. We study Bible together in English."

"And Jonathan is learning some Vietnamese," adds Carson.

Lien shoves her hand in front of me, asking me to admire the diamond on her ring finger.

"Very nice," I say, taking her hand in my own. A single large diamond encased in a silver band is surrounded by smaller diamonds glistening like stars against a night sky. "So how old is Jonathan?"

"He's twenty-four," Lien says as she draws her hand across the table back to her lap. "He is a bank manager."

"So he works with lots of money," I say with a slight smile.

Lien gets my joke. "Yes, he plays with money when he go to work every day."

I laugh, pleased with how well Lien understands my jokes in English. On a serious note, I ask, "When are you planning to get married?"

"November thirteen."

"A fall wedding," I say. "That will be nice."

"And I want to find my mother."

twenty-five

Immediately, I lean into the table, my elbow nearly knocking over my teacup. "You want to do what?"

Lien glances at Carson. "My mother. I need to find her."

I look around the restaurant, suddenly aware that neither her mother nor Minh are here tonight. "Where is your mother?"

"I don't know."

"She's not here? Is she at home?" How could she not know where her own mother is?

"I don't know. Maybe Chicago."

"What?"

Carson intervenes, understanding my confusion. Resting a hand against my arm, he says, "Sam, you know that Lien's mother gave her up when she was young."

I recall Beanie once telling Dovie and me that when her second husband left her, she felt she'd been hit smack in the head by a telephone pole. I feel like that right now. "What? What do you mean?" My questions sound foreign, like English is not my first language. "So . . ."

Carson offers, "Minh and Chi are her uncle and aunt. Huy's her cousin."

I stare at Lien.

She merely looks down at my teacup.

"I knew Lien's dad—I mean Minh—wasn't her biological dad. I knew some American soldier was responsible for Lien being conceived, but I didn't know that Chi wasn't the woman who gave birth to Lien. . . ." I let my voice hang heavy and murky like fog on a mountain road.

I'm left to my own stupor as Lien and Carson talk. I realize I should have put two and two together before this, but as my mother would say, *"Sam, you've never been good at math."*

Carson uses a Vietnamese word and soon the conversation is all in Vietnamese.

Lien sees my discomfort and says, "I am marrying Jonathan. I want my mother to come to the wedding. I want her to see me marry."

Carson nods. "We know. You have wanted to do this for some time."

"Do what?" I ask.

"Find her mother."

Lien says, "My uncle and aunt give me good home. I love them. They will come to wedding, but I want my mother, too."

"When was the last time she saw her mother? Why did her mom give her up?" I don't know why I'm asking Carson and not Lien.

"Thuy gave her up to be raised by relatives." Carson is annoyed with me. His brows are furrowed, his eyes like darts, and his jaw taut.

Suddenly, I am reliving those days at camp when Lien was

accused of stealing and Carson was certain she had not. I remember the way I felt misunderstood and how Carson avoided me after we disagreed about Lien. I cringe as I recall how that situation drove a wedge between us.

Lien once told me, as many of the Amerasians I knew at camp did, that she wanted to meet her father in America. *"I hope I find him,"* she'd said, *"when I go to America."*

I don't think these children understood how big America is, or how much the odds were stacked against them. The statistics were dauntingly grim. And when birth fathers were found, they often had wives and children and no desire to look at a flesh and blood "mistake" they'd brought into the world in the heat of their youth and between enemy lines in an uncertain war.

I do not know if Lien has searched for her father after arriving in the U.S. seven years ago. And I understand why she wants her birth mother at her wedding. But how feasible is this going to be?

"So," says Carson as he drives me back to Dovie's, "we have a lot of work ahead of us."

"How do we start? How do you go about finding a missing person? I can't even find my mom's cat." The task seems huge. I think of Taylor and wonder if he could help.

"We've always worked well together," Carson says as he slows to stop at a red light. With his eyes on mine, he adds, "We can do it."

"I don't know. I'm not sure I can trust you."

Carson seems perplexed, the very reaction I was going for. "What do you mean by that?"

"At PRPC you gave up on me after we disagreed. We were supposed to work on a project then, too. But you ignored me after Lien was accused of stealing." I pause, not sure how he'll respond. Perhaps he thought I'd forgotten all about this.

"Sam, that was long ago."

"I know, but I still don't know why you weren't up front with me."

"We were spending too much time together. We needed to be more involved with other aspects of the camp."

He thinks I should be happy with this explanation, I can tell by the look on his face.

The light turns green, and we curve down the streets, passing city signs for Old Salem. I decide I will thank him for taking me there and tell him the date was fun but that I cannot help with this project for Lien until I get more answers from him. I see myself standing in the admin room so many years ago, waiting. Carson and I were assigned to decorate the room together, and I can still feel how sad and disappointed I was when he didn't show up.

I swallow, dig my nails into my palms, and say, "It hurt me that you told Dr. Rogers you didn't want to work on that project with me." When he doesn't respond, I aim to clarify his memory. "Remember how you sent someone else to take your place?"

"I did?"

I let out a snort. "Did you really forget that, or are you just pretending you have? How would you have felt if I suddenly decided I didn't want to be friends with you anymore?"

The silence between us is long, but I refuse to be the one to break it. I asked him questions; he needs to find a reply. Carson has a habit of being evasive.

At last. "Sorry."

"That's it?"

"Sorry for all the times I messed up, Sam. I was dating Mindy. I planned to be faithful to her. And there you were . . ."

"And?"

"Things got complicated." He pulls the car over to the side of the road. Putting it in park, he turns to me. I watch his face glow momentarily from the headlights of a passing truck.

"Let's start over. We get to be together again." His smile is the lopsided one I've missed seeing over the years.

Even so, I am not in the mood to put a mere bandage on my seething feelings. "Start over?" I push the words past my closed throat. "Just what does that mean?"

"Like the refugees start over. A new life. We get to live as Sam and Carson here in America in 1993." He seems pleased with his explanation.

"What is that going to be like?"

He takes the car out of park and starts to slowly drive again, turning back onto the road. "I'm looking forward to finding out."

Unsure how to respond, I turn on the radio, grateful the song playing is one that has no meaning for me. For us.

twenty-six

December 1985

I rarely saw Lien after she was accused of stealing. Huy told us that Minh demanded that she keep to the Hongs' billet, wash clothes, prepare meals, and clean. Huy said his dad and the elders in the Vietnamese community were shunning her because they believed she was guilty. Huy said that people had stepped forward and said they'd seen Lien in the past with articles of clothing and jewelry that did not belong to her. I often wondered how much of what I'd said had influenced the elders.

"Minh wants me to stay away from Lien," Carson told Brice and me one evening. "When I told him that Lien is innocent, he told me that I have no business interfering in the neighborhood's decision, that just because I'm white doesn't mean I know everything."

Minh realized that many of the Vietnamese continued to hold doubts about Lien due solely to her half-breed status.

Prejudices died hard, even in the camp. The Vietnamese loathed the Cambodians and were not fond of the Laotians, either. All of these refugees were war refugees, having left their countries due to fighting and mayhem, and yet fights often broke out among the three ethnic groups in the camp.

One night a Cambodian man waved a butcher knife at a Vietnamese boy, threatening to cut his heart out. "What caused the reaction?" I'd asked when our director told us the news at the staff meeting the next morning.

"Hatred and tension" was the reply. "A long line of historical events has caused disharmony among these people. When you're taught to hate, you learn how." His sigh was deep. "Only in Heaven will we all really be united in love."

"I heard the boy was causing trouble in the Cambodian neighborhood," said one of the teachers.

"We live in a broken world," Dr. Rogers said, his eyes dark with remorse. "Let's just do our best to show God's love to each refugee. God loves them all."

While there were plenty of horror stories told by the Vietnamese and the Laotians, the one that bothered me the most was told to me by a Cambodian student's father. The Khmer Rouge under the leadership of Pol Pot had killed his friend simply because the man was of Chinese descent and had an extensive education.

I looked at the young faces of my students and wondered how they could continue on so happily when they had already seen so much brokenness. Yet they did, always showing up to give me bottles of soda and angelic smiles.

twenty-seven

Natasha and I choose a Mexican restaurant because she's avoiding the handsome waiter at the Native Thai. This restaurant is one we've been to before, and she likes it, if only for the décor. Sombreros with tassels line the plum-colored walls, and there's a life-sized donkey over the bar. When you pull its tail, it brays "Viva Mexico!" three times. The music filling the establishment is the kind you can salsa to, if you choose. Neither Natasha nor I feel like dancing.

Natasha slips a finger around one of her curls as she scans the menu. She orders the special, and when it arrives at the table, piping with steam, it's on a plate the size of a sombrero, filled with five different kinds of meat, chunks of pineapple, and grilled onions and green peppers. Three warm tortillas in aluminum foil are brought on a separate platter. I nibble at a soft taco and wonder why I bothered to order anything.

"Tell me about your week." Natasha cups a soft tortilla in one hand and spoons the meat into it with the other.

I start to say something about Carson, then reconsider because I know that's what she expects to hear. I decide to start with Dovie. "My aunt has a new boarder."

"Okay, let me guess her name. Ummmm . . ." Natasha pretends to be in deep thought. "Let's see. Greenie?" She smiles. "Or Stringy?"

"Oh yeah, Greenie Beanie or Stringy Beanie." Natasha thinks Beanie is the most peculiar name.

"Not even close?"

"No. It's Pearl."

"Pearl! I had an aunt named Pearl. She wore three-inch heels and grew radishes."

"Really?"

"We always thought she should have grown onions." Natasha notes my confusion. "You know, pearl onions."

"Oh."

My thoughts slide to Lien's request. I sip my Pepsi while Natasha chews a forkful of meat. When she finishes, she says, "What are you thinking?"

"Nothing."

"Tell me."

So I decide to tell her about Lien.

"So she didn't really steal anything?" Natasha wipes her mouth with a napkin.

"Apparently not."

"And Carson believed all along that she was innocent?"

"That's right."

"And you?" She adds some hot sauce from a bottle to her food. She claims that most food needs a kick of hot sauce.

I add a little to mine, too. "At the time, I thought she was guilty. Lien was a handful."

"Her mother gave her up?"

"Yeah. When she was three or four."

"That had to be painful."

"For whom?"

"I would imagine for both of them."

Natasha tells me I should confess to Carson that I care about him.

I laugh. "When you tell that waiter at the Native Thai how you feel about him, then I'll say something to Carson." I know I'm safe; she'll never tell this waiter her feelings.

"At least I don't think about him every minute."

"I didn't say you do."

"Not like you think about Carson."

Mom is glad to be back at work. She hums a tune as she moves some pencil-straight skirts to the clearance rack. After a while I recognize that it's Elvis's "Always on My Mind."

I help a customer who tries to convince herself and me that she wears a size five when I can see she is more like a size ten. After trying on three pairs of jeans that do not fit, she accepts my suggestion to try on a pair of petite-length size-ten Levi's.

"How are they?" I ask her from outside the dressing room.

After a few incomprehensible mutters, she comes out modeling them.

"Nice," I say. "They look fabulous."

Mom winks at me, pleased that I have, at last, learned the art of making a customer feel good about herself. The woman purchases the jeans.

When the store is clear of shoppers, Mom tells me that she found a new kind of licorice sold at a little store on Sandbridge Beach and bought six boxes. After lunch she talks about a retired Navy man she and Maralinda met one night on a scenic boat ride.

"He made us lobster and steak the next night," Mom tells me.

"So he invited the two of you over for dinner?"

Mom picks up the feather duster. "No, we invited him over."

"Really?"

"Yes, he seemed lonely. Maralinda said he's not her type."

"Is he yours?"

"Oh, heavens no!"

"Why not?"

"I like men who like to go to the theater. I like men who enjoy the classics." She dusts the picture frames with a few swift dabs. "You know, who can quote Hemingway and Melville."

"And he couldn't do that?" I recall that Daddy couldn't, either.

"He didn't know a thing about *Moby-Dick*. Thought it was a ship."

"Well, at least he got the water part correct."

"He smelled of talcum powder." She puts the duster on the counter and adjusts the bow of her apron.

"Better than smelling like a gym, right?" I scan her face for a smile, but there isn't any trace of one.

"He cooked us a lovely dinner, but he wouldn't eat it."

"Why not?"

"How should I know?"

"Was he not hungry?"

"No, he wasn't my type." She stands at the front window now, staring out like she's checking the weather. "But he was very handsome."

Why would a man cook and not eat? "Had he already eaten?" I ask, insisting on a reply.

Mom doesn't give it. Dreamily, with one hand on the blond-haired mannequin that is dressed in a suit the color of caramels, she admits, "His hair was peppered with red streaks. It was sorta nice when the light caught it."

"What was his name?"

"How should I know?" She turns to the rack of new fall dresses, a finger resting alongside her nose.

I wonder if the chemo from years past has made her a little loopy.

I'm still thinking about my mother's comments about this handsome man she met at the beach. If she were to find love again, would I get along with my new stepfather? The thought hits me every so often. There was a time I wanted her to remarry like other friends in my high school whose parents got married for the second and even third time. In tenth grade I thought she might like my psychology teacher until I realized that this teacher didn't believe in using crock pots. His aversion to this appliance was so strong that I thought he had psychological issues about it. My mom relied heavily on her Rival crock pot to do her cooking while she was at work all day.

As I view the sizzling sun setting outside my window, I'm reminded of all the times I wanted her to find a good man. My recent date with Taylor spins around my mind as I think about the time we spent together. He could be the one for me, I tell myself as I smile into my dresser mirror. I bet it would be fascinating to be married to a private investigator. I seldom get second dates, and he's already asked me out again for this Saturday.

Lifting my hair, I pull the thick brown layers back into a ponytail and, seeing a few bumps along my chin, decide to try the new peach mask I bought at the grocery store. I squeeze the creamy contents of the floral tube onto my nose, forehead, and chin. I dab some across my cheeks. After making faces in the mirror, I pause to see how long I'm supposed to keep this stuff on my face. The directions say fifteen minutes.

My skin is like plaster from the cleansing mask when the phone rings. I consider letting the answering machine pick up.

On the fourth ring, I answer.

Carson's voice glides sweetly into my ear. "Hey, how are you?"

"I have another date."

"Really? One of those filled ones you get at Christmas?"

"What?"

"Aren't they filled with cream cheese?"

"No." Is he trying to be funny or did he really think that I was speaking of food? "I'm going out on a date with a man."

"Oh?"

With my skin about to crack from the substance I've put on it, I am not in the mood to talk to him. Carson is not the right man for me. I need to put him aside.

"So where are you two going?"

"Out to dinner at Donatello." I make the name of the restaurant sound swanky and sophisticated, hoping that Carson will feel I've landed a man who wants to take me to nice places. "It's in the Georgetown district."

He pauses before saying, "Okay . . ."

"Carson." My breath feels hot and thick.

"Yeah?"

"Don't call anymore."

"What?"

Slowly, I add more words to soften the roughness. "Please don't call me anymore, okay?"

"Sam, we're friends."

"I know. But you're a guy and my P.I. guy is awfully jealous."

"P.I. guy?"

"Yes, he's a private investigator. Like Magnum." I don't know why I throw in that last part—perhaps I want Carson to know that what this guy does for a living is as exciting as Tom Selleck's TV job.

"Does he have a name?"

"Of course. You don't think that his mama named him P.I., do you?" Sarcasm and a sassy attitude rise within me. In a minute, if I'm not careful, I'm going to feel that quiet ache in my heart.

He sighs. "How long have you known him?"

"A while."

"How long is that?"

I am not about to tell Carson that I met Taylor recently at a wedding I was not even invited to. "A while."

"Be careful."

"Why?"

"Because you're a flirt, and I know you give your heart away quicker than it takes for a mosquito to bite."

Carson, it seems, knows exactly what to say, or write, to hurt me. I tell him good-bye and hang up the phone, reluctance in my fingers.

I run the bath water, filling the tub with half a bottle of cranberry-vanilla bath salts, and as the foamy concoction rises, I consider calling Natasha. As I settle into the tub, I decide against talking with her. I don't need to hear her say that she knows I will start talking to Carson again because deep down I'm in love with him. I let the suds cover me up to my chin by sinking deep into the bath. Using a washcloth, I scrub the mask from my face, hoping it did what the container said it would—tighten pores and make my skin smooth.

Once I'm in my pajamas—cotton with silk, a line we used to carry in the boutique before Mom became annoyed with the manufacturer for unethical child labor in Malaysia—I turn on the late show and pop a bag of microwave popcorn. Uncle

Charlie gave me a silver-plated bowl that is in the shape of a motorcycle, and I pour the hot popcorn into that. I chew and let the butter run over my tongue, wishing that I were like my great-uncle, able to outrun anything, especially these wretched, tangled emotions.

Although I know better, I pull out the box of old photos from their hiding place in my closet. Of course, I shouldn't give in to the desire to look at them, but it's too late. With the box open on the floor of my bedroom, the photos are freely visible. I look over photos of students—some smiling, some looking serious—and I remember them. The timid Cambodian group of teens had been a delight to teach. A small class, they studied hard and were well disciplined. For their graduation party, their mothers brought chicken curry and rice. I shuffle through photos of the curry meal, the students receiving their certificates, and myself. Picking up another stack, I flip through pictures of my one and only class of Laotian students, the marketplace on a Saturday filled with the wares the refugees made to sell, me in a sarong, me at a staff meeting, and me with Lien and Huy. Then, as though the pounding of my heart has paralyzed my hand, I stop.

I see a picture of Carson and me that one of the photographers took and gave me as a gift. Sealed in the clear plastic wrap the camp photographers often placed pictures in, the photo is one of us seated at the wedding reception we attended the day Lien was accused of stealing. I have on a cotton sleeveless red dress dotted with swirls of cream. Carson is dressed in a tan shirt and pants. He leaned in close when the picture was snapped. Our smiles are content, happy. Over the years, it's hurt me to look at our faces. Because each time I viewed mine, I saw hope and love spread across each portion of my skin. Every time I hold this three-by-five-inch piece of glossy paper, I have not been able to hide from what is blatantly evident. The young woman in the photograph is in love with the man sitting beside her.

twenty-eight

January 1986

Carson and I both were at the departure area when the Hong family left. I'd been at the camp for seven months and had seen my share of arrivals and departures in that time. I taught myself not to get too attached to any of the refugees. Transition was a large part of the place, and the purpose of our camp was for each refugee, regardless of how he or she had arrived in the Philippines—by plane with the Orderly Departure Program, or by a crafted boat, stealing away into the night—to leave. Each refugee came to the processing center to learn English, get needed medical attention, and then to get their name on The List. When their name appeared on this sheet, it meant preparations had been made for them to resettle somewhere else, usually the United States. Even so, saying good-bye to favorite families never grew easy. "See you in America" was the resounding phrase used, but we knew the chance of seeing any of them in the U.S. was slim.

Lien and her family boarded the dirty white bus with fifty others whose names were on The List. The bus bulged with their belongings. I thought of the knitted sweaters to ward off the cold in places such as Chicago and Detroit that mothers created in their billets. They'd never seen snow or felt the cold of a blustery wind, and looking at the sweaters, I knew they had a shock coming. There was no way that a simple sweater would keep them warm when the snow lined the streets in front of their new homes.

Lien hung out an open window and waved as the bus was pulling away from the departure area, heading to the airport in Manila many long miles away. "I never forget you, teacha!" she cried.

I was not sure if she was referring to Carson or to me.

Huy smiled and called out to us and to his friends—two boys his age who had come to bid him good-bye. Huy's parents were subdued; their eyes focused on the bags on their laps. I wondered what was going on in their thoughts. I wished they would let go of their anger toward Lien and the shame she'd caused them. I asked God to let them leave their anguish here and not take it with them in their luggage to America.

Carson and I stood side by side with our arms waving until the bus was out of sight. Half of what Carson spoke to the refugees I could not understand. By this time, his Vietnamese had improved considerably.

When the departure area was silent again, he and I went back to the staff housing, hoping and praying that the refugees could and would adjust well to America—and realize the value of what we'd tried to teach them. In time, I knew that they would be able to grasp that we'd been honest when we'd said it was rude to urinate on the street or blow your nose in your sleeve.

"They still think she stole," Carson said as we ate dinner in the mess hall. He stared at his plate of pork *pancit* as though it were the guilty one.

"She probably did." I'd finished my helping of chicken *adobo* too quickly and my stomach felt queasy. "I saw her with that bracelet that didn't belong to her. She could be sweet, but also devious."

Carson stood up. "You assume things, Sam. Always." And after glaring at me, he left me alone with my food, the rice noodles congealing as I bit my lip.

twenty-nine

Mom lets me have a dress from the clearance rack for my date tonight. She knows that I've been eyeing a short black one with spaghetti straps—a new item for the store, with a brand name that I could never afford. "Not for you, Samantha," she told me one afternoon as I pressed its soft fabric against me and smiled into the mirror. "You don't want to wear black. Black dresses are overrated." From the curve of her mouth, I almost thought that she was ready to spout out a line she often whispers when we are out in public and she disapproves of what someone has on. *"Just because the model in the catalog is wearing it doesn't mean you should."* I found the phrase funny the first time I heard Mom say it when we saw a lady in a mini pumpkin orange smock with purple trim.

The dress I'll be wearing is light blue, reminding me of a clear spring morning. It has a moderate neckline and zips in the back. Mom says my pearl earrings will go well with the dress and she lets me "borrow" a few bracelets to adorn my arms.

At home I take a long shower, lathering up with a bar of honeysuckle soap. I paint my fingernails a frosty coral and hum along with Crosby, Stills, and Nash as their song "Southern Cross" plays on the radio.

Taylor is just as cute as the last time I saw him. He asks about my day and how the shop is doing and if my mother has found her cat.

"No," I say as we are seated at a table to the left of the bar. "You never know. There's still hope about that cat."

It's been over six months, so I doubt that Butterchurn is ever going to drink milk from the dish Mom has sitting out for him in the garage. That cat has found a new owner or been eaten by the proverbial wolves that lurk. I want to be hopeful, but my misgivings loom larger than hope.

We look over menus filled with tasty-sounding Italian special-ties. When Taylor asks what I'd like to eat, I'm at a loss. I've been too busy concentrating on our conversation. He tells me he's going to have a shrimp dish, Gamberi Alla Caprese, and by the time the waiter approaches our table, I realize my time is up so I order the same.

Over our dinner I ask him what I've been planning to. "Can you find anyone?"

He smiles. "Just about."

I want to ask him all the tricks and tools he uses, so I can tell Carson what I've learned. For once, I'll know more about some-thing than him. "What made you want to be an investigator?"

"Too much TV." Warmly, he says, "Now, tell me how you became a boutique owner."

"I don't own the shop. It belongs to my mom."

"But do you like working there?" He lifts his fork filled with shrimp to his mouth and chews.

"I enjoy seeing the way the right clothes can make people happy, and finding items that fit them. My mom wanted a shop where tall and short women have a chance to get quality clothing that fits them in all the right places."

"That's right—you told me that she's tall. Six feet?"

"Yep, and look at me, I'm only five-five. Her mom was short, so I guess I got that gene." Wanting to steer the conversation back to finding missing people, I say, "Taylor, I really want to talk about you." I make my voice flirty.

"Me?"

"Yep." I sip from my water glass.

"Well, I'm not that interesting."

"I think you are." Lowering my lashes, I slowly raise my eyes to meet his soft glance.

"Really?"

"Oh, yes." My Flirty Sam side has this habit of showing up at times like this. Natasha tells me this side of my personality is going to get me into trouble if I'm not careful. "Did I tell you that I was at a refugee camp years ago?"

"No, I don't think so."

"But you already knew that, right? Since you're a P.I., you probably did a background check on me."

"Not yet." His smile shows I am amusing him, and that is exactly what I want to do. "Do I need to do a check?"

"A thorough one. I'm wanted."

"I bet you are."

I turn the conversation back to where I want it. "So, I need to find a Vietnamese woman."

"Okay." His expression invites me to continue.

"Last we heard she was up north somewhere. Her name is Thuy. In Vietnam the last name goes first, and it's Pham." I make the *ph* sound like an *f*. "So Pham Thuy, or the American way, Thuy Pham."

Taylor sips his Coke. "Thuy Pham," he repeats.

"She was born in 1950. I think."

"Friend from the past?"

"I've never met her."

"Oh?"

I suppose I should tell him, so I begin with a little Amerasian girl who showed up in my classroom one day, and work my way through time to her upcoming wedding. "She's asked for my help." I still haven't decided if this is a blessing or a curse. I suppose I should feel honored that Lien has confidence that I can find Thuy. "Lien hopes to find her in time to invite her to the wedding."

Taylor nods. "Sure," he says. "I can certainly try."

When he reaches for my hand with his warm fingers, I am sent back to another time, half a world away.

thirty

January 1986

The moon was a globe the color of waxy butter that night. The air was moist and stirred by a faint breeze. Carson and I sat in the lounge of the admin building long after the video ended, talking. Our voices were sleepy, but we made no movement to leave the room.

Our knees touched. He told me how he missed iced tea and fried okra. "You know, Bojangles has great sweet tea. Have you ever eaten there?"

A surge of desire came over me. The next thing I knew I'd put my fingers on his jaw and leaned in to kiss his mouth. But before my lips met his, he jerked away. His eyes were like darts, artillery barricading the enemy forces.

Up until that moment, I was certain he dreamed to kiss me. Yet here was his chance and he wasn't interested. I didn't know what to say, so I stood up and muttered, "Fine, be that way," and stormed out of the room.

He ignored me after that. When he saw me walking toward him, he'd rush into the dorm. The rides to our neighborhood to teach consisted of empty stares out the window, at the floor, anywhere but at each other. During staff meetings, when he sang and played his sax with the other musicians in our group, his eyes never met mine. He quit stopping by my dorm room to ask if I wanted to walk through the neighborhoods with him and eat a Vietnamese sandwich or bowl of noodles at one of the outdoor cafés.

Thinking that we still got along so well, Dr. Rogers asked Carson and me to decorate the administration building and paint the front door, hoping that we could give the drab place a makeover. "You can put some of your photos of the camp on the walls," he told me, making me feel good about my photography.

Dr. Rogers set a time for Carson and me to meet when the admin building would be vacant of staff. Getting there a little early that evening, I turned on the overhead light, anticipating time alone with Carson.

After fifteen minutes passed, I wondered where he was. I waited and waited, twisting my fingers and biting my lip.

When I was about to head over to Carson's dorm to see what was taking him so long, one of the female Filipino teachers entered the building. With a tight smile she walked over to where I sat. "Sorry to be late. I just got out of another meeting in my dorm."

I asked what she meant. That's when she told me that Carson was off the project. "Carson asked me to replace him," she said innocently.

As she and I hung the bright and happy posters we'd made, I felt far from bright and happy.

"Apparently," Dr. Rogers told me in private, "Carson doesn't feel the two of you work well together. I'm sorry, Samantha."

I couldn't believe that Carson wanted nothing to do with me and was letting others know that. Tears burned my eyes and I wanted to crawl into a hole.

I hated Carson after that. Actually, I wished I could hate him, but he occupied my heart—a constant reminder that you don't always get what you want.

Eventually, we did talk to each other again. It was like a waterspout that has been blocked and is slowly freed from congestion—a trickle at a time. I asked to borrow a pen and he lent me one. He needed to know what time we'd been invited to a Laotian family's billet for a Saturday dinner. I avoided his eyes but replied, "Six." Seated around the wooden dinner table with the refugee family, Carson and I conversed, acting like we were still the close friends we'd been weeks ago.

But it was not the same. You can't go back. What's done is done. Unrequited love is never easy. Time heals all wounds. I kept repeating such clichés to myself, hoping that they, like medicine, would take away the sting.

They didn't.

thirty-one

When I get to the shop, out front are two police cars with their emergency light bars flashing red and blue. A stream of yellow caution tape is plastered around the vicinity. This is a scene right out of a TV detective show.

During the five-mile drive over, my mind pounded from Mom's phone call. I'd stumbled out of bed. My digital clock read 12:49 a.m. Realizing the phone was ringing, I grabbed the receiver from the cordless on my bedside table, knocked over the stack of mysteries, and immediately heard Mom's words: "Someone broke into the store."

At the shop, I park my Honda beside one of the police cars and survey the situation. The door to Have a Fit has been broken with the force of some tool, and with the help of my criminal knowledge that comes from watching shows like *Magnum P.I.*, I know it was probably a crowbar.

Mom, dressed in a pair of gray sweat pants and a dark blue *Virginia is for Lovers* T-shirt, stands by the front door. I hear her say to a cop that she's okay. Even so, my words tumble out as I hug her, "Mom, are you okay?"

She smells of cold cream. I wonder if she was sleeping when she was alerted that the boutique was in trouble. "We have been robbed," she tells me.

I hate hearing the truth from her lips.

"The people from the security company called. I was in such a deep sleep."

I don't want to ask, but I must know. "What's gone?"

"They took money out of the register—but only fifty dollars was in there."

I'm relieved and yet frightened in the same breath.

Gripping her arm, I guide her into the boutique. Together, we scan the store in its disarray, and she notes more items that are no longer there.

Two gowns are gone, the black dress I wanted to wear, and some shirts. Whoever did this knocked over a clothes rack and hit the walls with something that put holes in the plaster.

"At least they didn't set it on fire." Mom leans against the one wall that is not damaged.

We watch as a gloved officer dusts the cash register with a powder. "I should be able to get some prints off of this," she tells us.

The policeman who enters next is handsome. He reminds me of Starsky on *Starsky and Hutch*. "I'm Officer Garner. I'd like to ask you some questions," he says to Mom and then smiles at me. "Shall we sit down?"

I pull a folding chair from the back room for her as the policeman grabs two more from the tiny cardboard table where Mom and I often sit at lunchtime, sharing a sandwich. We place the chairs near a rack of silk blouses.

Opening a large memo pad, he begins to write. "Now," he says to us, "what time did you close the store last night?" He glances up at Mom. "It's Mrs. Bravencourt, correct?"

"Yes, Officer Garner." She clears her throat. True to form, she has remembered his name. "We closed at seven. Like we usually do."

Although her tone is cordial, I note that her fingers are clenched into fists.

"And who closed the store?"

"We both did," I answer. "We always walk out to the parking lot together."

He scribbles on the pad, balancing it against his thigh. Looking up, he asks, "Does anyone else have a key or work with you?"

Mom shakes her head. Then she says, "Sometimes Natasha works here, but she doesn't have a key."

"Who is Natasha?"

"My friend," I tell him.

He adds to his notes. "And you two are mother and daughter?"

"No, sisters." I laugh, trying to add some humor to ease Mom of her tenseness.

He smiles. "I should have realized that," he says.

Mom isn't smiling.

I'm suddenly ashamed. My mom's store was robbed and I'm flirting with the policeman.

"Now, did you have a security system?" He looks at me; he really is much too handsome.

Mom says, "Yes, I set it. That's how you got here."

"Oh yes, the alarm went off when the door was forced open, and we were called." He scribbles some more.

"Looks like they struck the walls with a crowbar." Mom motions toward the wall in front of her. "Knocked the pictures down, too." She gives a nervous glance toward the officer and then asks, "Who would do something like this?"

"We'll try our best to find out, ma'am," he assures as the policewoman checking for fingerprints lets him know her work is done. "Did you get anything?" he asks her as she carries her black bag across the room.

"I was able to lift about three fingerprints," she tells him before heading outside.

With that, Officer Garner thanks us for answering his questions and, looking at Mom, says, "You might want to call someone to fix the front door."

We call a locksmith immediately; Mom complains that he is stealing more than the thief by charging such an enormous fee.

I try to appease her by saying she should be glad that someone is available to repair the door and change the lock in the middle of the night.

My mother merely grunts. She walks over to the pictures, now strewn on the carpet, their glass frames shattered. "Uncle Charlie gave me those."

I join her to examine the damage. "We can get new frames. The prints look like they haven't been ruined." The prints are, in my opinion, nothing more than globs of orange and pink paint, the colors of Dunkin' Donuts. Mom says they are rare pieces of modern art; I guess I have yet to understand why they are called modern and, more important, why they are called art. "Be careful," I warn. "There is glass everywhere."

Stepping over a large triangular slab of glass, she says, "I suppose we should get the broom."

"Tomorrow," I tell her. "I'll clean it up first thing in the morning."

She acts like she hasn't heard me at all. Surveying the store once more, she murmurs a few unintelligible words. When the locksmith finishes his job, she says to him, "The evil in our world. Just miserable."

Standing, he runs callused hands over the knees of his dark

blue uniform. "I agree with you completely." He hands Mom two sets of keys. "There's a new lock and the door is secured again." Then he picks up his metal toolbox as Mom writes him a check.

We test the key a few times before the man drives off in his company's truck. Again Mom muses, "The evil that prevails in this world. People have no business invading others' lives."

The word *invading* sparks memories. I think of how countries are invaded and lives are damaged. I think of the countless stories I heard from the refugees. I search for something calming to say to ease her but can't come up with a thing.

I stay at Mom's house. I add sheets to the guest bed, wondering if I will be able to sleep at all. I know that Mom won't. I hear her toss and turn until dawn fills the guest room window, peeping through the white blinds. Glad that the night is over, I get out of bed to prepare for another day at the boutique.

Mom greets me in the kitchen, dressed for work in a pair of cotton slacks and a black blouse. "I hope they caught whoever broke in."

I hope so too, of course. But I also know that only on TV does law enforcement work that quickly. In real life, as in love, the good guy does not always win, nor does the girl always get the guy.

She tells me I can wear some of her clothes today since all I have is what I had on yesterday. "There's a Ralph Lauren shirt in the left of my closet that should fit you," she says as she makes her way toward the door, the soles of her shoes heavy on the hardwood. Over her shoulder, she says with resolve, "Sam, we will get through this."

I give a weak smile. "We will. I'll see you at the shop soon."

thirty-two

The next night I order takeout from the Chinese restaurant I like and then take a long walk around my neighborhood. Sometimes I find taking a walk a good opportunity to not only get exercise but to pray. Frustration that someone would have the audacity to break into the shop gnaws at my insides. *Calm down*, I tell myself. *You're going to have a heart attack over it*. The words *heart attack* sear my heart, and I feel tears ready to surface. I walk faster, the tears large and hot against my cheeks. I can't help but think that if Dad hadn't had a heart attack, Mom and I would be better off. "God, at least if she's going to have to be lonely without Dad, please give her cat back to her," I pray.

Rounding a corner, I see two Asian kids on skateboards, gliding across the pavement. Thinking of Lien, I ask God to change my attitude toward her, ashamed that I've been stuck in recalling how she used to be instead of the new woman she is now. She's still on my mind when I enter my apartment to a ringing phone that interrupts my prayer.

Carson wants to know how I'm doing. At first I want to remind him that I told him not to call me ever again, but instead I tell him that the boutique was robbed.

"Robbed?" He says the word like it's foreign.

"We're not sure who did it, but they stole some clothing and money after breaking the lock."

"Are you all right?" The genuine concern in his voice reminds me of when I sliced my finger with a knife in my dorm's kitchen and he administered medical attention, wiping away the blood and wrapping the wound in a bandage he rushed to get from our agency's secretary.

"Yeah, it's been messy. We feel so violated."

He insists on driving up here to see me. "I'll book a hotel room. Let me call Jason and see if he can cover my shift at the station."

He arrives at the shop at ten forty the next morning and, noting the damaged walls, says he'll go out and buy plaster and paint.

Mom's eyes grow wide. She stops chewing the licorice morsel. "Really? You would do that?"

"I came to help out," he says, tall and grinning. "Where is the nearest store to get the supplies, ma'am?"

Mom looks like she is going to faint from his kindness. She studies him a moment, sort of like she's in a trance.

"And I'll need some new frames for those two pictures." He winks at me, warming my heart. When he called last night, I told him about how much those two blobs of paint on canvas mean to my mother. Earlier today, I cleaned the glass from the carpet with our store's broom and vacuum cleaner. Then, carefully, I removed the prints from the broken glass and carried the destroyed frames to the dumpster. I was proud that I didn't even nick myself at all.

Carson takes our measuring tape from the drawer and writes down the dimensions of the pictures. "What color frames would you like?" he asks Mom.

"Silver," she says without any hesitation.

An hour later he returns with a large container of plaster and a gallon of creamy rose paint. "The paint should match pretty well," he says, his voice exuding confidence. When he brings in the picture frames from his car, he hands them to Mom, and I watch her unwrap them with delight.

As customers enter the shop, Mom has me wait on them. She's in the back storage room, placing the gifts from Uncle Charlie into their new homes. I know that there must be a story behind these so-called works of art, but I have never heard it. When she reenters the main part of the shop, her smile is large. "They fit perfectly," she whispers to me.

"When did Uncle Charlie give those to you?"

"You don't know?" She sounds disturbed, like something is wrong with me for not knowing, the same kind of reaction a history teacher might give when a child doesn't know who George Washington is. "Haven't you heard the story?"

I confess that I have not but get ready for another Uncle Charlie story.

"He got them for me at the state fair."

"Legally?" I ask with a smile. I know that my uncle was rarely on the right side of the law.

"Yes, Samantha," Mom says.

"Well, with Uncle Charlie, you never know."

"They were being sold at a booth for a quarter apiece. I thought they were beautiful."

I turn my head to try another angle—perhaps now I'll be able to find the beauty in the blobs. I can't seem to, so I think to myself that I now know why the expression *beauty is in the eye of the beholder* was coined.

"I was just a young girl, and he took the time to think about me."

Suddenly, I get it. Right here in the shop, I now understand. Mom was drawn to her Uncle Charlie—despite his strange antics—because he cared about her. He took her to the fair and bought her something of value. Her own parents didn't show affection for her, yet this man made her feel cherished.

Morning slips into afternoon, and sunlight shimmers through the front window. We try to act like it's business as usual as Carson, dressed in a pair of worn jeans and a radio station T-shirt, fills the holes in the walls, sands them when the plaster dries, and adds a coat of paint. As if we're used to having a man work closely beside us every day.

At seven, Carson rinses his roller and paintbrush in the bathroom sink. I watch the pinkish white water dissolve into the drain. After drying them, he sets the roller and brush on the card table in the back room.

I leave him to walk over to the front door and lock it for the evening.

Mom counts the money in the register's drawer, writing numbers on a slip of paper. Since the robbery, she no longer leaves any money in the register overnight.

"Let's all go out to dinner," Carson calls out to us.

"What?" I make my way to the back room where the bathroom is.

Carson dries his hands on a paper towel from the metal dispenser. "I'd like to take you and your mom out to dinner."

"You would?"

"Yes, I would."

Standing in front of my mother, he asks, "Where would you like to eat tonight?"

She's speechless; again she looks ready to faint. As Beanie would say, *"She's all kinds of flustered."*

Moistening her lips, she calmly says, "I have stew in my crock pot. I tried a new recipe with chicken and tomatoes. We could go home and eat there."

Carson smiles demurely. "You can have the stew tomorrow. I'd like to take you out to dinner tonight."

Before the waiter asks if we want dessert or coffee, Mom says she's heading home.

Carson sputters, "Now?"

Mom says, "I'll leave you two alone."

"I hope we haven't bored you with our refugee talk." Carson's concern is genuine, and I can tell that my mother is enjoying the attention he's giving her.

Mom and I went to our homes to get ready and arrived at the Peking Gourmet Inn just minutes before Carson's car entered the parking lot. There was no wait to be seated; it helps that it's a weeknight and not the weekend when the restaurant is swamped.

Now, Mom places a narrow hand on the linen tablecloth. Her ruby bracelet that Dad gave her glistens under the lanterns that adorn the ceiling of the restaurant. "I've enjoyed your refugee conversation," she says.

I see that her eyes look sleepy, like she's ready to drink a cup of warm milk and slip into bed. If Butterchurn were still with her, she'd be adding milk to his bowl, as well.

Using her hand to push herself up from the table, Mom stands, her eyes on Carson. "Thank you for this evening," she says in a regal tone.

He pushes his chair back and rises. Touching her arm, he says. "Be careful driving."

Mom smiles warmly. "I usually am."

"Is she okay?" Carson whispers after Mom's slipped out, her purse secured under her arm, the Chinese waiter wishing her a good evening. Carson's seated next to me again, his right shoulder inches from mine.

"She gets up early, so she's probably tired by now."

"She didn't eat much." He eyes her half-eaten plate of walnut chicken.

"The robbery has her uptight."

"I bet it will for a long time. My dad was mugged in New York City a few years before he died. He had nightmares for a while after that."

Our plates are cleared by a lean waiter with a congenial grin. Carson and I order coffee, and when the waiter brings the cups to our table, we continue our conversation about Lien.

"Huy thinks she might back out." Carson stirs sugar into his cup.

"From what? Meeting her birth mom?"

"Yeah."

"No way!" Adamantly, I say, "She's anxious to meet her again."

"She refused eight years ago."

"Refused?" The word tastes bitter on my tongue, a contrast from the sweet sauce I had with my order of Szechuan beef.

"Before Lien and Huy and his parents left Saigon, Lien had the chance to say bye to her mom."

"But she didn't?"

"Her mom gave her up, and not saying good-bye was Lien's way of showing her anger."

Feeling like I'm the last to know everything, I ask, "How come Lien didn't tell me this?"

"I think she's a bit embarrassed that she was so belligerent. You know how she is. She suddenly decided that what she said and did was wrong."

"Why is it that she tells you everything?"

Avoiding my eyes, he picks up his coffee cup. "She says I remind her . . ."

"Of what?"

"Her father." The words come out solemnly. He places his cup down without drinking.

"Really? Does she remember him or does she just want to believe he was like you?"

"She has a picture. She showed it to me."

"And?"

"It was a blurry black-and-white photo. He's in uniform and about my height." After a few seconds, he adds, "A mound of curly hair. I guess that's where Lien gets her mop."

I focus on drinking my coffee, hoping its strong flavor will soothe the envy that always seems to surface when I come face-to-face with Lien and Carson's friendship. "I think it's interesting that she hasn't tried to search for him."

"She knows the chances of finding him or that he'd want to be found are slim."

"But has she tried?"

Carson shakes his head. "I've discouraged her."

"And she always listens to you." The sarcasm in my voice catches me off guard. I suppose the coffee isn't strong enough to soothe my tone.

Carson doesn't let it affect him. "Sam," he says, "sometimes you have to fight one battle at a time."

As I let Carson's words sink in, I take another sip from my cup. My gaze runs over the wall to my left that is crammed with photos. There are more pictures of George Bush Sr. on this wall than anyone else who has eaten here. Apparently, this is one of his favorite restaurants, the Peking duck being the dish he always enjoys. "She'd love seeing this wall," I say, my mind still on Lien. " 'Miss Bravencourt, I know famous people come to my restaurant. Movie stars.' " I make an attempt to mimic the young girl's voice.

With a smile, Carson joins me in observing the pictures. "She does like to claim celebrities have eaten at the Saigon Bistro. If she finds out about this place, she might want you to take pictures of all the patrons that come to her restaurant so that she can display a wall of fame."

A little after ten, the restaurant prepares to close. Carson pays the bill and then he and I linger in the parking lot. I search for the moon; in the Philippines my fellow teachers teased me because I found comfort in gazing at the moon.

"Do you know how to get back to your hotel?" I locate the moon, obscured behind a tree, glowing like a lantern on the streets of Old Salem.

"I think I can find it." He was good at driving the agency's van amid the chaotic traffic of Manila. I suppose the suburbs of D.C. won't be too much of a challenge for him.

At my car, he hugs me. "Sam, it's been nice."

My heart feels like gelato—soft and vulnerable. Quickly, I pull from his embrace. "Thanks for dinner. Mom enjoyed it."

"Did you?"

"What?"

"Enjoy dinner?" Giving me a boyish smile, he opens my car door for me.

I slip into the seat. "Yes, I did." *Don't make me say that I always like being with you, Carson. Because I am not going to admit that to you now.*

Deciding I need to check in on her, I drive to Mom's, the moon's brightness making a trail along the road. Mom's lights are still on when I park in her driveway.

I call out to her as I enter the ranch house, reprimanding her for leaving the front door unlocked.

I find her in her bedroom, dressed in a matching nightgown and robe the color of holly berries. "I was about to head downstairs to lock the door," she tells me.

Sprawling out on her double bed, I watch as she sits on a puffy backless chair, brushing her hair by her vanity mirror and dresser.

"I just don't know," she says as the bristles from her hairbrush make their way down the shafts of her hair. After this, she'll apply Pond's cold cream to her face and throat and then remove the white film with a damp washcloth. I think the first recollection I have of my mother is in a lavender nightgown, smelling of cold cream and sleep.

"What?" I rest my head against a satin pillow.

"I don't understand."

"Don't understand what?"

She turns to face me. "Why you haven't snatched Carson up and made him your own."

"Mom!"

"Yes?" She draws out the word so it almost sounds Southern.

"That sounds so . . . so possessive!"

"And your point, darling?" That sounds *very* Southern.

"People don't snatch people and make them their own."

"Why not?"

"Sounds like slavery."

"Love." She breathes the word.

"Well, I know you think I got your good looks, but that doesn't mean I can just decide who I want to like me and make him fall at my feet."

Placing the brush in a drawer, she takes out a large jar of Pond's. "He's charming and genuine."

Swinging my legs over the edge of the bed, I frown. "You just met him!"

"I know what I see."

I change the subject. "Are you okay here alone?"

"He's got a nice smile. Very charming."

I leave after that, locking her front door with my key.

thirty-three

February 1986

W hen Carson left the camp, I was clueless. True, I knew that his sister was sick with something the doctors were still trying to figure out and that his mother had asked him to come home. But he loved teaching and being with the refugees, and his one-year contract still had six weeks left.

I wanted him to confide in me like he did whenever we talked of our fathers. I liked it when he would single us out—*"We know what it's like, Sam, to miss our dads."* Instead of asking me what he should do, he spent time in Dr. Rogers's office.

The day he left PRPC, I was inside the admin building planning a lesson on the expectations of being a student in an American school. I planned to tell my new class the rules they'd be expected to follow in their new schools.

I looked up from my notebook at Brice, who stood in front of me. "Gonna be lonely here without him," he said.

My stomach cramped. "Without who?"

"Dr. Rogers drove Carson to Manila today."

I didn't want to ask why, yet even so, the word came out unbridled. "Why?"

"Carson's flying back to the U.S."

I just sat there and felt my heart turn to mush. The room was stuffy, the air thick with sadness. I left the building and longingly looked over at the dormitory where he had lived. He was gone. I would not see him entering or leaving that rustic building's door ever again. Blinded by tears, I rushed into my dorm and went straight to my bedroom. The tropical air dried my tears, causing my cheeks to stiffen. I knew more would come; I could feel them building up behind my eyes. But they didn't find their way to my cheeks. Instead, I pounded my pillow and sobbed, "I will never ever think about you ever again."

Which was a promise I knew I could never keep. I thought of him the rest of the day, remembering all the places we'd talked and walked together.

I was surprised later when I got a letter from him, postmarked Raleigh, North Carolina.

His sentences were filled with how much he'd missed sweet tea, fried chicken, and hiking the Blue Ridge Mountains. How nice it was, he said, to be back in air-conditioning and experience the blooming of the azalea bushes in the spring.

I replied, a lengthy tome about all the happenings at the camp, answering his many questions about refugees he was friends with who were still in Bataan. I gently reprimanded him for not telling me good-bye, a reprimand he never commented on. He wrote a few more times, and when he didn't mention Mindy, I hoped that she was no longer a large part of his life. I imagined him as he visited his sister in the hospital, wishing I was with him to comfort him as his sister went through tests, wanting to feel my arms around him as they had been when we were together in his classroom.

With Carson gone from camp, things were not the same for me. The anticipation of running into him at the mess hall or riding with him to our classrooms was gone. Each time I went to the marketplace to buy bean sprouts, onions, and cabbage for the stir-fry dinners I cooked in my dorm, I wished Carson were with me to share the meal.

After his fourth letter to me, I waited for another. One night I realized that anticipating his letters was consuming me. I was here to teach the refugees. I was supposed to be praying for my students and their families. Instead, I scanned my mailbox for a letter postmarked from Raleigh.

The letters stopped. The fourth one was the last one I received from him, and I reread it many times, saving it along with the others in the back of my closet.

It didn't take much time until I was counting the days before my contract ended and I was scheduled to leave the refugee camp. When my sun-starched calendar on the wall of my bedroom showed that there were only forty-two days left, I began to prepare my good-byes. The heat was getting to me, as well as the torrents of rain that came during the rainy season. I was tired of living in a fishbowl with either fellow teachers or students constantly at my side. Even the thrill of being in Manila on weekends lost its luster.

Brice's year in the camp was nearly over too, but he decided he'd extend his contract for another. "I like it here," he said one evening as "Borderline" blasted from someone's tape player. "I'm feeling more at home."

I nodded, because I did understand. But I looked forward to not having to boil drinking water on the stove, and being able to drink soda with real ice cubes, enjoy Hershey's chocolate, and even my mother's crock-pot meals. Although I would miss aspects of the camp, especially the laughter of the children, I was ready to leave.

thirty-four

Carson's eyes are shining and warm, a look I haven't seen since our days at PRPC. After greeting each other in the parking lot with a hug, we step inside Sanjay's bakery. The air-conditioning is working today, and within minutes I feel chilly.

"You got it fixed," I say to Sanjay as Carson stands at the glass counter filled with tasty treats, looking over the menu. A few days ago, Sanjay asked Mom and me for the name of a trusty HVAC repairman, saying the air-conditioning in his shop was not cooling no matter how low he set the thermostat.

Sanjay gives me one of his wide-eyed grins. "Venya said she must have it cooler or she would stay her entire pregnancy at home."

"Venya's pregnant?"

"Oh yes, very much so. The baby is all she talks about now, all she talks of every day."

I congratulate him and then Carson orders a breakfast bagel with egg and bacon. I choose a gooey pastry topped with raspberries and cream cheese—one of those baked goods that leaves your mouth and fingers sticky.

"Something to drink?" Sanjay asks.

"Coffee," I say, hoping it will warm me, and Carson says he'll take some, too.

We sit side by side in wicker chairs, away from customers entering the shop to pick up styrofoam cups of coffee and bagels to go.

I take mini bites, making sure to wipe my mouth frequently. The coffee is stronger than usual, and hot.

"Do you think your mom's at the boutique yet?" Carson asks after chewing some bacon.

"If it's nine, she is. She always gets there early before the store opens."

He turns his wrist to view his watch. "It's nine thirty."

"She's there, looking at the paintings and grateful for your help with making the walls look restored."

"You think she'll be okay?"

"My mother?" I let out a low laugh. "She always seems to land on her feet."

"Glad I could help."

"Me too." I meet his eyes and am happy to see that they are still shining. "Thank you."

"I meant to hang the paintings back on the walls."

"Don't worry about them. I can do it."

He nods, then suddenly says he needs to get on the road.

My reaction is the same as it was years ago in the refugee camp, a need to protest. I start to say that I wish he could stay longer, that I'd like a refill of coffee, that I'll miss him when he leaves, but I simply drain my coffee cup.

"I've got to work at the station at four this afternoon."

With a hand on the small of my back, he leans in and kisses my forehead. Then he stands, clears the table of napkins and cups, and waits for me to get up.

My knees wobble, but I manage to make my way out of the shop with him.

He hugs me before getting into his car. Without another word, he drives away.

I listen to the songbirds in the nearby oak trees, feel the joy and sorrow in my own heart, and eventually go to work.

"Ahh, Sam," says Sanjay when he enters the boutique later in the day. "I see you have a man."

I'm dusting while Mom attends to a tall woman with lots of tattoos on her legs. Dusting and thinking that Carson will lose interest in me. Why shouldn't he? What does a forehead kiss signify? Was it a kiss of friendship? Was it a promise of something more?

"Sam, he is good man, no?" Sanjay lets his eyes lock with mine. His lashes are long; I bet he was teased as a child in Bombay.

Swallowing, I say, "He's a good man."

Sanjay's smile captures the light from the front window. "You need a good man. What the world needs now is love sweet love."

Sanjay then tells a story about a customer who complained that the muffin had too much chocolate in it and wanted a refund.

"How can anything have too much chocolate?" I ask.

"I don't know."

"Did you give him a refund?"

"No, Venya would have been angry with me." I cannot imagine an angry Venya. His wife is a tiny soft-spoken woman who wears marigold silk saris. And now with her pregnancy she might actually gain a few maternal curves.

"So what did you do?" I ask, dusting the freshly painted wall where the two pictures used to hang, my thoughts feeling affection toward Carson.

"I gave him a blueberry muffin and wished him a good day."

Amused, I laugh.

"That is the American way, is it not?" Sanjay's face is solemn. "Have a nice day."

"Did you smile when you said it?"

"Yes, that is also the American way." With a hand on the doorknob, he says, "I need to get back to the bakery. A bride and groom want a carrot cake." Turning back to look at me, his eyes narrow. "Is this normal?"

"You mean, is it American?"

"Yes. That's what I want to know."

"I think that as far as weddings and cakes go, in America couples do whatever they want."

"It does seem that way."

"And in India?"

"We follow whatever our parents want."

"And your parents wanted you to come to America?"

He finds the humor. "No, they protested, but Venya and I were stubborn. I better go back to the shop. The cake is going to take many hours to decorate. They want martini glasses and green olives on the top layer."

Not sure I've heard Sanjay correctly, I say, "Martini glasses and olives?"

"Yes. That's what they ordered."

"That's plain strange."

"Only in America, no?"

When he exits, I hang the pictures for Mom. Just like they were before, the heavier blob of orange and pink on the left, and the lighter one with a twirl that looks like a pig's tail on the right. Stepping back and squinting, I search for beauty in these prints. Perhaps, as I concluded earlier, the splendor is in the giver.

Mom joins me to view the paintings. "The frames are perfect." Her face brightens. "What a nice man," she says with emotion in her voice. I'm not sure if she's talking about Uncle Charlie or Carson.

That evening I appreciate the air-conditioner as the outside world swelters with humidity. With a new Busboy mystery, *Armed in Amsterdam*, and my soft sofa, I curl my legs under me and start chapter one. But I don't get far. Touching my forehead, I think of how Carson leaned in to kiss me, replaying the whole scene in my mind.

The phone rings into my thoughts and as I go to answer it, I hope it's Carson.

A female voice responds to my hello with, "Hello? Is this Samantha Bravencourt?"

"Yes."

"Hi! It's Avery Jones."

"The real Avery?" I suppress the urge to giggle. "Hi, how are you?"

"Great! I got your number from the phone book. Not too many Samantha Bravencourts in there."

I'm tempted to tell her that there are more Avery Joneses listed in the Winston phone book than I would have ever guessed.

"I called one Samantha and I knew right off it wasn't you. She had a real Southern accent, and I didn't think that would be you." Her voice bubbles, words spilling into each other as she tells me what she's been up to. She married Perry a year ago in a Methodist church in Fort Wayne. She tells me she's an ER nurse and that Perry's an intern at the same hospital. They want children, a boy first, and then another boy because Perry enjoyed his brother. Then, a girl. She really wants a girl.

I watch robins in the scarlet crepe myrtle outside the window. I try to push aside the feeling of hurt that expands inside my chest. Avery got married and she didn't invite me.

"My cousin just had twin girls. Now that would be fun." Her light tone continues as she tells about the twins. I have never understood why anyone who has spent any amount of time with an infant would wish for twins.

"And how are you?"

Looking around my apartment, I answer, "Fine, fine. Yeah, I'm doing well."

"Where do you work now?"

"My mom's clothing store. She opened it just after I returned from the Philippines." And before she was diagnosed with breast cancer, I almost add, but I don't. I consider telling her about Taylor, knowing she would appreciate the funny story about how I thought I was going to her wedding and met him there. I consider telling her about Carson. But I don't.

"I've got some guy friends," I say and again wonder what the kiss from Carson meant. A forehead kiss is only a kiss of friendship, is it not? "No one special," I tell her.

"You'll meet someone."

Eager to change the subject, I ask, "Do you still eat Twizzlers?"

"All the time."

When we end the call, I laugh. Then I laugh because it's funny to hear myself laugh in the darkness of my apartment. If I hadn't gone to the other Avery's wedding and reception, where would I be now?

A professor once told our history class that if you changed one thing in the course of your day, your day would end up differently. He explained with an example. "Say I would have left the house on time to get to work. I would have stopped for coffee on the way. But because I was running late, I didn't stop. Since I didn't have my morning coffee, I needed a cup and was dragging by noon. So after my last class, I went to the break room to get a fresh cup. I never went to the break room at noon; I was usually in my office eating a bag of Fritos and grading papers. In the break room stood a most beautiful girl. She was the sister of my colleague down the hall, and she was visiting him and attending his classes just for fun. Now, if I hadn't missed my coffee that morning, I would have had no reason to enter the break room and I then never would have met Julie."

"So did you ask her out?" a kid with thick glasses in the front row asked.

"Many times," our professor said. "And then she became my wife."

thirty-five

Searching for a missing person is even harder than searching for a missing cat. Of course, Carson reminds me that Lien's mother is not missing. Hiding, perhaps.

"Why do you use the word 'hiding'?" I ask.

"Didn't you hear the story?"

Again I realize that I have not been told everything.

We're seated in Dovie's kitchen. She asked me to come down for a butterfly release, wanting me to take pictures. I told her that anyone can take pictures of the event, but she insisted that I was the one with the creative eye and good camera. "Besides," she added, "we are making pound cake, using one of Uncle Charlie's recipes he brought over from France when he was stationed there. You'll love it."

I stocked up on film, packed my camera bag and a suitcase, and filled my Honda with gas for the southbound trip.

After an afternoon of capturing butterflies creatively, I enjoyed the dinner of omelets and hash browns Beanie had waiting for us. We ate and talked, and right at dessert time, Carson appeared. I knew Dovie had been on the phone with him, enticing him with the promise of homemade pound cake with fresh whipped cream.

After he arrived, Pearl, Dovie, and Beanie left us alone in the kitchen with the ticking of the wall clock.

Carson rests his arms on the kitchen table and explains. "Lien's mom was with the American soldier until after Lien's birth. Then he went back to the U.S. She was shunned. She couldn't handle the shame. Her parents told her to give up her baby. Actually, Lien was almost four at the time. Lien's mom then decided to give Lien to her relatives."

A pain in my left temple causes my eye to pulsate.

"Thuy, Lien's biological mom, had a hard life in Saigon. After she made sure that Lien could be taken care of by the couple that was much more financially stable, she went to her hometown in the country to be with her parents. She wanted to pretend she was a single woman again and tried to live as normally as possible. But her past reputation caught up with her. Locals wrote nasty slurs on the wall of her parents' house. One man tormented her in the marketplace."

"Why?"

"I thought you—"

I stop him right there. "I am tired of you thinking that I know everything."

His mouth droops; his eyes lose some of their color. "I was actually going to say that I thought you possibly didn't know about that story."

"Oh." Coughing, I look away.

"Sam, don't be angry."

My face feels warm. "Why not?"

"I'm sorry."

"For what?"

He sighs. Cupping my hand in his, he says, "I am on your side."

I want to pull my hand away. I want to stand up and leave like I did a few times in the refugee camp.

"We seem to apologize a lot to each other."

I nod. "I have this problem with flying off the handle." Looking at him, I add, "And so do you." At one time, my words would have been delivered with a fierce blow, and Carson would have retaliated with the same force. But we are older now; the years have softened our attitudes.

"I just want to know all there is to know about the Hongs and Lien. I don't want you to call me unintelligent." I do not meet his eyes.

"I'd never do that."

"You did, though."

"When?"

"In PRPC. I read your letter to Mindy one night. The part where you said I wasn't intelligent." I suppose that now is just as good a time as any to let Carson know that I'm the type of person to invade one's privacy.

Carson's face sinks like a pothole. "No . . ."

I listen as the clock ticks and Milkweed drinks from her bowl.

Carson says, "I'm sorry, Sam."

I find his eyes, soft and gentle, like he really means what he says. I suppose I need to confess something else to him and what better place to do it than in Dovie's kitchen? "You know, about Lien . . ."

"Yeah?"

"It was me who told Van and the others that I thought Lien was a thief."

Carson sighs. "I know, Sam."

"Did they tell you?"

"You made it clear that you didn't think much of Lien."

All my tirades against her parade before me, and I'm ashamed and guilty.

Firmly, Carson says, "She didn't take that jewelry, Sam."

"I know you think that."

"I *know* that. It was a man who did. Not a refugee, but a Filipino. They later caught him trying to steal again from the billets."

"How do you know this?"

"Filipinos entered the camp and stole from the refugees from time to time."

I think of how the entrance to the camp was always protected with guards on duty with guns. "Why was Lien's uncle so certain that she took the jewelry, then? Why was she blamed for everything?"

"She was mischievous. You know that."

Under my breath, I blurt, "She didn't stand a chance."

"You're right; she was discriminated against because of who her father was."

"I always wondered why the full-blooded Vietnamese admired us but couldn't be decent to someone who was half white."

"People are strange," Carson says without any trace of animosity. "They have their prejudices."

"It seems like coming to America is what has helped her family."

"True," he says. "Some Amerasians are much better off in this country than they were in their own. And some end up in gangs just like they did back in Vietnam."

"But Lien is on a good path," I say with certainty. "And she has Jonathan. He's a decent guy, isn't he?" *Please tell me he is.* I want to hear that he is a great match for her. I see Lien's effervescent smile and know she has always just wanted to belong. Somewhere. "Her family will accept her if she marries an American, won't they?"

"Oh, yeah, they will."

With a small meow, Milkweed jumps into my lap, settling into a small bundle, her eyes closing as I stroke her soft fur. "Did you move to Winston because of them?" I ask Carson.

"The Hongs? No, I moved to work at the station. Lien wrote a few times when they lived in Chicago, and I knew that they were unhappy up there. I guess it was about two years ago when I saw them again."

"You went to Saigon Bistro and there they were?"

"That's just the way it happened. I went in for a bowl of pho and the past surrounded me." There is lightness to his voice.

"Were they happy to see you? I mean, was Minh still mad at you for defending Lien?" I recall Minh's cold stance on the bus when they departed the camp.

"I worried about that, too. But the minute he shook my hand, I knew he'd put that behind him."

thirty-six

On Sunday afternoon in Dovie's kitchen, the iced tea tastes a little bitter, but perhaps it is due to what I'm hearing. Little is worried about her daughter because, although Liza followed her dream and went to Paris, Little has yet to hear from Liza. The hostel where Liza said she'd be staying has never heard of her. Little will call the U.S. embassy in France on Monday.

Pearl enters the kitchen, ready to make a rhubarb pie, her weekly routine. She massages her fingers, one hand caressing the other.

"Bothering you, Pearl?" asks Beanie.

Pearl fumbles with a sack of flour, unable to open the bag. Beanie reaches over and tears the top portion of the paper for her. Pearl tries to flex her index fingers.

"Why don't you just sit for a spell?" Beanie motions toward the empty chair to the left of me at the kitchen table.

"I was going to make a few pies." Opening the pantry door, she reaches up and takes an apron off a hook.

Beanie says, "I was going to give you a little therapy."

"I could use some." With the apron balanced over her shoulder, Pearl stiffly makes her way to the table.

Meeting her halfway, Beanie takes her by the hand and pulls out a chair for her to sit in. Then she takes a clear bottle from the cabinet over the sink and plants herself across from the older woman. With care, she removes the cap and pours a white creamy substance into the palm of her hand.

Gently, Beanie rubs the lotion from her palm onto Pearl's fingers.

"Ahh," sighs Pearl and closes her eyes for emphasis. "That is remarkable."

The trust between the two women tells me that this therapy has been done before.

"What is it?" I ask. The contents of the bottle give off a heavy odor of ginger and orange.

"If I told you," says Beanie, "I'd have to kill you."

I laugh.

"Ancient Chinese herbs?" The strain in Pearl's face has lessened.

"Old family recipe," says Beanie. She takes Pearl's other hand and repeats the rubbing. "Cures everything from senility to beestings, especially good on stiff joints."

Pearl nods, her eyes still closed, her head hung against her chest. "I feel my arthritis pain going away." The apron slips from her shoulder, easing silently onto the tile floor.

Beanie rubs her thumb over Pearl's knuckles. "Now, you go watch a show or two on TV."

Pearl's eyes pop open. "My pies," she says reluctantly.

"We can have leftover pound cake for dessert tonight."

Pearl extends her fingers. "I think I could roll out a crust now."

"Go rest," Beanie insists. "Go on. Enjoy feeling better."

After she leaves, Beanie puts the cap back on the potion. "Cures bruises, too," she tells me.

"Do you get bruises often?" I think of how Mom says she can bump into almost anything and obtain a bruise, her skin is so thin.

"About once a week when I fall."

As she picks the apron off the floor and hangs it back on its hook, I look at her face to see if she's joking. "You fall that often?"

"Sometimes more." She lifts her pant leg to expose a greenish blob on her shin. "Got that a week ago."

"How?"

"No one's told you?"

"About what?"

"I have seizures." She takes the lid off the bottle again and adds some of the lotion to her bruise.

"You do?"

"I've been on all kinds of meds. Nothing has really helped."

I know so little about seizures. "How long have you had them?"

"Epilepsy? All my life."

I piece together what I know about Beanie. She was married to an abusive man, left him and was homeless for a while. I know her son from her first marriage is currently in jail for drug trafficking. Now she's on disability, although she'd like to work to make more than her monthly check offers. I look her over. She's probably only forty-five or so and yet it seems her life experiences have been more daunting than most I know, except for the refugees. "Beanie, you've had a rough life," I say with feeling.

"Wouldn't know how to handle anything but rough."

Standing from the table, she refills my tea glass, asking if I want more ice cubes.

"No, thanks. I don't need any more ice."

She sets the pitcher of iced tea on the counter and then takes two red onions from the fridge.

"What does Dovie say to do about your dizziness?"

"She prays." Beanie searches for a knife.

"Do you mind?"

"Mind what?"

"That she prays for you."

A snort follows. "I would think that if she wants to take the time to ask God to help me, I should be all kinds of grateful."

I smile.

As she slices the first onion, she says, "She prays for all of us. I hear her talking to God every morning. Some wake to birds singing. I wake to Dovie's prayers."

"I know."

"I have no problems with prayer," she adds. "I have no problems with God, either. I just don't like those people who look at me funny. Like I'm not good enough for them because I'm different. You know, don't nobody want to be judged."

"You're unique," I say.

"Unique." She rolls the word over in her mouth. "Is that better than different? 'Cause I like the way that sounds." Adjusting the collar on her oversized shirt, she proudly repeats, "Unique."

After we eat a dinner of bacon potato stew, oatmeal bread, and tomatoes, Beanie turns the radio on to Carson's station. She, Dovie, and I clean up the kitchen. At our insistence, Pearl takes her yarn and needles into the den to watch *Jeopardy*.

Carson asks for requests on his show. "This is Carson Brylie, and it's your turn to tell me what you want to hear." His voice fills the room like a familiar scent, relaxing all the senses.

He plays "Saturday in the Park" by Chicago. Beanie and Dovie do a few dance moves around the kitchen, dish towels flung over their shoulders. Beanie looks professional, while my aunt as usual doesn't pay attention to the beat of the music.

"Remember the cha-cha?" says Beanie, but Dovie says she never learned that one.

When that song ends, the station goes to a commercial break. Dovie and Beanie are still dancing, laughter flowing about them.

I'm sweeping the kitchen floor when Carson says, "I want to dedicate a song. This one is an old favorite of mine. It goes out to Samantha Bravencourt."

My heart freezes as I stop sweeping. Why is he dedicating a song to me? At this point, I don't know if I should be pleased or annoyed. Then I hear the music for "Fifty Ways to Leave Your Lover" and let a smile replace the tension in my face. I sing a few of the words, letting the broom handle act as my microphone.

When the chorus begins, Beanie claims, "Not very romantic, is it? 'Set yourself free'? 'Hop on a bus, Gus'?" Her forehead wrinkles as she frowns.

"Oh, sometimes a song can have more to it that makes the heart flutter than meets the eye. Or should I say more than meets the ear?" Dovie gives a nod my way and then begins to dry a glass bowl with her towel. She hums, just like her sister—my mother—hums when she does tasks around the store, a little off-key but with gusto and feeling.

I swallow a few times.

Beanie says, "Sounds like a breakup song to me." But now there is a smile on her face, as if she has heard Dovie and gathered that there is more than meets her ears.

When the kitchen is "put back into place," as Dovie says, the two women join Pearl in the den to watch a movie. They ask if I want to join them, but I know my heart is tugging at me to do something else.

I sit on the porch in a wicker chair, drawing my knees up to my chest. The night is cooled by an intense wind, the little butterfly wind chime bouncing on its perch and clanging like a fire alarm. Over that noise, I listen as rain glazes the tree leaves. There are no crickets and bullfrogs singing their songs tonight.

With my arms wrapped around my legs, I close my eyes and immediately see Carson's face. Actually, I see it in various situations. Like a slideshow, images come to me. Carson with a smile under the trees at the snack shop when he and I sang a silly song together, when I tried to kiss him and he turned away, and today as he told me not to be angry. How can I help but be a little angry? He has kept so much from me.

It is then that I realize the tugging at my heart is an invitation to pray. I should talk to God. As Dovie would say, "It's time to have a heart to heart."

In the Philippines I'd sit outside my dorm on a grassy knoll and watch the fields below. Occasionally, I would see a water buffalo or a farmer in a large straw hat harvesting his rice. The bullfrogs would sing and the sky would display an assortment of purple clouds as the day signed off.

I talked to God those evenings. Even though it was hard to find time alone among the refugees and other teachers, this sanctuary behind the dorm building became my respite from the long and sticky days. I wrote in my journal and created my newsletters to send back home. I thought about new ways to reach my students, sensed the anguish they'd faced, and prayed for my classes.

I missed Mom, too. There were times I felt I was selfish to have let my adventurous travel-loving side take over so that I had to leave her. She was alone except for a few relatives scattered here and there. At the time, she was working in retail, managing a clothing store in Fairfax County. I suppose that's when the desire to run her own shop came into play.

Talking to God tonight with a cat by my side and a thunderstorm brewing in the east feels perfect. There's calm mixed with stress as Milkweed meows and the thunder crackles.

I release my fears. They bounce before me as I name them. Inside my heart, I've kept them like shackled prisoners in bondage. First comes the fear of the past: the pain of being rejected by Carson. Then there's the present: not knowing how he feels about me now, not wanting to give away my heart only to get it smashed again. And lastly: the unknown future. Is there even a future designed for us to share? I close my eyes as Pearl did earlier today, just letting Beanie soothe her aches and pains.

When the rain pelts against the roof and fills the gutters, I stroke Milkweed's fur and feel an odd yet tender sense of satisfaction. I spoke to God. God heard me. Sometimes that is all I need to know.

thirty-seven

The new alarm system at the shop has an annoying beep whenever anyone touches it, but at least Mom feels safe. I catch her checking it every hour, pressing the top of the keypad with a finger. Once I even saw her running the feather duster over it. She's been sold on Burtel protecting her dresses, coats, pants, jewelry, scarves, and the freshly painted wall.

On the first few days following the robbery, it seemed all the security companies called to offer their best deals. Mom soon stopped answering the store phone and just let the answering machine pick up the missed calls. I'm not exactly sure why she chose Burtel except that when Sanjay came over three days ago, she did ask him what system he used at the bakery. When he told her he used Burtel, she asked if he'd ever been robbed.

"Robbed of my dignity a few times," Sanjay replied.

"What do you mean?" she asked.

"You know, the customers who want something for nothing or fret and curse at you when you can't get 150 turkey sandwiches made for them on a two-hour notice."

I thought Mom would be horrified to think that people expected that kind of superhuman feat, but instead she said, "I didn't know your bakery served sandwiches."

"We do. We used to only have the breakfast baked goods, but now we are more known as a deli and a café."

"Rye bread?" Mom asked.

"If you like."

"Provolone cheese?"

"We have that, too."

"Tomatoes and lettuce?"

"They are the freshest this side of the Capitol."

With that information, Mom ordered two turkey sandwiches for our lunch. "Light on the mayonnaise and mustard. Add some pickle relish if you have it. No hurry," she said. "Just call when they are ready and Sam will come over to get them."

I rolled my eyes as Sanjay laughed and left the store.

After she and I ate lunch in the back room, she picked up the phone and called a Burtel representative. One of their technicians installed the new security system Mom wanted the next afternoon.

Sanjay pours me a cup of hazelnut coffee and listens to me talk about the phone call I received from Taylor last night. It's a Thursday, and every Thursday the bakery has a different coffee special. Mom's already been in the bakery to get her cup.

"Taylor found out Lien's mom is here in town."

"Here?" says Sanjay. "In D.C.? I thought you said last week that she was in Chicago."

"That's where she resettled at first. But Taylor said her last known address is here."

"Well," says Sanjay as he hands me the styrofoam cup, "I guess that's why he is the investigator. So did he give you the address?"

"He had one. But it's old." Taylor told me he actually called the phone number that went with the address only to find that the number was no longer in service.

"Old?" Sanjay's forehead wrinkles. "How is an address old?"

"It means it's not current. You know, no longer up-to-date."

"Sounds like fashion. So what do we do?"

"What do you mean?"

"If she is here, maybe someone knows her. We talk and see who else talks." His dark eyes shine from the light coming in the front window.

"Who do we talk to?"

"We do like on the TV detective shows. You know—Magnum. He goes around asking the right questions."

I smile and sip the coffee.

"How is it?"

"The coffee? Great, as usual."

"You need to make a flyer. Like you did for the missing cat."

Sanjay points to the flyer for Butterchurn. When he heard Butterchurn was lost, he wanted a flyer for his store, too. His doesn't have an actual photo of the cat—instead he drew a fat cat and gave it a collar with *Butterchurn* on the tag. "I will put one up here." He motions to his bulletin board that has assorted advertisements from faithful customers.

"Okay."

"Do you have photos of this missing woman?" he asks.

"Carson and I made some photocopies of the one picture Lien salvaged." Carson and I had spent some time at the Office Max in Winston. After we finished there, he took me to his house to play Ping-Pong for old times' sake.

"Get to work," says Sanjay, breaking into my thoughts of how Carson won two games and I won two games. "There is no time like the present. If your investigator friend has tracked her to this area, then someone who comes into your shop might know her."

You accused her. I berate myself with the words until finally I beg my guilt to evaporate. True, I told Van and the councilmen that I believed Lien was a thief. She was, in my mind. Partially due to guilt, but mostly due to my desire to help a young woman who has been through more difficulties than anyone should face, I'm fueled up to help Lien now. At my kitchen table, I continue with the flyer, adding a photo of Lien and Thuy to the middle of it. In the black-and-white photo, Thuy's face looks no older than her daughter's. They have the same eyes—eyes that have seen too much sorrow and anguish. Lien's and Thuy's full names are written by the pictures. Underneath, in a smaller font, is my number to call if anyone has any news of Thuy's whereabouts.

I run my finger over Lien's photo, over her wayward hair and her lips from which I've heard many a wayward word. "O God," my voice cries out into my small kitchen, "please let it be soon that Lien will be reunited with her mother."

After that, my heart feels exposed, and as the cliché goes, my conscience gets the best of me. I dial Taylor's number. First I thank him for all the effort he's put into the search for Lien's mom. Then I close my eyes as tight as I can like I did when I was a little girl in red tights and patent leather shoes. This is what I did when I had to confess to my parents that I'd gotten a bad grade on a spelling test or that it was me who broke the cookie jar. Awkwardly, I let the words out. "I still like him, Taylor."

"Who?"

I realize then that I was so preoccupied with how my words were going to sound to him that I've left some important ones out. "Carson." I've already told Taylor about my year in the Philippines and how I "ran into" Carson recently.

After a brief silence during which I dig my nails into my palms and wonder why I had to give in to truthfulness, I hear Taylor say, "The man you were with in the Philippines."

"Yeah. He means a lot to me."

"So you're thanking me and then telling me that you don't ever want to see me again, is that it?"

"No!" I'm too adamant. "I just want to be honest." Quickly, I add, "But I have this friend and she's great."

"A great friend." His voice is flat.

"Yes. You'd like her." I'm too enthusiastic.

"So let me get this straight. Not only are you dropping me, but you're trying to set me up with your gorgeous friend?"

"She's not gorgeous." Oh, I hope Natasha will forgive me for being this honest. "She's cute."

"Kittens are cute, too."

"She likes kittens. And dogs. In fact, she loves Boxers."

"Well, sounds like we have a lot in common," he says, but he doesn't sound happy at all.

I don't know what else to say, but I do wonder why being truthful sometimes hurts so deeply. "I have to go," I tell him. Then I hang up, bumping the receiver against the phone cradle.

thirty-eight

Today the boutique is filled with women of all sizes, spread out among the tall and petite sections. I pick a gum wrapper off the carpet, annoyed that people think littering is acceptable behavior.

"I'm ready," a voice says, and I see a tall, slender woman twice my age standing at the counter by the register. I ring up her purchase for a pair of khaki pants with an inseam of 33.

"You'll enjoy those," Mom tells her as I slip them into our trademark beige and pink shopping bag. Mom would know; she owns three pairs of pants just like them. In fact, she's wearing her newest pair right now.

Soon only one short lady is left in the store. The woman approaches me with a pair of navy pants. "Can you alter these a bit?" Her frosted blond hair makes her face look younger than she probably is. But her narrow hands show age spots. Mom always says you can tell a woman's real age by her hands.

I ask if she'd like to try on the pants in one of our dressing rooms, but she pays me no attention. Her eyes are fixed on the flyer that is taped to the wall behind the counter. Dropping the item of clothing onto the countertop, she continues to stare.

"Her name isn't Thuy anymore."

"Excuse me?"

She looks like she's debating whether or not to say more. After an awkward silence, she mumbles, "She goes by the name of Sophia."

My gaze darts behind me to the flyer. "Sophia?" My voice cracks. "Are you sure?"

"I'd recognize her anywhere."

"She has a daughter. Had a daughter."

Crisply, she states, "You don't ever 'had a daughter,' love. Even if your daughter is buried, you always have her. Even if the daughter doesn't ever want to see you again, you are still her mother."

Cringing at her tone, I take a step back.

"I take it this daughter is still living?"

"Yes."

"And she wants to be found?"

"Oh, yes."

"Hmmm . . ." She looks back at the flyer.

"Do you know where Thuy . . . I mean, Sophia, is?"

"I might."

As my heart leaps, I pull out an extra flyer from under the counter. Handing it to her, I ask, "Do you want money?"

"Money to tell you where she is?" She laughs. "If only money was enough! I have a feeling that all the money in Vietnam couldn't make me tell you where Sophia is unless she wanted you to know."

"What do you mean?"

Taking the flyer from me, she clasps it to her chest. "I will ask." Her eyes hold mine in a steely lock. "That is what we do for each other, is it not? Ask."

"Do you think she'll want to see Lien?"

"That I do not know."

"Is she in the area? Does she live nearby?"

Although she doesn't say a word, something about her expression causes me to believe that Lien's mother is still in town.

I'm about to toss out another question, but my own mother, who has made her way to my side, places her fingers against my arm. Firmly.

We watch the tiny woman leave our shop; the bell jingles. Only the scent of her Chanel No. 5 and my flattened ego linger.

"Find out where she's going!" I rush to the front window, almost colliding with one of the mannequins as the woman walks along the sidewalk. I look to see which vehicle she gets into, ready to take down the license plate number.

"Samantha," my mother says, approaching me. "You can't make this happen."

"But—"

"You just have to hope she'll get back to you and want to see her daughter." Mom's tone is harsh. "That's all."

Tears sting behind my eyes.

"Did I ever tell you about your great-aunt Ruthedale?"

I close my eyes, my eyelids acting like barriers for my tears. I hope she won't go into a tangent like she does when she tells the stories of late Uncle Charlie.

"She tried to run the world."

"Isn't she the one who died of a heart attack at age thirty?"

"Exactly. She wanted to control everyone all the time."

I try to blink back a tear but it's too late; it has curved down my cheek. Walking toward the counter to put some distance between my mother and myself, I somberly say, "So she had a heart attack and died."

"Yes."

"And you're telling me this because you want me to stop wanting to have things go my way?"

Mother pauses and then, "No."

Pulling a tissue from the box we keep under the counter, I wipe my nose with it.

"I am telling you this because I don't want to see you get hurt."

The front door opens and three customers enter our shop. It opens again and one more comes inside, removing her sunglasses and pushing them on the top of her head. Mother greets them, calling a few by name. Regulars, I presume, yet I have no idea who they are.

One smiles at me and says she enjoyed the Elvis Night we had. She hopes we'll do that again soon. The dress I convinced her to buy that evening has been a wonderful addition to her wardrobe. "Thanks for that," she says as she heads over toward the scarves, now marked at twenty percent off. "I wore it to a soirée last Friday and got many nice compliments."

I still don't recall ever having seen her before. Sniffing, I decide sometimes your eyes don't see well when your heart has been ruffled.

thirty-nine

When I tell Carson that I'm coming down for another visit—mainly because of the wedding shower Dovie is hosting for Lien—he says he hopes he'll get a chance to see me. I'm in a semi-state of elation, having just found out that Lien's mother is in D.C. and that we are one step closer to reconnecting her and Lien.

I ask Carson, "Hope you'll get a chance to see me? Are you not going to be in town?"

"Oh yeah, I will."

I let silence enter our conversation, waiting for him to clarify.

He doesn't, so I say, "Will you be busy or something?"

As the words leave my mouth, fear lodges in my throat. This fear's nothing new when it comes to this cute Southern gentleman. He brushed me off in the Philippines. He could be about to do it again.

Suddenly I realize these months of thinking he's matured and letting my heart grow fond of him again could end with me getting my heart broken for the second time.

"Well," I finally say, my words coming out in a rush, "I hope I get to see you."

"Do you have any news?"

I told myself that I would not share the news of Sophia with Carson until we were face-to-face. "I could and I could not." I let this sentence come out slowly, like the way Pearl removes a hot pie from the oven. Then something comes over me, and I firmly state, "I have to go. Now. Bye."

I want him to protest, tell me not to go yet. But he doesn't. "All right. See you soon, then."

Every night since the woman at the store said she knew Lien's mom's whereabouts, I've hoped to get a call from Carson. Yet, now that he did call, I've held back. Something tells me to be cautious. Perhaps it is my own mother's voice in my mind, warning me not to get my hopes up and not to try to control the situation.

When I arrive in Winston on Friday evening, my mother allowing me an early exit from the shop, I'm surprised to learn from Beanie that Carson is coming by to see me at nine fifteen, after his radio shift.

I'm in the kitchen at the table with Beanie, eating a slice of Pearl's rhubarb pie with a scoop of vanilla bean ice cream, when Carson rings the doorbell. Pearl and Little are watching a rerun of some movie with Dovie. I hear gunshots and the clomping of horses' hooves, so I assume it's a western.

Beanie asks Carson if he'd like a slice of pie. She holds the pie out for him to see; three-quarters of it has already been consumed by Dovie's tenants.

Carson sits across from me, his long legs slipping under the table. He thanks Beanie for her offer but says he and a friend shared a pizza at the station and so he's too full to eat anything else now.

Right then I know that something is wrong, and the juices in my stomach start to sour. I push the plate of pie away and sip from a glass of ice water.

"Where'd you get the pizza?" asks Beanie.

"Mario's."

"Did you get their marinara sauce to dip the crusts in?"

"Yeah. That's the best part."

The two chatter on about the pizza place and someone they both know who used to work there. Finally, Carson looks back at me and smiles. "Going to finish your pie?"

"No, why?"

"Just wondering if you're ready to go."

I sip my water. Coolly, I ask, "Go where?"

"How about a walk?"

Carson knows I love going on walks, but tonight I want to decline. If he knew that I gave up a perfectly good guy because I love him, what would he say? Part of me is afraid he'd laugh and say, "Sam, why'd you do that?"

"It's not bad out there. Nice night." He takes my hand.

I search my mind for an excuse. Maybe I have to help Dovie with the butterflies or chickens. But Dovie's in the den, still watching the movie. The truth is, neither the butterflies nor chickens need me.

Beanie clears my dishes. "Go on and walk. You've been driving all day," she tells me as she loads the dishwasher. Then she winks at me and I feel embarrassed by her gesture; I'm sure Carson saw it.

Minutes later, Carson and I walk along the sidewalk in front of Dovie's neighborhood. The air is tolerable with little humidity. Carson was right; the night is a nice one, the stars popping out against a charcoal sky. I search for the moon and see a sliver of light masked behind a violet cloud.

I plan to walk to the end of the block and then tell Carson
I'm tired and need to go back to Dovie's. I know I'm being
childish, but there are times when that is all I know how to
be. Our inner child never leaves us, a sociology professor once
told our freshman class. How right he was.

When Carson asks how things are going and if Taylor has
made any progress on the search for Lien's mother, I stop walking. He stops too. I feel the irritation that was choking my heart
disappear. Excitement now replaces it. I'm eager to release the
news. Finally, I get to share something about Lien's family
before Carson knows anything about it.

Carson eyes me. "So, what have you got?"

"I know where she is."

"You do?"

"A woman came into the shop and recognized Lien's mom
from the picture in the flyer."

"And?"

"She knows her. She knows where she lives!"

As Carson grins, I think to myself that I will never forget
the relief on his face. Then I add in the missing pieces to the
story of that afternoon. Of course, my enthusiasm wanes as
I say, "I'm not sure if this woman will get back in touch with
me, though."

I try to cheer myself with the message I've been mentally
repeating over the week. Wouldn't any mother want to be reunited with her child?

Continuing our walk, Carson says, "Too bad she didn't leave
her number. Did she write yours down?"

"No. She was a bit distant. But she did take the flyer I gave
her."

We turn left and walk past a house with two gnome lawn
ornaments.

Carson says, "She could be upset."

"Who?"

"Lien's mom. The woman who wants to be called Sophia now."

"Upset about what?"

"Remember I told you that Lien had a chance to see her mom years ago, but she refused?"

"I know, but that was then. That shouldn't play a part now, should it?"

Carson's arm brushes against mine as I try to ignore the electricity I feel between us. I move to the left, onto the curb, to create a wider space so that our arms won't touch. I tell myself that I should go back to Dovie's and sit in her air-conditioned den and forget Carson. I want to be old like Pearl, crochet baby booties, make pies, and not have a romantic bone in my body so that I won't desire moonlit walks and dinners for two.

Carson watches as I balance along the narrow curb. Then he says, "Thuy found out that Minh and the family were able to leave for America under the Orderly Departure Program, their first stop being the processing center in Bataan. She came from her village to say good-bye. Lien didn't want to see her. Lien called her horrible names, just like everyone else had done because Thuy had a half-breed daughter." Carson pauses and then says softly, "It hurt Thuy badly, I'm sure."

I see a vehement Lien, behavior like she exhibited in the classroom when teased about her freckles or the unusual color of her hair. And I can imagine her being nasty to her mother. "She's different now," I breathe. "She can only be kind."

To avoid the spray of a sprinkler watering an ample lawn, Carson and I move to the center of the street.

"Should we tell Lien about the woman who came into the shop who knows Thuy?"

After a moment, he says, "Let's wait and not get Lien's hopes up."

Based on his logic, I agree. Lien doesn't need to know yet.

"Are there more secrets?" I ask, after a neighbor calms a yelping dog in her backyard.

"No. You know everything now."

"Except for what's going on inside your heart," I say lightly, although once I say it, it costs me. I feel immediate pain surge under my rib cage. I cannot bear that I've given him room to trample on my heart once again.

"You could know that, Sam. All you have to do is ask." His tone is mellow, and he places his hand on my shoulder.

I'm still not sure if he thinks of me as a potential girlfriend or as a sister.

As we circle around the neighborhood toward Aunt Dovie's house, streetlights flicker on around us, casting shadows on the pavement. Carson says, "She wasn't who I thought she was."

"Lien?"

"No, Mindy."

Slowing my stride, I prepare to hear about this past girlfriend. Although I don't want to appear too eager, I certainly don't want Carson to think that I haven't wanted him to talk about their relationship.

A sigh leaves his chest. "She wasn't at all interested in what I wanted. I guess she was jealous."

"Jealous?" I see her picture in my mind, that glossy print that seemed to threaten me whenever I entered Carson's room. Now I want him to say that Mindy was jealous of me and all the time he and I spent together. That he confessed to her in letters that he was really not in love with her, but in love with me. My thoughts leap all over themselves but are suddenly interrupted.

"Jealous that I got to experience Asia. She's never been out of the South."

Oh. "That's crazy. You said her family was wealthy. She could have traveled."

"I don't want to talk about her."

I'm unable to stifle a snort. "But you brought her up."

"I shouldn't have."

"I've always wanted to know what happened between the two of you. Why can't you tell me?"

"Let's not talk about her."

Fed up, I blurt, "Keep your secrets, Carson. I'm getting so tired of all this mystery." I consider leaving him alone under the streetlight, reconsider, and stop. "You know, if I want a mystery, I'll read my Busboy books. The rest of my life should not be one puzzle after another."

Carson clenches his jaw. His neck muscles tighten.

I start to walk, tiny steps that morph into larger glides. I can see the edge of Dovie's house and the azalea bushes that line her driveway. I will go inside her home and go to bed. And as I let sleep consume me, I'll ask God to remove my feelings for Carson.

"Sam, look, I don't want to let anything get between us. I really want us to be friends." He rushes to catch up to me.

Friends?

I'm at Dovie's now, and I make my way down her dimly lit driveway. Over my shoulder I say, "We are friends, Carson. Nothing ever changes." I curve around his car toward Dovie's front door. I look to see if anyone is seated on the porch, but not even Milkweed occupies a space there tonight.

As I grab the doorknob, ready to yank the front door open and go inside, away from Carson forever, he is behind me. His hands embrace my waist.

"Sam." I feel his breath on my neck.

I tighten my grip on the knob.

"Do you know how much I care about you?"

I take a breath. "I think you've let me know that we are friends."

He spins me gently to face him as I release my fingers from the door. His lips touch my nose as his arm cradles my shoulders. "I'm no good at this. I want to say so much to you."

"Like what?"

"I don't want to lose you again."

Something tells me I should push him away and run inside, bolting the door behind me. Something else tells me to lift my lips to his. Tonight, the something else wins.

After all, the urge to kiss Carson has never left, even after all these years.

forty

Something's wrong. The minute we enter Dovie's hallway, I sense it, like the suffocating feeling you get from the clamminess after a summer rain. For one thing, the TV is off and no radio station is playing. It's only ten twenty, too early for everyone to be asleep.

Dovie appears in the hallway, Milkweed at her feet. She's carrying a glass filled with ice cubes and water. Her face is drained of its usual rosy color. When she sees us, she stops and says, "It's Beanie."

Fear rises in my mouth. I turn to Carson.

As he takes my hand, he and I follow my aunt upstairs to Beanie's bedroom. Inside, a solitary lamp casts light upon the twin bed where Beanie lies. Her eyes are closed and I realize I never knew she had such dark and long eyelashes. Her quilt tucks her in, pulled up to her chin. Pearl is seated on a chair, and Little is hovering near Beanie's feet.

"What happened?" I ask after I see Beanie's chest rising with breath and catch my own.

"She had a seizure and fell," says Dovie, her voice barely audible.

"She went up to her room to listen to the radio." Little explains in her slow manner as I see the lump on Beanie's forehead. "We heard a thud and rushed up here."

"What did she hit?" asks Carson.

"The footboard," says Dovie, her hand gripping the edge of it. She places the glass of water on the bedside table next to Beanie's radio and then sits on the bed. Reaching under the quilt, she lifts out Beanie's hand and holds it, her fingers laced with her friend's. "Now, Beanie, I know you can hear me."

There is no response from Beanie. She appears to be oblivious to our commotion.

"Who moved her into her bed?" I ask.

"A joint effort. I never realized how many muscles it takes to carry a body." Pearl wheezes and then places a plump arm against her own chest.

"Do we need to call someone?"

Quizzically, they all look at me.

"I mean, does she need a doctor to help her?"

Dovie says, "We know what to do. We know how to care for her. The first time this happened, I did call an ambulance and I don't think that Beanie ever forgave me." My aunt strokes Beanie's motionless hand.

"Does she usually take this long to come back to herself after a seizure?" I whisper.

"She was talking a moment or so ago."

"Really?" I scan their faces and add, "That's good, right?"

When Dovie nods, I ask, "What was she saying?"

Little and Pearl giggle.

Pearl says, "She said, 'Get that thing off of me.'"

"We put an ice pack on her forehead and she was livid." Dovie brushes the woman's hair from her face as she speaks.

"I heard language I hadn't heard since my husband died," Pearl says with a smile.

I'm not ready to laugh or smile. "So she's going to be okay?"

"Yes," says Dovie. "Beanie always is."

Carson leaves the room shortly after Beanie opens her eyes and cries, "What is going on? Why are you all here?"

We all laugh then, too loudly, but I guess it's because we're so relieved.

In the hallway, Carson draws me to him. "I'll see you tomorrow," he breathes into my ear and then kisses me. I feel that I could just stand here being kissed all night, sheltered in his arms.

After getting a drink of water, I find Beanie's potion to cure ailments, the one she used on Pearl's arthritic joints. Remembering how she said it helped with bruises, I take it upstairs.

In Beanie's room, Dovie is the only one left. Seated on the bed, her eyes are closed, her head bowed toward Beanie's. I know she's praying.

I stand by the open door with the bottle until Dovie raises her head, indicating that her prayers have finished.

Beanie's eyes flicker. Seeing the bottle in my hand, she says, "Good girl."

I trade places with Dovie and open the lid to the herbal lotion. Tipping the contents onto my fingertips, I use my other hand to carefully set the bottle on the bedside table. With my index finger I smooth the concoction onto Beanie's forehead. I feel the bump and see the colors of a bruise forming. "Does it hurt?" I ask as the fragrance of oranges and ginger rises to my nostrils.

"Like fire. But I know the ointment will help, so keep going." Her voice is raspy and strained.

I motion for her to stop talking. I add some more of the potion, smoothing it out along her hairline, amazed at how soft her skin is. I suppose I thought that after the life Beanie has led, her skin would be rough and callused. A dollop of the white balm runs near her crooked left eyebrow. I rub it into her temple. "Feel better yet?"

She sighs. "Makes you tired, those seizures. I'm too old to have to put up with them."

"You're not old," I say. I suddenly realize that I've never been this close to Beanie before since I know she doesn't accept hugs and silly sentimental displays of affection. Beanie likes to appear tough, yet when she's sick, she's just as vulnerable and dependent as the next person.

At one fifteen, when Dovie leaves to get ready for bed, Beanie shifts to sit up and take a sip from the glass of water. Then she slowly eases down onto her mattress, her head against the cotton pillow. "Promise me, Sammie Girl."

"What?"

"When I go, you take care of your aunt."

"Where are you going? You're not going anywhere."

She coughs. "Dovie needs to be told how entertaining her butterfly stories are. She needs to know that we are fascinated with those specks that dart all over creation."

When her eyes flutter and then shut, I wonder if she's going to sleep. After a brief respite she says, "Don't waste time with the bitty things of life, Sam."

"What do you mean?"

She finds my hand and squeezes it. "When you find what you want, don't ever let go."

Wondering where she is going with these thoughts, hesitantly I say, "All right."

"I chased after the wrong bottles—the kind that have Johnnie Walker on the label. That led me to the wrong men, which led me to . . ." Her voice trails off, perhaps lost in memory. Lines of anguish are imprinted on her face.

I seal the bottle of lotion and place it on the table. "Tell me about your son."

At first I think she won't, but after a moment her mouth opens. "He got into a mess. But he's gonna be okay."

"When does he get out of jail?"

"In about nine months. He's a handsome boy. Takes up after me. The day he was born, I couldn't believe that I could love someone so much." Releasing my hand, she says, "Ah, look at me." She says no more, as though embarrassed at being sentimental.

Feeling my throat start to weld, I look away from her at her shelf of colorful candles, all of them created by her from a kit she bought after going to some home party that charged too much for candles. I recall the day she said, "I can make these myself and not spend all that money." Then, with great excitement, she showed us how to make the candles, dipping the wick into the hot wax so many times my head grew dizzy. She let me try my hand at it, and the slender form I made looked like the tail of a muskrat.

"Not to worry," she encouraged me. "Art has no boundaries, just like love. If it's in the heart, you can claim it."

We had to hold the formations until they dried, and then she placed them in brass holders that Dovie purchased at a yard sale.

She's watching me, her eyes now open. "When I go, you can have those."

Turning from the shelf, I look into her dark eyes. "You're not going anywhere, Beanie."

She yawns. "You may leave now, Sammie Girl."

"No, I'll sit here a little while longer."

"I'll be here tomorrow." She yawns again. "And the next day. And the next. Not sure about the day after that one, though." Amused with herself, she lets a smile break over her lips. I watch it fade as sleep takes over.

I head to the basement, to the lumpy bed there, even though I know there are only a few hours until I'll need to wake to get ready for church. The drip of the faucet puts me into a deep sleep.

In my dream, Beanie is standing in a field of sunflowers, and as Dovie's butterflies leave their cage for a world of freedom, Beanie says, *"Don't judge me. Just love me."* She says it over and over so that when I wake, I am ready to love and not judge.

I check in on Beanie, thinking she'll be amused by the dream. She's asleep. "Beanie," I say, "I dreamed of you last night. It was like a broken record."

She continues to sleep.

"You kept saying 'Don't judge me. Just love me.'"

I stand at her doorway, waiting for a response. After a few minutes, I start to get worried. Just then I see a weak smile form on her lips. "Thank you," she says. "Thank you." Then she lets out a snore.

The bridal shower takes place at Dovie's the next day at three in the afternoon. This means that Pearl will have to forgo her customary nap, but Pearl says she thinks for a celebration, she can manage.

Between checking on Beanie and getting the refreshments ready, Dovie, Pearl, Little, and I are moving at a steady pace.

Leave it up to my aunt to hold a bridal shower for Lien. When I told her that Lien was engaged with plans to be married in November, Dovie's mind was clicking like a cash register.

"Do you know if anyone has planned a shower for her?" asked my aunt.

"I don't know," I said, trying to think if Lien's friends would be the type of folks to do this.

Without wasting another minute, Dovie grabbed a calendar to see which dates she had to offer Lien for the party. She asked for Lien's number, and while I stood by her side, she told the young woman that she wanted to have a shower for her. "I'm Samantha Bravencourt's aunt, and I live in Winston. I want to have a little party for you."

Lien was speechless, and Dovie thought something had been lost with the language barrier. But Lien understood perfectly; it was just hard for her to respond when tears were stifling her throat.

Lien's two bridesmaids arrive a little before three, and then Chi and Lien join the gathering. Lien is wearing a navy dress with large white polka dots, a pair of ivory sandals, and a smile that won't stop. Chi has on a light green ao dai and her hair is swept into a bun. She even has on a shade of frosty lipstick.

Four women walk up the driveway, each with gifts. Lien tells me that they go to her church.

When her friend Grace pulls up in a dented Toyota, Lien squeals. "Grace, you come to see me all the way from college in Georgia! You surprise me so good!"

I snap photos of the decorated table with paper plates, napkins, and a wide vase of roses and carnations. I get a few pictures of the stack of attractively wrapped presents that are placed on and around a wicker chair on the porch.

Lien wraps an arm around me and says, "Miss Bravencourt, you please take pictures at my wedding. Please be the photographer."

"Me? At your church?"

"That's right, and you and Mr. Brylie are invited, of course. I want you to invite everyone you know."

Before we fill our plates with the treats on the table, Dovie offers up a prayer, asking that Lien be reunited with her mother and for joy in the upcoming marriage. "Amen and amen," she wholeheartedly offers at the end.

"I done bad stuff," Lien later confesses to me as we eat cheesecake and dainty ham sandwiches, prepared by my aunt, Pearl, and Little. "I not been good. I was not a good student for you." Her eyes are tender under the lids of gray shadow, and they pull me in.

I reach for her, and as we hug, I take this opportunity to give her my own confession. "I thought you stole all those things in the camp. I'm sorry for not believing in you."

She rubs my shoulder with her slender fingers and eyes me. "Oh, many people believe I am not worthy because I am Amerasian. They call me names. But Jonathan tells me that I'm a beautiful creation made and loved by God." She smiles and then adds, "And forgiven. Forgiven by God. That is an awesome thing, isn't it, Miss Bravencourt?"

"Yes," I say. It's all I can say. My throat clogs, right along with my eyes. I look at Lien's sparkling ring and wait for tears to disappear.

They won't; one dampens my left cheek, and seeing it, Lien says, "You cry for me? You too kind."

"I am happy for you," I tell her.

She grabs my hands and, holding them tightly, says, "My heart is beating with gratitude." Then she laughs in her typical fashion. "I never believe I get married and that you, my teacher, would be here to help me celebrate."

Years ago, in a sun-baked classroom, I never would have believed it, either.

forty-one

Carson comes over after the shower ends. He helps carry the used plates and cups into the kitchen and then sweeps the porch. Dovie, Little, and Pearl are all kinds of impressed. Their faces are brighter than marigolds under a clear autumn sky.

After eating a slice of cheesecake because Dovie insists, Carson suggests that he and I go out on the porch. We sit on the love seat, holding hands and talking.

As he caresses my fingers, I tell him about the shower and how I asked Lien to forgive me. He pulls me close and whispers, "You've come a long way with Lien. She's lucky to have you in her life."

As evening approaches, we're aware of the warmth in our bodies and our breathing. Milkweed sits at our feet, purring every so often, like she's happy that we have found each other again.

When Carson says he must leave, I don't want him to go. I dread having to be away from him but know I must leave tomorrow to head back home.

Being apart from Carson has never been easy for me. In the Philippines, there were times he would be in Manila for the weekend getting some R and R, and I looked forward to Sunday night when the agency van would pull into the administration building's driveway and he would step out with a wry smile. Once, we both ventured to Manila on the same weekend. That was a magical two days, even if Carson spent the majority of Saturday looking for a piece of jade jewelry for his beloved Mindy.

I head upstairs after watching him pull out of the driveway, and stop by Beanie's room.

Beanie's eyes spring open when she hears my footsteps. Looking at me from where she lies in her bed, she whispers, "I heard there is a boyfriend and girlfriend together at last."

"Not everything you hear is true, you know that." I give her a sly smile.

"I have reliable sources that tell me these things."

"How are you?"

In a whisper, she says, "I called my boy."

I ask how that went; she merely looks at her assortment of candles. Again, I ask, "How was it talking to him?" I know she has not called him in years.

"I told him I'm sorry," she says, making room for me to sit on the edge of her bed. "I haven't been the best mom for him. Too many issues in my own life. And too much disappointment he's given me."

I stroke her palm, which is lying open like she's released something.

"Life is just too short to let our pride get in the way, Sammie."

I think of my own pride and how it has been like a boulder

in my path—large and obtrusive—keeping me from being more giving and loving.

She asks for some water and then wants me to turn on her radio for her. "Music soothes, you know."

"I know." I turn on the radio to her favorite station—Carson's station—and listen to the last verse of "Morning Has Broken" by Cat Stevens: "Morning has broken like the first morning . . ."

Once Beanie's eyes close, I lean in to kiss her forehead. Then I leave her room with the hope of sweet dreams that will usher in a new morning with promise.

When I enter Have a Fit at noon the next day, Mom says, "You're back from the South. I thought you'd stay this time." She looks like she's lost weight since I saw her last, a tall and thin frame in a sage apron.

Bothered that she would think I wouldn't return to her, I act like I didn't hear her comment. "How was your weekend?" I ask and give her a hug.

"The store was busy. Natasha came by to help."

I owe Natasha another dinner for her efforts.

With a pair of scissors I start opening a box UPS sent days ago filled with winter fashions, and place sheath dresses and wool jackets on hangers. I reprimand myself for forgetting to wear my tennis shoes.

From across the room, Mom asks, "How is Carson?"

"He's great." *I miss him already.*

Mom smiles and fingers a piece of licorice. Before putting it into her mouth, she says, "I want you to know that I think he's right for you."

Glad to hear her say this, I grin.

"I pray the two of you will love each other more each day."

Love? Could Carson *love* me? The word sounds strong. I know I love him. That is one of those things that will not change.

Dismissing my thoughts, I get to work. I find the smell of new clothing irresistible. Each item is wrapped in plastic. Gently, I pull out a maroon dress, dangle it in front of me, and then study it for flaws. Mom taught me how to note the stitching, the hem, the sleeves, and the texture of the fabric. She calls this "quality control." It took her a year before she believed that I was capable of performing this task.

Mom dusts the new alarm system. "And the Vietnamese girl?"

"She was really happy about the shower Dovie had for her."

"Has anyone heard from her mother?"

"No, not yet."

I'm hoping that Mom will say the frosted-haired woman came back to the shop with Thuy's contact information. But she only looks at me, a finger alongside her nose. "Are you okay?"

"Why?"

"Because you're mixing the size petites with the larger sizes."

She's right; I'm doing what she does that annoys me.

"I can tell that you had a good weekend."

I smile.

"How is Dovie?"

"She's doing well." I straighten the dresses and then remove the smaller sizes to another rack on their correct side of the shop. *She worries about you, me, Beanie, Little, and Pearl. She has a large heart, a tremendous faith in God, but she's still human and she frets over us.*

"And those others she keeps?"

"Beanie had a seizure, but she's recovering."

"A seizure! That sounds awful. How does Dovie deal with all of this?"

"It was scary. But we all took good care of her." I think of how we sat around Beanie's room, tending to her needs.

When a woman enters the shop with a soda from Wendy's, I hope Little hears from her daughter Liza soon. The American embassy in Paris said there was no record of Liza having traveled there. If she remains missing, I might have to ask Taylor to do some more detective work.

After the customer leaves the shop with a black dress, a pair of triangle earrings, and a plea for us to discard her Wendy's cup, Mom says to me, "Why don't you go on home?"

"Why?"

"You look sleepy."

Again, at a little before five, she tells me to go on home. "Take a hot bath. I'll be all right without you."

But I want you to need me, I am tempted to say, but I don't because the door chime jingles against the doorjamb and I know we have a customer. I turn to see a man in a dark uniform walking toward us. He looks vaguely familiar.

"Hello." He nods at me, then addresses Mom. "Hello, Mrs. Bravencourt."

Mom's about to pop another piece of licorice into her mouth but halts the action by keeping her hand in her apron pocket. "How are you?" There is a smile in her voice.

"I just wanted to make sure things are going well with your business. I heard from Officer Garner that you were robbed a few weeks ago."

"Why, thank you. It was awful. Have the culprits been caught?" She places her fingers along the glass countertop.

I finally realize this is the officer who came when we had the fire in the dumpster.

Officer Branson edges closer to the counter and leans his large frame against it. "We are trying our hardest. I wanted you to know that I'll be patrolling this strip mall a lot more closely now." His hands are inches from Mom's.

"Well, that is nice of you." I expect her to protest, but she doesn't. She smiles instead. I note how her lips curl in a coy way.

The policeman rubs his mustache, then, using two fingers, smoothes the hairs. "Sorry for all the trouble you've had with the fire in the dumpster and the break-in."

Mom nods. "I just don't know what is happening to our world."

The policeman agrees that it is a rough world filled with malice. "But there is lots of beauty in it, too."

"Oh, there is much beauty," says my mother as she twirls the jewelry display around once, and when it stops, straightens a pair of dangly mauve earrings.

He notes the flyers on the wall. "A missing person *and* a missing cat?"

"Yes," says Mom. "My cat has been gone since February and the Vietnamese girl's mother has not been spotted in years."

The officer asks a few questions and the two continue to chat, their voices filled with warmth, their eyes animated.

I'm greeting a customer when Officer Branson asks Mom if she's ever read *Moby-Dick*. After she recites a few of her favorite parts of the book, he asks if she's ever been to see a play at Folger Theater.

I've been at home fifteen minutes when Mom calls from the shop. Convinced she's going to say she needs me after all, I swing my purse over my shoulder.

"That lady was here."

"Which lady?"

"The one who said she knows about the girl's mother. She gave me a phone number."

"What? Really?" This is what I dreamed would happen. I can't believe it has happened, yet I am still suspicious that Mom doesn't know fully what she's talking about.

"Do you want the number?"

"Yes, yes!"

She gives it to me, and I quickly write it on an old grocery store receipt I've pulled out of my purse. I read the numbers back to her to make sure I've heard them correctly.

"Now, be careful," she says before hanging up to greet a customer. "Your heart is like Dovie's, and the two of you cannot save the entire world."

After a few deep breaths, I call the number. There is no answer.

I take another breath and steady my heart.

To pass the time, I put on a pair of shorts and a JMU T-shirt and head out for a walk. I check my mail at the mailbox, make my way around the block, and then come back to my apartment. Gritting my teeth, I dial the number on the receipt once more.

"Hello?"

"Hello. I'm calling for Thuy." Remembering the woman at the shop said that Thuy was now going by a different name, I make the correction. "Sophia. I would like to speak with Sophia." I brace my free hand along the kitchen countertop.

After a pause, I hear, "Yes."

"Is this Sophia?"

forty-two

"What do you want?" the muffled, accented voice asks.
Gathering my courage, I dive into my soliloquy.
"I'm Samantha Bravencourt. Back in the eighties I taught English at a refugee camp in the Philippines." My mouth goes dry and, swallowing, I continue. "One of my students was Lien Hong." Then I make myself stop and wait.

When there is no response, I raise my voice. "Is Lien your daughter?"

"Lien?"

"Your daughter. Right?"

The silence is heavy.

I try to dig my fingernails into the Formica.

"What do you want?" The words sound angry.

I press on. "She's your daughter, isn't she?"

"Where is she? She in some kind of trouble?"

"She's in America. In Winston-Salem."

"Winston?"

"Winston-Salem. It's in North Carolina."

"North Carolina." She repeats the state like she's not sure it is real.

"She's getting married. She wants you to come to the wedding."

"Wedding." Again this is stated like she's not sure of the reality.

"Yes." I say the word for wedding in Vietnamese and then feel foolish—like my shaky Vietnamese is really going to help her understand any better that Lien is getting married. "Lien is getting married in November."

"I don't travel. North Carolina much too far."

How can it be too much of a distance for her? Her daughter is getting married. Don't families put these events above all else? "Where do you live?" I ask.

"Sorry," she mumbles.

Fearful she might hang up, I clamor, "Lien misses you. She wants you to be there at the wedding in North Carolina. Please come."

"I live in Washington, D.C."

"I live near D.C. I'm going to the wedding."

"I cannot. Good-bye."

Something comes over me. Like a gust of wind, I blurt, "Then we will have it here."

"I am sorry."

Quickly, I repeat, "We will have it here. Here in Falls Church. Falls Church is right beside D.C." I feel like I'm back in the refugee camp, trying to make a point in English when no one is listening because Lien is causing a ruckus. I provide the name and address of my church in town.

Finally, she says, "When?"

I choose the same date Lien has planned for her ceremony. "November thirteenth."

"November?"

"Yes. At three in the afternoon."

"Three o'clock?"

"Please come. We will see you November thirteenth." I don't ask if she can be there. I don't plead, either. I demand that she will be present. "Lien will be so happy. Thank you." I'm about to add that I'll tell Lien about our conversation and that she'll be so excited she'll be calling, but I don't get a chance to do that.

Thuy has hung up.

I suck in air. What have I done? Again I've taken control of a situation I have no business taking control over. I place the receiver in the cradle and make my way to the sofa. Lien's already got the caterer, florist, and others lined up for her wedding ceremony and reception in Winston. Most likely she's also sent invitations. In one of her rare attempts to speak in English, I heard Chi tell Lien that she needed to get them out so that people would be aware of the upcoming event. "No invitation—how will everybody know to be there?" the woman demanded.

Walking back into the kitchen, I pick up the phone and call Carson. I count the rings, and when his answering machine comes on, I listen to his voice.

I don't leave a message as he requests. I call Lien. She answers right away, and when I tell her about the conversation with her mother, she gushes, "Thank you, thank you."

Gripping the receiver so tightly that my fingers turn numb, I confess, "Uh, I told your mother something else . . ."

"That I am a troublemaker?" She laughs, and as she does, I hate that what I'm about to say is not funny.

"I told her that you are getting married in Falls Church."

"What?"

"She says she can't travel long distances."

"Why not?"

"I don't know."

"But Miss Bravencourt, I don't have a church in Falls Church."

"I do."

"You do? A church for my wedding?"

"Yes." And as soon as I say the word, I know I am now committed. How is it that this child I wanted nothing to do with has now become my life?

Lien's voice is hopeful. "Will you call your church?"

I suppose I will have to.

Mom suggests that I meet Pastor Jed at the church in his office. She is a firm believer in face-to-face talks. At first I don't want to go. But after a quick bagel with cream cheese at Sanjay's bakery, I drive to my church. Sanjay has listened to the story and agreed with Mom. "More convincing when you talk with faces in view," he says as he slips a cheese Danish into a paper sack and hands it to me.

Puzzled, I look at the bag.

He smiles. "You will need it. Energy for your task."

"Oh," I say. "I thought it was for me to give my preacher. You know, as a gift."

"If you think that would work in Lien's favor, then use it as a gift." With another smile, he sends me on my way.

I feel apprehension spread through my neck. I've never done anything like this before. Carson is better at advocating for others. He should be doing this instead of me.

At that moment, I remember words I learned in Sunday school: *God gives us grace and strength for each task.*

I water my planters of ivy and think about what to eat for dinner. There's the new Italian restaurant not far from here, and if their flyer is correct, they offer takeout, even delivery. I'm thinking about a cheesy slice of lasagna when Carson calls. Without a proper hello, he tells me Lien is in tears. Her mother has changed her mind and will not come to the wedding.

"What?" My voice ricochets off my kitchen walls.

"She has M.S."

"What?"

"Multiple sclerosis."

As I walk into the living room, I feel my heart pump vigorously, and I find respite on the sofa in case my body decides to give out from the rapid increase in blood pressure. "But why does that mean she can't come to the wedding? We are having it locally for her benefit." I think of my long talk with Pastor Jed last week about having the ceremony at our church. I had to explain the whole story. He was interested in details. He suggested that Lien and Jonathan come to him for some premarital counseling. "That's my standard," he said. "I like to offer this to all the couples I marry."

I left his office with mixed feelings. On the one hand, I was grateful that the church had nothing scheduled for November 13 so the wedding ceremony could take place in the sanctuary. On the other hand, I wondered how in the world I was going to get Lien and Jonathan to agree to be counseled by my pastor. Later, I called Pastor Jed and asked if he would be willing to talk with them via phone. He said that would work, although he preferred face-to-face. I guess we are all a viewing-faces generation in spite of telephones and computers.

Now Carson tells me that Lien's mother isn't even going to show up for the wedding. "She says she can't come."

"But why?" I cry.

"All she told Lien is that she's unable to be there."

"No, no," I moan. I let the receiver slip from my weakening grip.

"Sam. Sam?"

I pick up the receiver off the sofa cushion. "I'm here."

"Don't give up so quickly. I think Thuy is worried."

"About what?"

"She's in a wheelchair. I think she's not sure she wants to be seen."

"Can't she think about how much her being there means to Lien?"

"We are working on that."

I swallow. I must release this hold on wanting things to go my way at this wedding. Gulping, I lower my voice and say, "Okay. I'll trust God to make it happen." Yet my heart is packed with doubt.

I try to read from where I left off in my Busboy mystery, making myself comfortable on the sofa with a cup of coffee and a light quilt over my legs. When the coffee grows cold, I reheat the mug in the microwave and again think about what to eat for dinner. While my stomach craved Italian before Carson called, now I think it wants something Asian. A steamy serving of pho would be tasty tonight, but I don't feel like getting into my car to drive to the local Vietnamese restaurant, and I certainly am not in the mood to dine alone in public. So I heat a bowl of ramen and add a few fresh carrot slices to the broth and watch the news on TV. I rethink the whole pet concept. If I had someone else living with me, I would never have to eat alone.

When Dovie phones me an hour later, she cries, "They found her." I think she means Lien's mother, but my aunt is talking about Little's daughter, Liza. "Liza wasn't going to France. She went to England. Little got it mixed up."

How does one get France and England mixed up? I wonder silently. And then I ask it. "How do you confuse France and England?"

Dovie laughs. "Little doesn't quite know."

"Has she lost her hearing?" I know she has a speech impediment, but I always thought her hearing was fine.

"No. I think the truth is, Little has always wanted to go to Paris to see the Eiffel Tower. She has Paris on her mind. 'Course she's too afraid to fly there, so I'm not sure how she'll do it."

Just because you have a country on your mind doesn't mean you panic when your daughter isn't there. I wonder if the women at Dovie's have found some of Uncle Charlie's old moonshine in the basement.

"Little wonders how she got confused, too. I guess old age makes you silly."

"Is Liza okay?"

"Yes, she's really in love. With a Frenchman. She's happier than happy."

I try to get this straight. "So Liza is in England but in love with someone from France?"

Dovie chuckles. "Child," she says, "there is more to the story."

Yes, I think, the stories of our lives are never simple. There are complicated feelings and situations, and humans with complicated feelings in complicated situations. Like Thuy and Lien. There has to be more to their history than I will ever grasp—those hidden components, things that have gotten "pushed underneath all the living." Those components are what chronicle our lives, providing the vibrancy, sorrow, and frustration that can sound illogical to an outsider but make sense to the people involved. "Okay. Tell me more," I say.

"Liza is in England and her boyfriend is coming over to see her from Paris."

I run what she just said through my mind. Not sure I have all the facts, I prod my aunt to continue. "And?"

"Do you understand it now?"

"No, I don't. Why is Liza in England?"

"They are meeting there because that's where her job is."

"I thought she was interested in the convent. You can't have a boyfriend if you are going to become a nun."

"It was me who wanted to become a nun."

My mind swirls faster than waves during a hurricane. "Well," I tell Dovie, "I'm glad everything has worked itself out." *Now, Lord, please let the same happen for Lien and her mother.*

"Me too. Little will just have to get used to the idea of flying."

"Where is she going?"

"To meet the boyfriend and her daughter in Europe. And so," my aunt says without any more explanation, "when will we see you again?"

"I don't know."

"How is the search going for Lien's mother? I know Lien must be excited to be getting married."

"She is."

"We got an invitation today. Not the typical kind, but a homemade one. Had a little flower stamped on it. Beanie says that it's very Asian-looking."

"That's good," I say because I don't know what else to say.

"I guess we'll see you for the wedding."

"Yes." The word sounds weak.

"Will Cecelia be there?"

My mother will be there. In fact, Lien pretty much asked if I could add my family and friends to her guest list, wanting to "make sure lots of people come to see me be married."

But before I can reply, Dovie says she must go feed the chickens. Apparently, Breakfast and Dinner have been ganging up on Lunch, keeping her from getting her share of feed. Ready to discipline, my aunt hangs up.

forty-three

When I told Mom that Pastor Jed said he'd perform the ceremony for Lien and Jonathan, I watched her face brighten, her eyes shiny behind her glasses. I bet she was thinking, Well, I guess my daughter is capable of working this all out. In spite of the fact that I told her to be cautious and not get so involved.

Today, I see the gears inside her head churning as she prices a rack of silk blouses. After a few minutes, she asks, "Does Lien need a dress?"

"You mean as in wedding?"

"Yes, a bridal gown." The words flow off her lips like satin.

"I don't know."

"Ask," my mother prods.

So I call Lien at Saigon Bistro and find out she does not have a dress yet. She says she looked for "an American dress" with her friends at a store, but all the ones she thought were pretty were so expensive. "Expensive!" she cries again.

Figuring that Mom has something up her sleeve, I tell Lien not to worry.

After I put down the phone, a flock of women enter the shop and I begin to assist one who wants a wool skirt with a blend of polyester in a size two. I take her to the rack of skirts in her size, and after looking at them she decides that perhaps she's really a size three, or six.

"Do you think I'm a six?"

I can tell she's holding in her tummy; I've seen this sucking in of air and standing erect many times. "You could be," I say as I escort her to one of the dressing rooms.

Minutes later, she groans through the rose-colored door. "I guess I am a six after all. I used to be a two. It's having all those babies."

After she buys a size six skirt, I hope that everyone else will leave because I'm eager to hear Mom's plan for Lien. I want to talk freely with her without interruptions from customers.

Yet the customers are in no hurry, unaware of my urgency. A round woman with five pairs of slacks flung over her pudgy arm asks where the dressing rooms are. Mom unlocks the door to one for her and pleasantly informs her to call out if she needs a different size. Then Mom pulls me to her side and says, "I am going to do what we did growing up in North Carolina."

"What was that?"

"Making sure every bride had what she needed."

Never have I heard Mom say that line. Growing up, I listened to plenty of Uncle Charlie tales from Mom, Dovie, and even from my uncle himself, but no one ever mentioned that the state of North Carolina took care of her brides.

Mom and I debate how to dress the two mannequins that occupy our store's front window. I complain that I think we need new mannequins; these have always looked like they came over on the Mayflower. The white paint has chipped off the brunette's left hand, making her look like she has a skin disease. Mom pulls a beige tweed coat from one of the racks and drapes it over the blond doll. "I think it's a nice coat and will draw customers in."

From my years of working with her, I know that drawing customers inside is important, and therefore the way the wooden lifeless forms are dressed needs to be taken into careful consideration. I like her to think that I am capable of understanding the value of an eye-catching show window.

When Mom says, "This coat has a few wrinkles," I know she wants me to get the clothes steamer from the closet and get the wrinkles out. As I plug in the machine, my mother considers what else the plastic lady needs to entice passersby. "A scarf?"

"I think she needs a gray one with turquoise spots." I fit the coat onto the stiff model, pulling the fabric over her cold arms.

As Mom straightens the skirt, I move the arm of the steamer over the clothes, watching the vapor of steam soak into the fabric.

With a finger on her nose, Mom says a blue scarf with gray ovals looks better.

"Really?" I ask over the hiss of the steamer.

She waits for me to finish my task and then holds the blue scarf up to the doll's neck. "This scarf looks good with anything. That's what they say in the catalog I ordered it from."

When the door to the shop jingles and is thrust open, neither of us expects to see who walks inside. It's Lien; Lien is right here in the shop.

I move from the window to greet her.

Lien is an array of smiles. "Miss Bravencourt, I have made you do too much. I told Minh and Chi I had to take days off of work and come help you. It is my wedding, and I make you already do too much work."

Impulsive as always, I think as she throws her arms around me. Her bracelets rub against my neck. What will she do next?

"I ask Carson for directions," she says, looking me in the eyes. "And I drive and drive. It's a long way. Almost as far as Vietnam." She giggles and hugs me once more.

I introduce her to Mom, who says, "Your dress arrived."

I'd sent Lien one of our suppliers' catalogs, telling her to pick what she liked. She phoned to say she liked them all and for us to choose. After much deliberation, Mom and I decided on a satin ivory gown with Queen Anne's lace and a V-neck. The dress was sent with a half-off price tag, which my mother quickly removed and then carefully hung the gown on a rack.

From the back of the boutique, Mom brings the garment, which is sealed in a clear plastic coating for protection.

We watch as Lien's eyes resemble saucers. "For me?"

Mother nods and carefully removes the plastic, exposing the soft fabric for Lien to view.

"Oh!" cries the young woman. "I never imagine it would be so pretty."

Mom produces one of her *I love it when customers are elated* smiles and guides Lien to the dressing rooms.

Entering one of the stalls Mom opens for her, Lien shuts the door. "What if I am too fat?" she jokes.

I dismiss her worries. "The dress is your size."

When she opens the door and steps out, timidly at first, Mom and I are both caught off guard. Quickly, I find a spot on the carpet and look at it until I've blinked away tears.

Mom makes Lien turn around a few times and then says, "Now, that is stunning."

Lien asks what that word means, and together Mom and I say, "Beautiful."

Smiling at her reflection in the dressing room mirror, Lien runs fingers over the beaded neckline. I note how the gown clings to her narrow abdomen and around her hips, its train cascading over her legs and onto the floor like a frothy stream.

Mom takes a hair clip with a glistening pearl on it from the display of accessories and, brushing back Lien's hair from her forehead, inserts the clip along the side of her head. Mom actually laughs as the young woman exclaims with enthusiasm, "Oh, now I look like real American bride."

Lien hugs my mother, and as she does so, I see a combination of pride and affection in Mom's reaction. Mom's always saying that Dovie's heart is large, and when I decided to go to the Philippines, she claimed I was the "charitable type" like my aunt. Yet, in this moment, I see that my mother has her own style of being charitable.

When Lien has slipped her jeans and T-shirt back on, she joins us at the counter. "You go with me," she then says, looking me in the eye.

"Where?"

"I go see my mother."

"Where does your mother live?" asks Mom.

Lien digs into her worn Gucci bag and produces a slip of blue paper. She hands it to Mom, who, after reading the address, nods and says, "That's not far from here." Then Mom tells me, "You take her."

"Oh, no . . . I don't think . . ."

Lien's smile evaporates as Mom's eyes work like darts into mine.

With Mom's insistence and Lien's forlorn look, how can I deny what I'm asked to do?

"It's just past the little Greek restaurant on the corner by the store that sells those army clothes." Mom hands me my purse from behind the counter.

Taking my purse, I nod. "All right, I'll go."

Lien and I hop into my Honda.

"I never drive with you before, Miss Bravencourt," Lien says as she pulls on her seat belt. "You good driver?"

"Of course." But today, my nerves are tight and I wonder how I got involved in this scenario. Thoughts dash against my mind. What if Lien's mother doesn't want to see her? What if she's not home? What if they fight? What will I do? What should I say?

Lien chats as we drive, commenting on the area, the fall colors, and about the things she misses in Vietnam. I remember how I once asked my students if they could go anywhere—anywhere in the world at all—where would they like to go? I started the dialogue by saying I wanted to go to Egypt and see a pyramid. The class was quiet; even the rats remained silent.

Eventually, one small student raised his hand.

"Yes? Tell us, Bui."

Timidly, he said, "I want to go to Vietnam."

All at once, the children came alive. "Yes, I want to go to Vietnam," they chorused.

I couldn't understand why they would want to return to the war-torn country, a land they had just left. Some families had left under the Orderly Departure Program, but others had escaped by boat, paying large sums of money to operators and risking their lives.

"But it's our home," Van explained to me. "We are Vietnamese, and we want to go back. We left our hearts there."

The afternoon sun is fading as I approach the address Lien jotted down on the piece of blue paper. Slowing down, I make a left onto a street lined with massive oaks. My stomach twists like a pretzel sold by the vendors near the Smithsonian.

"It's 607 Amelia Avenue," says Lien as she looks out the window.

"Do you see it?"

"She said there is a sign for Laurel Archibold Apartments."
With her nose to the window, Lien searches the road.

I look to my left and see that the numbers on the mailboxes
are odd ones and, thinking that the apartment will be on my
side of the street, continue to read all the mailboxes, steering
my car away from trash containers and potholes.

With a cheer, Lien shouts, "I see the sign for the apartments!"

Sure enough, there's a large wooden block with *Laurel Archibold Apartments* printed on it in curvy blue letters. Both
of the *l*'s and the *a* and *e* of Laurel have worn and faded over
time, and the first five letters of Archibold are barely visible so
that at a glance, the sign reads, *ur bold*. Smiling, I pull my car
into the parking lot; gray apartment buildings surround us.

We circle around until we find one that has 607 in bold
numbers over the door. My first thought is, we made it. My
next is how bleak this place is.

Lien unfastens her seat belt. With a hand on the door she
looks at me. "Come on, let's go."

Paralyzed, I sit.

She opens the door and thrusts her legs out. "Miss Bravencourt, hurry."

Something comes over me. I feel it start in my head and
move down my whole body, like a blanket being pulled over
me. I hope this isn't what having a seizure feels like. From the
way Beanie has described the ones she has, I'm probably safe.
I turn toward Lien. "Look at me," I say.

Confused, Lien slides back into her seat. She eyes me.

I conform my tone to that of a teacher, to the voice I used when
I wanted to make a point in the classroom. "You go by yourself."

Immediately, Lien replies just as I knew she would. "No.
No. You come too." Her voice has gone back in time to that
of a little girl's in a *Hello Kitty* T-shirt.

I take my eyes from hers, not wanting to see her desperation. "No, I'll wait here."

"Why? Please, Miss Bravencourt."

Before she can continue, I place my hand on hers. "Listen," I say. "Will you listen to me?"

"Yes." Her hand trembles.

"You are a woman now, Lien. You are brave. Look at all you've done! You came to America, learned a new language, got your high school diploma, work in a restaurant, met a man, fell in love, and have searched for your mother." I pause and give her a weak smile. "After doing all those things, you are capable of meeting your mother. On your own. Without me."

"Without you?" She frowns. "I need more courage." Squeezing two of my fingers, she pleads again. "I need you."

"Go. I know you can do this."

"I'm frightened."

Clamping my mouth so I won't say anything I shouldn't, I release my hand from hers.

Huffing, she says, "Okay. Okay."

I hold my breath as she climbs out of the car. She takes a few steps and then turns to say, "You pray to God for me?"

"Yes, I will do that."

As my heart beats with fear for her, I watch from my car window. She leaves me, walks up the uneven path toward the main door to the building, and then pauses.

When she gets to the door, she looks back at me. She waves. It's not one of her wild waves that she so often produced in the camp's marketplace when she saw Carson or me. This is a feeble movement of her arm. She looks so tiny against the stark edifice. Lien, who used to make us all quake with her powerful arm that hit many a teasing boy or girl. Lien, who showed no fear.

I ball my fingers into fists to keep myself from running to her and calling, "Wait! Wait! I'll come with you." I know this is something she must do alone. I know I cannot intrude on this moment.

When I look up from my fists, she's out of sight. I hope she made it inside; the child Lien would have hidden behind a bush. I scan the two scrawny bushes by the door and realize they are not big enough to hide a woman. Remembering my promise to pray, I begin. I pray for Lien to have courage, for Thuy to let her inside her apartment, for understanding, and for a good reunion.

As I become aware of my strenuous breathing, I wonder how else to pray. I watch a thin mother in an oversized plaid jacket push her toddler in a stroller from one of the apartments to the left. As the two come closer, I note how bright with love the mother's eyes are as she stops to stroke the child's hair and tie his shoe. I bet Lien's mom looked at her like that. I bet she hated to have to give her up.

On the sidewalk embedded with weeds, a man sails by on a bicycle. A young boy on a smaller bike follows. I wonder if Lien ever had a bicycle. There are so many things I don't know about her. My eyes grow moist; I dig through my purse for a tissue.

When the air in the car gets stuffy, I roll down the window and, sticking my head out, watch crimson leaves rustle in the wind overhead. I count the windows on Thuy's building, noting the chipped paint on the shutters.

Forty-four minutes later, my heart swells with gratitude as anxiety dissipates. Lien exits the concrete edifice. Quickly, I dry my eyes.

She opens the car door and slips into the passenger seat. Giving me a hug, she cries, "I saw her! I saw my mother."

I let tears consume me again.

"She nice," Lien says. "She have photo of me when we were in Vietnam."

"That's great."

"We drink some tea."

Smiling, I repeat, "That's great."

"I tell her not to worry about the M.S. She think I might get sick like her, but I just say, 'Never mind, never mind, we don't need to worry. We are together now. Just be happy.'"

We do grow up, don't we? I think as a gust of wind causes golden leaves to find resting spots on the milky pavement. This self-absorbed child has become a woman, and I get to experience this amazing chapter of her life. I feel privileged and unworthy at the same time.

We ride in silence for a few miles, until Lien says, "She sorry about everything. Just like me."

forty-four

The day we have all hoped would happen has arrived. The bride has yet to walk down the aisle but already I'm exhausted. Having the wedding at my church instantly put me in charge. By no means am I a wedding planner, yet I feel I've done a commendable job.

The church is decorated with crystal vases of pink roses and white lilies. The organist doesn't sound too bad. And Taylor and Natasha have met, shaken hands, and are seated on the same pew in the sanctuary. Dovie, Pearl, and Beanie are dressed in matching hats with short golden plumes and seated in the second row on the bride's side. I must get a photo of Beanie—finally inside an actual church. I wish Little could be here, but she's in Europe for two weeks, visiting her daughter and meeting her daughter's boyfriend, who really is from France.

After seeing that all seems to be under control in the sanctuary, I head down the hallway to find the bride.

Lien is adding mascara to her eyelashes in one of the preschool Sunday school rooms. She's seated at a low table in a chair shaped like a bunny, a compact in one hand and the mascara wand in the other. The faint scent of perfume surrounds her. Seeing me, she says, "I take my shoes off. They hurt my feet." She wiggles her bare toes.

I stand off to her side and snap some photos—first her face and then her feet.

She giggles. "My bridesmaids leave me to do this on my own."

"You look really nice," I say. Then I adjust the pearl hair clip Mom gave her to wear. Smoothing her hair to one side, I place the clip in her brown locks. Her hair smells sweet, like cherry blossoms.

She eyes herself in her compact mirror. Putting the makeup into a white bag that is on the table next to her bouquet of flowers, she asks if it's time to head to the sanctuary.

I've left my watch at home but am sure that it's time.

"Miss Bravencourt, you help me so much. I never be able to do this without you." She stands and slips on a pair of white pumps. In the shoes, she's taller than I am. I hand her the bouquet Natasha made for her. She sniffs the arrangement of red roses, baby's breath, yellow carnations, and white gardenias, and then tells me, "I am happy."

When we leave the classroom, we make our way to the vestibule, where we can hear the organ music and the conversations of the assembled group in the sanctuary.

Lien walks slowly as though practicing for her walk down the aisle. Her gown's train swishes against the carpet. At the vestibule she suddenly trips, and I help to steady her.

"I'm nervous," she says, catching her breath. Like a child, she then peers through the crack in the door separating the vestibule from the larger room. I think she's looking for her mother, but she says with relief, "I see Jonathan. He did show up." I wonder if she thought that at the last minute her fiancé would bail from the ceremony. "I see his parents and brothers." His two brothers are the groomsmen, so I'm glad they are standing, as they should be, next to the two Vietnamese bridesmaids.

I get a couple of shots of Lien as she holds her bouquet. When Carson appears, I ask if Lien's mom has made it. He gives me a worried look, and I know that she has yet to arrive. I take a few pictures of Carson and Lien together.

Swallowing panic, I look at Carson's watch. It's five minutes to three. I swing open the front door and scan the street. I don't know what kind of vehicle to look for, but even so, I keep watching for Thuy. The organ music continues to play, tender tunes that cause me to worry that any minute they will change into the bridal march. *Not yet, not yet,* my mind echoes.

Carson's jaw is tight when I return to his side. So only I can hear, he says, "She better get here now."

Minh has arrived and shifts from foot to foot beside his niece in the vestibule. He sucks in his belly, runs fingers over his hair, and looks like he might pass out.

Lien's face is beaded with sweat. I recall how during the rehearsal last night she couldn't stop giggling. I search her face for a smile now, but there is none. I take a tissue from a box on the table and blot her cheeks. Next to the tissues sits a clear box containing a corsage. Two tiny red rosebuds sit between a white carnation and a spray of baby's breath. It's waiting to be pinned to Thuy's dress.

Minh adjusts his tie, fiddles with the neck of his starched shirt, and gives us an apprehensive smile. He looks at his watch. "It is time," he tells us.

I think of the importance of the day and want to say something significant, something warm, truthful, and kind. I wonder what I would want to hear from my friends on my wedding day. I have no clue.

The organist has stopped playing. In seconds, she will begin the famous tune that will send Lien and Minh down the aisle toward the waiting groom. I only have a second. With my hand on Lien's arm, I whisper the Vietnamese words for *You are beautiful* that suddenly like a flash come to mind: *"Dep gai."*

Smiling, I know that she gets it; my pronunciation must not be too bad.

Embracing her lightly so as not to smudge her makeup, I whisper, "I am so happy for you."

It is then that Lien's bottom lip quivers. With a hand to her mouth, she says, "Thank you for all you always do for me."

I have to look away as my eyes turn damp.

Carson opens the door that separates uncle and bride from the gathered crowd in the sanctuary. As the music begins, everyone stands.

Lien gulps as Carson nods, and with her arm slipped around her uncle's, Lien starts to glide down the aisle with him. This kid who only knew how to rush into my classroom, scaring the rafter rats and everyone else in sight, is now gracefully making her way down the aisle toward the next adventure of her young life.

I grab my camera and am ready to slide in after them to get a few shots when I hear one of the double doors pulled open behind me.

Carson and I turn at the same time to see a woman appear. Her face looks vaguely familiar and then I recall exactly where I have seen her before. She's the one who came into the shop that day so many weeks ago. "Is this the right place?" The sunlight plays against her frosted hair.

I walk to her side, a finger to my lips.

Dismissing my gesture, she booms, "Is Lien getting married here?"

"Yes," I say.

She turns and heads outside, the door banging behind her.

Carson and I share a moment of anticipation, and then a small Asian woman in a metallic green wheelchair is brought into our view. Carson helps hold the door open, saying a few lines to the woman in Vietnamese. Assuming it is Lien's mother, I grab the corsage, remove it from the box, and swiftly pin it to the lapel of her blue silk dress.

"Welcome," I say, relief filling every pore. I don't know if that is the appropriate thing to say or not, but it is all I can come up with for an occasion like this.

Lien and her uncle are now at Jonathan's side next to the two bridesmaids and two groomsmen. Jonathan's leg is twitching, just like he told us earlier that it would.

Not wanting Thuy to miss any more of Lien's life, I motion for her to wheel her chair down the aisle. She presses a button on the console in front of her and the chair springs forward. The wheels squeak over the carpet as the other woman follows closely behind.

Lien glances over her shoulder to view what she has been hoping for all these months.

I expect to hear the little girl who is still very much alive in Lien shout in her native tongue to her mother, a greeting of glee. Perhaps even a boisterous wave and a loud hyena-sounding laugh. But the woman in Lien merely smiles demurely and turns her attention to the minister and her groom.

I steady myself and enter the sanctuary, my camera at my eye. I snap a few pictures and, as the music ceases, scoot over to the left of the room where poised guests reverently sit.

Thuy has stopped her wheelchair at the edge of the front row, her corsage lopsided, a handkerchief shielding her eyes. I use my camera to hide mine, suddenly blinded by this happily-ever-after.

forty-five

When I asked them, Sanjay and Venya said they'd be glad to have the reception at their bakery. Sanjay let customers know that he would be closed for the day, encouraging me to create a sign with my Sharpie markers for him to place on the front door.

With the help of some enthusiastic ladies in my church, I arranged the tables in rows and added white linen tablecloths to each one. In the center of the tables, we placed bud vases with single red roses. Then we prepared the lime sherbet punch and filled crystal dishes with mixed nuts.

Sanjay made the wedding cake, a three-tiered work of art decorated with baby-blue beaded icing and six pale pink roses piped on the top layer. He joked that he had thought about adding martini glasses and olives but decided against it. Carson and I offered to pay him for the cake as well as for the use of his store. He refused any monetary compensation. "I just like to see people find each other," he said, exposing his romantic side.

Chi, Minh, and Huy stayed up well past midnight on Thursday making hundreds of spring rolls and mixing the special dipping sauce to get the right consistency. They placed their fried creations in large sealed Tupperware containers for the trip to Virginia. Once in Falls Church, I arranged for them to put the chagio in Sanjay's deep freezer until Saturday morning when they took them out to defrost. Sanjay offered turkey sandwiches, although we protested. "You don't like turkey? I can make chicken salad."

"No," I'd said. "We like sandwiches, but you are already making the cake."

"Venya can make the sandwiches."

I thought of how tired Venya seemed lately with her pregnancy. She's in her third trimester.

"She needs something to do when she can't sleep at night. The baby kicks every night from ten until three in the morning." Sanjay sounded weary.

After more convincing, we accepted the offer and let Venya make turkey sandwiches for the reception.

Pearl wanted to know if we needed some rhubarb pies, but I told her the wedding cake would be enough. She, Dovie, and Beanie drove up from Winston last night and got a room at the Hampton Inn, saying that the breakfast this morning was one of the best hotel breakfasts they'd ever had.

As the church ladies turned Sanjay's bakery into an elaborate reception hall, Carson set up an old turntable and CD player on a table in one corner of the store. He was instructed by Lien to play old records her mother might like—some classical selections like Bach, some Beatles, Michael Jackson, Carly Simon, and Bread. Carson was willing to play whatever she requested, carrying in a large crate of vinyl records and another of CDs.

Sanjay locked his shop at two, telling us we needed to get out so that we could head over to the church or we'd miss seeing his favorite part of the day—when the groom kisses the bride. Carson and I rode together, the fingers of his right hand laced with mine as he drove us across town.

After the ceremony, all the guests convene in the church parking lot where a butterfly release is to take place. Once, after showing Lien photos I'd taken of one of Dovie's butterfly releases, the girl said she wanted my aunt to do this at her wedding.

"I want butterflies because they are symbol of freedom, and besides, they are so pretty."

I agreed with her.

Of course, Dovie is in her element this afternoon as she educates us about the monarch butterfly, its life cycle, its colors, and what it means to release yourself to God to let Him work in you. "Jonathan and Lien," she addresses the newlyweds, "I hope that in your marriage you will strive to freely share from your hearts with each other. Be free like the butterfly."

"Well said," Pastor Jed comments with a smile.

Even my mom marvels as the tiny insects spread their vivid wings and dance into the autumn air. I overhear her telling Dovie to bring herself, Beanie, and Pearl over to the boutique tomorrow to find some clothes. "We have a new line of scarves with butterflies on them you might like."

Dovie says she'll be happy to come to the boutique and that she's sure Pearl and Beanie would like to shop there, as well.

Once the last butterfly has slithered to freedom, a splash of color against a blue autumn sky, Carson and I rush over to Sanjay's before the line of vehicles makes its way from the church to the bakery. From the parking lot, I get a picture of the cars. Inside the bakery, I take photos of the flower arrangements, the cake, Carson at his D.J. post, and Huy in a waiter's outfit. When the guests enter the reception, I capture their smiles.

The first song Carson plays is for Jonathan and Lien to slow-dance to. It is Bread's "Lost Without Your Love."

As the song fills the bakery and I note the sugary lyrics, I lean against the wall and get three close-ups of Lien and Jonathan. Both seem relaxed; Jonathan's leg has stopped twitching. Lien closes her eyes as she rests her cheek against her husband's shoulder. I capture Thuy looking on, her face soft and gentle.

The next dance is open to everyone, and without too much prompting, both Beanie and Pearl move to the beat of "Celebration." Carson catches my glance and smiles from his D.J. corner, most likely recalling the day we requested this song at my aunt's.

The sandwiches and chagio are on one table, the punch and cake on another. Lien instructs me to be the one to tell people when it is their turn to eat. After the young couple entertains us with one more dance, I encourage people to move toward the food. I help Lien's mother get a plate with chagio and a turkey sandwich and then guide her over to a table where there is room for her wheelchair.

Carson plays some Beatles songs, and Lien coaxes her bridesmaids to dance. Soon a dozen people are swaying to "All You Need Is Love." Jonathan swings Lien in a circle until she grows dizzy and topples into his arms.

"Sam?" Carson is at my elbow.

"Hey," I say. "They do look nice together."

"Lien says that after this dance, you and I need a break from our work. She wants her bridesmaids to just play some Vietnamese songs on their flutes."

"And she doesn't want pictures?"

"She says that you are entitled to a break."

Jonathan twirls Lien around slowly this time and then catches her as the audience claps. I quickly get a few shots of that on film.

Carson places a hand over my camera lens. "Sam, let's go outside for a bit."

"Don't you know that you're not supposed to put fingers on a camera lens?" I scold. I pretend to be upset, but as usual, Carson's smile is enticing, even more so than Sanjay's cake.

"At least they're clean. Come on."

The bridesmaids are taking their instruments out of their cases and assembling them. I am glad that Lien wants some of her culture to be part of this special day.

Carson whispers, "I have something to ask you."

With that, I leave my camera on the counter, giving a quick smile to Lien's mom as she smiles back, her corsage still teetering on her lapel. I follow Carson out the front door of the bakery, away from the sound of flutes warming up to play.

The sun is a soft glow against a paling sky. We had cringed when we first heard the meteorologist's forecast of rain, then cheered when two days ago the prediction changed to clear skies with unseasonably high temperatures.

Carson takes me to the back of the shops by the dumpster. He walks to the railing by the parking lot where the trucks make their deliveries.

Standing under a canopy of branches toppling with yellow leaves, I say, "Don't tell me that Sanjay thinks there's been another dumpster fire?"

"No." His voice is low, almost worried.

"So what is the question?" I squint into his eyes. They are the color of emeralds today.

He takes my hands in his and rubs one of my fingers with his thumb. I note the movement of the thumb, let my heart enjoy how being close to him makes me feel. Sometimes you just want to bottle certain moments in life so you can keep them forever. I'll remember this feeling, I tell myself. One day when I'm old and still single, I'll still have this day of celebration to cherish and be grateful for.

Looking intently into my eyes, Carson asks, "Do you want to get married?"

I steady myself, quite aware that I just might fall over the railing.

forty-six

The first happy words that come to mind do not jump out of my mouth. Instead, caution fences me in and I hear myself saying, "I suppose one day I could get married. If the right guy ever came along."

"Who is the right guy for you, Sam?" His eyes hold questions as his hands continue to hold mine.

"There was this guy . . . once."

His jaw stiffens.

"Carson and Samantha!" The loud voice calling to us belongs to Sanjay. When he draws closer to us, he says, "Lien is going to sail up her bouquet. Come inside."

Reluctant to be pulled away from our seclusion, Carson and I leave the back of the shops and enter the bakery.

The women are leaving their seats to stand against one of the walls. Lien walks over and stands with her back to them.

"Miss Bravencourt," she coos at me. "You single. You stand in line, too."

Natasha makes room for me next to her and Pearl. She gives Taylor, seated at a table with Dovie, Thuy, and Mom, a bright smile.

Taylor smiles back, his eyes flashing contentment. I think back to how I met him and find it fun that he agreed to come to this wedding. I told him he needed to come since he had assisted in helping Lien be reunited with her mother, but he knew that I really wanted him here to meet my cute friend Natasha.

"Dovie, Mom," I call over to them. "They are single," I tell the group. "Now come on over here."

Both women give a little shrug and then amble toward the rest of us.

"Beanie!"

Beanie shakes her hat-covered head from where she is adding more punch to her cup. "I beg to sit this one out." I know that if she were in the comforts of Dovie's kitchen, she would add, "Too many marriages already for me, thank you."

The women stop talking as Lien raises the bouquet over her head and shouts, "Ready!"

Turning, she catches my attention and then with an energetic movement, throws her bouquet for a lucky someone to catch. With a look of anticipation, Natasha leans forward, reaches up, her body blocking the others. With a snap of her wrist, the flowers are hers. I should have warned everyone that they didn't stand a chance, as Natasha is quite the athlete.

The group cheers at a smiling Natasha as I scan the bakery for Carson. Not spotting him, I decide to look outside.

Taylor gets my attention as he refills his punch glass. Motioning toward Lien and Jonathan, who are now sitting with Thuy, he says. "Looks like you did a good job."

"Well, I suppose I do have some investigative skills of my

own." I don't go into any more detail about the situation; I am more interested in something else at this moment. "I'm glad you could be here." I give him a warm smile.

"Dear, come here a moment." Dovie stops me before I can reach the front door.

I stand between her and Thuy at their table where they are eating from a bowl of mixed nuts. "Yes?"

Patting my arm, Dovie says, "Tell Thuy what a wonderful house I have."

Uncertain as to why I need to do this now, I say, "Dovie's house is really nice. I love being there."

Dovie nods. "Thank you," she says. Turning to Lien's mother, she beams, and with a heap of affection in her voice, adds, "And there is room for you at my home."

Thuy raises a limp arm for more nuts. Her hand misses the bowl and knocks over a glass of punch. "Oh. Sorry," she mutters, clearly annoyed at herself.

"No worries," says Dovie, taking a few stray napkins to mop the spill from the tablecloth. "These kinds of things happen to me all the time."

I help by finding more napkins on the next table and then, pulling Lien away from Jonathan, say, "Lien, Dovie wants your mother to move in. Would you like that?"

Shock covers Lien's face as she looks at my aunt. "With you? Live with you?"

Dovie says, "Yes. Thuy can live with me. My house is wheelchair accessible."

Beanie says, "If Thuy moves in, it will be like *Summer of Bloomsville.*"

Once again, she has named a movie I haven't seen, but Dovie has.

"That's right," my aunt says. "Only the woman's wheelchair was wooden in that one, wasn't it? And she had a nice man to push her. Perhaps you will find a nice man in Winston." Dovie gently pats Thuy's arm.

When Lien and her mother start a dialogue in Vietnamese, I make my move outside. I am not sure whether Lien and Thuy should live in the same town, and yet Dovie would be a great caregiver for Thuy. From my observations today, I can see that the frail woman needs a full-time care provider. Right now, Angie, the frosted-hair woman, comes to do her laundry, drives her on errands, and shops for her groceries.

The sun is setting, making its last imprints on the cars parked in the lot. The earlier heat from the day is gone, and a breeze rustles clusters of leaves on the ground. I consider going back inside to get my shawl, a lacy one that Mom let me choose from the rack for the wedding. Not seeing Carson by the storefronts, I stride to the back, my arms crossed against my chest for warmth.

There he sits on a stoop by the service entrance of Have a Fit. His eyes are focused on his folded hands.

"Carson." He glances at me as I sit beside him. When he doesn't say anything, I pick up where we left off before the bouquet toss. "What I meant was that I wanted to be asked by this man I met years ago."

"Old boyfriend?"

"No, he was never my boyfriend."

"Who was he, then?"

I'm amazed at my next words. "I loved him." Unable to meet his gaze, I look down. "But I never knew how he felt about me."

"Oh?"

"He had a girlfriend back home."

"He did?"

"Yes, but I cared so much for him. I even asked God to make him like me, to make him love me."

"And?" He lifts my chin and looks me in the eye. "Did this man marry the girlfriend?"

"No." I look down.

"Why not?"

"I don't know. I don't know his heart. He claimed he didn't love her."

Carson lifts my face to his. "Do you believe him?"

"I want to."

"And will you believe that God answered your prayer? That this man does love you, Sam?" His hands find their way around my shoulders, pulling me close.

This is what I've wanted, what I've dreamed of. I place my head lightly near his heart. Like Lien, like Beanie, I want to belong.

"Trust me, Sam," he says. "Please."

When my tears dampen his suit, he pulls away and from inside his jacket pocket produces a handkerchief. He hands it to me.

"What's this?" I ask, and as the words leave my mouth, my heart feels an odd soothing sensation, like it's been coated with Beanie's lotion. With the handkerchief in my hands, I go back in time. Laughter, a party, dancing, a walk, rain, and tears. I'd forgotten how intricate the embroidered yellow flowers were. I wasn't sure which kind they were, but today it's clear; these flowers are tulips.

With a smile he says, "This woman gave it to me. We shared a special common bond."

"Do you remember what it was?" I search his eyes.

"I do. Her father died when she was young. And mine had recently died."

I turn my focus back to the handkerchief. I loosely recall opening the box that held this gift. There had been so many more presents from students since that party. However, the memory of the night I used this cloth against Carson's face is one I've relived many times.

" 'You just keep pushing my love over the borderline,' " Carson says with a smile.

Playfully, I smack his arm. "You wrote that I wasn't intelligent."

"I wasn't intelligent enough to notice just how smart you were. I was fighting my feelings for you, Sam. You and I were—and are—so much alike. More than Mindy and I would ever be."

As a breeze cools the evening air, I shiver. Carson holds me closer. "I had promised Mindy that I'd be faithful to just her. In college, we'd made a pact."

"A pact? Really?"

"I guess it sounds sort of silly to admit it now."

"No," I say, clearly understanding now why the past played out the way it did. I recall the days of wanting so much to be with him, to have him all to myself without the tug he felt to go back to his dorm room and write letters to Mindy. But he had made a promise, and he'd kept it to Mindy until he realized their future was not to be. I run fingers along the edge of the handkerchief as I feel tears surface. I never thought Carson was the silly sentimental type. In a whisper I say, "You've kept it ever since."

"I only keep the things that matter to me, Sam."

I lean against him, burying my face in his shoulder, letting the weight from the past leave me. "All these years." The fabric feels light and even softer than it did when I first received it as a gift in my rustic classroom.

His lips feel soft, too.

"So are we going to make a pact?" I ask teasingly.

"Yes," he says as he kisses my eyelids. "For always."

forty-seven

Carson wants to get married tomorrow. I tell him that a girl has to have some time to plan. He says not if we elope. I stare at him, then run that option over in my head. If we ran off and got married at some county clerk's office, we wouldn't have to fool with a guest list, invitations, a reception, or flowers.

He grabs my hand and shakes me out of my deep thoughts. "I was only kidding. Seriously, we need to have a wedding."

"So can we ask Lien and Jonathan to do everything for us like we did for them?"

"Now you're thinking."

As Carson and I sit at Mom's dining room table on a Sunday afternoon in December, we look at a 1994 calendar and set a date: Saturday, May 28, a spring wedding.

"That's not far away," I say.

Mom says she'll start looking for the perfect dress for me.

"How about a veil?" I ask.

"Veils are overrated."

I'm about to ask her how she knows these things when there's a knock at her front door.

Mom stands up to answer it. As she swings the door open, all we hear is, "Oh! Oh!" A long gasp and then, "Oh, my."

I have never heard sounds like that come from her, so I jump up, rushing to the door. Carson follows.

There on the steps stands a robust woman wearing a tan jacket. I think I might know her. Cradled against her chest is a yellow cat, the color of butter. As the woman lifts the cat toward Mom, my mother takes the animal from her. "Baby!" my mother exclaims. "Oh, my sweetness." Looking up from the cat, she asks, "Where was he?"

The woman says, "There was a cry at my back door, and there he was."

This I cannot believe; Butterchurn is back.

"Where do you live?" I ask the woman. And how did she know that this tabby cat with green eyes and one white paw belongs to my mother?

"This is Mrs. Low, my neighbor," Mom says, and now I realize where I have met this woman before.

I watch my mother crooning and kissing her long-lost pet's head. "I'm Cecelia's daughter, Samantha," I remind Mrs. Low. Placing my arm around Carson, I say, "And this is my fiancé."

She notes the ring on my finger. "Lovely. Sparkly."

I smile, recalling the night Carson presented the ring to me in a tiny gold box with a black velvet bow.

"Where was he all this time?" I wonder aloud after we have all thanked Mrs. Low, closed the door, and Mom has poked and prodded to make sure her cat is without any medical needs.

"He looks good," says Mom, a smile filling her face. She

lowers Butterchurn onto the hardwood floor. "Someone's been feeding him. His collar is gone, though."

Butterchurn rubs against Mom's legs. Then, with a light purr, he gazes at the lit Christmas tree in Mom's living room and settles beside it in a cozy ball.

"It's been since February. That's ten months," says Mom, her mental calculator adding up the time that has passed. "What was he doing all that time in between?"

Gently, Carson places his arm around her shoulders and says, "Missing you. Trying to find a way back to you." Although his words serve as an explanation for my mother, I know there is more to his meaning. What he is trying to say is that the months in between were not lost. They were only a detour in his attempt to come back—to return for a second chance.

Mom assumes I will leave Falls Church and move down to Winston-Salem. Carson tells her he'll come up here and look for a job. "Why?" she asks him.

"Because Sam works here."

"Sam likes it in your Moravian town."

Carson looks at me as I think about where I'd rather live. I'd hate to be far from Mom and her shop.

As though reading my mind, Mom insists that she is fine and can manage the store without me. "You can get a job in North Carolina, be a teacher like you studied for in college."

"I like working at the boutique."

"I can get someone else to help me at the store, Sam. Pursue your teaching career."

"But what about you?"

She places a finger along the side of her nose and looks me up and down. "You will need a size five, I think."

I sigh. Already she thinks she's won the discussion and is now moving on to think about my wedding gown.

I let her change the subject, but on a cold day in February, when she's helping me pack some of my summer clothes into boxes for my move to Winston, I feel the need to bring up the topic again.

With boldness, I dive in. "I get a little tired," I say to her as I fold a shirt into a cardboard box.

She's been humming an Elvis song, "Love Me Tender," for the past half hour. She's unaware that she does this. Once I told her that she hummed often and she looked at me and said, "I don't know how to hum." Then, as if to tease me, she started humming once more. Today she asks, "What makes you tired?"

"Your independence."

"My what?"

"You're always acting capable, like you don't need me."

Her lips pucker like she's trying to hold back something. I watch her eyes to see if they'll turn wet. We can cry together, I think. Mother and daughter, a good cry in my living room. This is what movies are made of.

But my mother simply takes a backless sundress off its hanger and folds it into a large box in front of where she's seated. I wonder if she's thinking that she ordered that dress for me two years ago and she's never seen me in it. I've never let her know that the material—some man-made stiff stuff—irritates my skin when I wear it for longer than a few hours.

I keep watching her and waiting. As she continues to pick clothes off hangers and fold them into the box, I can't keep quiet any longer. "Dovie says that you are—"

Mom cuts me off, closing the lid to the box. "Dovie does not know everything about me."

"She wants to. We all want to know you." I edge closer to

her. Perhaps I can be the daughter who breaks her mom from her stoic mold.

"You are like your father."

I hate it when she says that because I never quite know what it means and how I'm like a man who was born in Scotland and spoke with a heavy brogue, often mimicked by my classmates. Does she mean that I'm like him because of my love of travel? If so, she has a point. Ever since that family summer trip to his home in Edinburgh, I've wanted to hop on a plane and let it take me to lands I've only read about. Yet, as my mind snaps back to the conversation Mom and I are having now, I doubt she is weighing any of my thoughts as her own.

Mom says, "You will see that everyone has their way of dancing."

What has this got to do with Dad? Did my father even dance?

"The dance of life. We all do it differently. But our movements and the music to which we dance are as unique as to how we survive."

In the movies Beanie and Dovie watch, the young heroine throws up her arms in despair or faints. I want to do one or the other right now.

Determined, I say, "I want you to care that I am moving to North Carolina."

She pats a pair of shorts with a graceful hand. "I do, Sam. I'll miss you. And yes, I will make the trip and come and visit you." She gives me a genuine smile. "You and Carson." Then as her eyes rove over the boxes, she confides words I have never heard. "I was told I had no skills. Told I needed others to make me succeed. Basically, as a child, I was led to believe that Dovie had talent and I was without any. Those are the things my mother said to me. I've had to fight her words. All my life."

I don't care if she doesn't want to be held, I step over boxes, trip on the edge of one, and wrap my arms around her.

We do cry together. She blows her nose with a tissue she produces from her pocket. I wipe my nose on my sleeve.

"Samantha," she says later as the moon glows in a starless sky, "you make Carson a happy man."

I want to ask, Do I make you happy? But it's late and she has her car keys and purse in her hands. So I offer a smile and then take her in my arms and hug her tightly again. This time she feels frail and small. "I love you, Mom," I breathe.

"I know you do, Sam." Pulling from me, she meets my eyes. "And I love you more than you will ever know." Then she leaves me. The clank of the door closing echoes through my apartment's walls.

After I brew a pot of coffee, I call her to make sure she's arrived home safely. She tells me not to worry about her.

"I'm the daughter, remember?" I say. "I'm allowed to worry." I give a light chuckle, hoping she'll join me.

She asks if I've noticed that Butterchurn has gained some weight and then tells me to sleep well. "And oh," she says as though her next thought is not really important, "I'm going on a date tomorrow night, so if you need me, I will be out."

"A date?" My voice squeaks.

"Yes, Samantha. Older women do go out, you know."

"Oh yes, of course," my words spurt. "And they should go out."

I want to pry with questions: Do you like him? Do you want to get married again? But I already know the answers. Yes, she likes him. Officer Branson is just her type. He enjoys the classics.

forty-eight

March 1994

I asked Carson what he thought our wedding invitation should look like and he said it didn't matter. "Can't we just call people up and tell them to come on over?" he said one day when I dragged him into a stationer's at the mall. I almost said that perhaps that's the way Southerners do it down in Winston or Raleigh, but the way I was brought up, I couldn't. But just as I got ready to speak, he suggested we get some ice cream at Baskin Robbins. So we left the stationer's for cones of chocolate.

Seeing that Carson didn't care about the invitation, I asked Natasha her opinion, and a decision was made. The wedding invitation is printed on ivory card stock with a white beaded border; the lettering is gold. The words on it make my heart sing:

> *Cecelia Bravencourt*
> *and*
> *Janice Brylie*
> *Request the pleasure of your presence*
>
> *At the marriage of their children*
> *Samantha Ann Bravencourt*
> *and*
>
> *Carson Lee Brylie*
> *Saturday, the twenty-eighth of May*
> *Nineteen hundred and ninety-four*
> *At four o'clock in the afternoon*
> *Lewis Memorial Church*
> *Falls Church, Virginia*
> *Reception at Le Rue to follow*

Inside a tiny envelope is a glossy card with green wording asking recipients to respond by May 1 for the reception. Le Rue is a restaurant near the Washington Monument, where apparently my parents dined on their tenth anniversary. Mom thought that would be a great place for the reception. I said I had no money for a reception of that caliber, and she assured me that there was money. "Uncle Charlie left me some," she said. "He told me to spend it on you when the time was right."

I guess there are some things I still don't know about my uncle Charlie.

At the Annandale Road post office parking lot, I open my car's passenger door to remove a large shopping bag filled with the addressed invitations for my wedding. I stayed up too late last night writing addresses and licking stamps while *The Sound of Music* played on my TV. Carson had his list of family and friends to invite. When Carson took me to meet his mother in Raleigh, she presented me with hers. I was surprised how many friends Mom had on her list, including Maralinda, who has agreed to help Mom in the boutique after I move. Carson thinks that all the time Mom now spends with Officer Branson might amount to another wedding in the near future, but I'm not so sure about that.

I hold the door to the post office open for a weathered man in a wheelchair. He is gracious, thanking me. One leg is missing, and just as I notice this, I see the sticker on the back of his chair: VIETNAM VETS.

My thoughts jumble as an ache brews in my heart. I think of war and how it destroys, divides, and damages. I see the faces of those in the refugee camp and those who found their names on The List and are now in America. I want to tell this wounded soldier that I am sorry for his loss and for the abandonment he may have felt upon his return. I want to say other things, but right now I'm just honored to hold the door for him.

Inside the post office, I wait behind a woman who is letting her child insert a manila envelope into the box. The child, a girl of about six, says with a toothless grin, "Grandmommy and Granddaddy are going to love my pictures."

The woman says, "They sure will."

"Excited is what they're going to be, right, Mommy?" Standing on her tiptoes, she gives the envelope a final push into the narrow slot and then claims, "I've gotten so big."

As I wait, I wonder how my aunt is doing trying to convince Thuy to move to North Carolina and board at her home. I've told Carson that between Lien and Dovie, Thuy might as well stop fighting. She does not stand a chance of staying in her meager apartment here. When it comes to being pushy about certain things, Lien and Dovie are not forces to try to stand against.

When the woman and child are finished, I remove an invitation from my bag and gingerly touch it. I am getting married, I almost say aloud to the woman, to the vet, to everyone. I grin as I wonder if anyone not invited will show up.

I note how easily the first envelope slides into the blue mailbox. It's addressed to the original Avery Jones and her husband, Perry. I add another into the thin slot, and then another one, until all ninety-two envelopes are safely inside.

When I walk outside, a breeze blows across the lawn, ruffling the American flag. I zip my coat and look at the sky. I think they've predicted snow again, although Mom says it's definitely not cold enough.

Walking toward my car, I think about all those invitations I've addressed and just mailed. Although I hope they make their way smoothly to their intended destinations, I know that there is always that margin of error. Perhaps a woman in need of a second chance will come to my wedding. Maybe she will let herself follow an unlikely script, written just for her. Being at the wedding might just place her in the right place at the correct time to set her next adventure in motion. She might even meet someone from her past who will change the course of her future.

As Beanie would say, *"Those kinds of happenings do happen, so I've heard."*

I know that they can. I also know that they are *right nice* when they do.

recipes

Dovie's Oatmeal Bread

1 cup of old-fashioned oats (not instant)
1½ cups of boiling water
¾ cup of molasses
3 tablespoons of vegetable oil
2 teaspoons of salt
2 cups of warm water
1 tablespoon of active dry yeast
4 cups of bread flour
4 cups of whole-wheat flour

Combine the oats and boiling water in a large mixing bowl and let sit for at least thirty minutes. Add the molasses, oil, and salt to the oatmeal mixture, combining well. In a separate bowl, dissolve the yeast in the warm water. Add to the oatmeal mixture. Stir in the flour, one cup at a time. Once the dough starts to pull from the sides of the bowl, turn dough onto a floured surface and knead in the rest of the flour until smooth. Continue to knead for about 8 minutes. Place the dough in a greased bowl, turning it so that all sides are coated. Cover with a damp cloth. Let rise until doubled in size—about 1 hour. Punch down and divide dough in half. Shape into two loaves and place dough in two greased loaf pans. Cover and let rise for 45 minutes to 1 hour. Preheat oven to 400 degrees F. Place loaf pans in oven for 5 minutes, then reduce heat to 350 degrees F. and bake for an additional 40 minutes. Loaves should brown and will be ready to take out of oven when they sound hollow when lightly tapped.

Pearl's Secret Family Recipe for Rhubarb Pie

For crust

3 cups all-purpose flour

2½ teaspoons sugar

¾ teaspoon salt

⅔ cup chilled solid vegetable shortening, cut into pieces

½ cup plus 2 tablespoons (1¼ sticks) chilled unsalted butter, cut into pieces

10 tablespoons or less of ice water

For filling

3½ cups sliced rhubarb

3½ cups hulled and sliced strawberries

1 teaspoon of lemon juice

½ cup brown sugar

½ cup white sugar

2 tablespoons of quick-cooking tapioca

1 teaspoon ground nutmeg

½ teaspoon salt

1 large egg yolk beaten to blend with 1 teaspoon water (for glaze)

Make crust:

Combine flour, sugar, and salt. Cut in shortening and butter until coarse meal forms. Blend in ice water two tablespoons at a time to form moist clumps. Form dough into ball; cut in half. Flatten each half into a circle. Wrap separately in plastic; refrigerate until firm, about 1 hour. Let dough soften at room temperature before rolling.

Make filling:

Preheat oven to 400 degrees F. Combine first 7 ingredients in large bowl. Toss gently to blend.

Roll out 1 dough disk on floured work surface to 13-inch round. Transfer to 9-inch pie dish. Trim excess dough, leaving ¾-inch overhang.

Roll out second dough disk on lightly floured surface to 13-inch round. Cut into 14 half-inch-wide strips. Spoon filling into crust. Arrange 7 dough strips atop filling, spacing evenly. Form lattice by placing remaining dough strips in opposite direction atop filling. Trim ends of dough strips even with overhang of bottom crust. Fold strip ends and overhang under, pressing to seal. Crimp edges.

Brush glaze over crust. Place pie on a baking sheet. Bake 20 minutes. Reduce oven temperature to 350 degrees F. Bake pie until golden and filling thickens, about 1 hour 25 minutes. Cool completely.

MOM'S CROCK-POT STEW

1 lb. lean stew beef, cubed
1 small onion, diced
4 carrots, diced
3 celery stalks, sliced
4 potatoes, peeled and cubed
1 packet onion soup mix
3 cups water
8 ounces beef broth
1 teaspoon sugar
1 8-ounce can of tomato paste
salt and pepper to taste

Place all ingredients in your favorite crock pot and cook on low for six hours.

questions for conversation

1. Have you ever tried to teach a child something? What was challenging about the experience? What did you learn about yourself? Have you taught a child from another country?

2. What strengths does Samantha see in Carson? Weaknesses?

3. What do you think of Beanie's character? Do you know anyone like her? How does Dovie help Beanie?

4. Have you ever received an unusual invitation or ended up at the wrong place at the wrong time?

5. What do you like or dislike about attending weddings? Share your favorite wedding experience.

6. Have you ever lost a pet? What happened?

7. Samantha takes time to just sit and meet with God. How does this affect her? Do you ever do this?

8. Many refugees have had to leave their homelands due to political unrest and are now scattered around the world.

Do you know any who live in your town or another nearby location? If you had to flee your home, where would you go? Would it be easy or hard for you to adjust?

9. Lien seems to have a large capacity to forgive. Is forgiving others easy for you? Who have you had to forgive recently?

10. Why do you think Carson wanted to be a part of the Hong family's life? Did he view his relationship with them differently than Samantha viewed hers? Why do you think Samantha decided to help Lien?

acknowledgments

During the writing of this book, I held a Name-That-Character Contest, asking participants to provide names for three of my characters—a Southern man, an Amerasian girl, and an older woman who collects butterflies. The contest winners were Sarah Palumbo for Carson, Shelly Epps for Lien, and Carly Kendall for Aunt Dovie. My thanks to these three!

Also, gratitude to my agent, Kristin Lindstrom; to the Serious Scribes—Kim, Martha, Katharine, Jen, and Catherine—who gave me insight into this work as it was in-progress; to my editor, Charlene Patterson, and the whole Bethany House team for the fantastic work they do to make a novel shine; and to the fans at the Alice J. Wisler Facebook Fan Club page who kept asking when this novel was going to be published (so that they can each purchase dozens of copies, I'm sure).

To my kids—Rachel, Benjamin, and Elizabeth—I appreciate your predictable and unwavering responses every time I asked if I could read some of my manuscript aloud to you: "Sure, you can read one chapter, Mom, but only one." And to my husband, Carl, for his encouragement and teapots of Earl Grey—both generously brought to my desk. How nice it is to belong to you!

About the Author

Years ago, when Alice J. Wisler's family moved into an old house with a magnolia tree out front, an ornate wedding invitation came in the mail. Only it was not for Alice; it was for the previous homeowners. Ever since she received that invitation, Alice has wondered what going to the wrong wedding would be like.

Although this is a work of fiction, Alice did teach Laotian, Cambodian (Khmer), and Vietnamese children in a dusty classroom with rats in the rafters at the Philippine Refugee Processing Center in the Philippines during the mid-1980s. The Amerasian children intrigued her then, and she continues to follow their plight in both Vietnam and after resettlement in the United States. As she wrote in one of her newsletters sent out by World Relief in 1985, "These children long to be accepted." *A Wedding Invitation* is about being accepted, being a part, being invited. God invites each of us to commune with Him, no matter what our roots are, the political status of our country, or what others think of us.

Alice lives and writes in Durham, NC. Ever since the death of her son Daniel in 1997, she's taught grief-writing courses. Learn more about her inspirational novels and her Writing the Heartache workshops at www.alicewisler.com.

More from
Alice J. Wisler

To find out more about Alice and her books, visit *alicewisler.com.*

When Jackie meets the handsome Davis Erickson—who happens to own the perfect place for a B&B—it seems her wishes might just come true. But when some disturbing secrets come to light, threatening her long-held dreams, will she risk it all to find the truth?

Hatteras Girl by Alice J. Wisler

If you enjoyed *A Wedding Invitation*, you may also like...

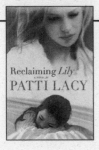

In the wake of a potentially devastating diagnosis, Gloria Powell and Kai Chang meet in a Ft. Worth hotel to discuss the future of Lily, the daughter Gloria adopted from China and the sister Kai hopes to reclaim. But is Kai an answer to prayer—or will her arrival force Gloria to sacrifice more than she ever imagined?

Reclaiming Lily by Patti Lacy

pattilacy.com